THE ARREST OF PASTOR PRATT

When Pastor Pratt is arrested and accused of a serious crime, what happens next shocks everyone to the core. Can anything good come out of the tragedy and heartache that unfolds?

THE ARREST OF PASTOR PRATT

by

Janet E Cooper

_DB_

DIADEM BOOKS

*To Dr Elinor Kapp, my healer and my friend,
without whom this book would not exist.
Thank you and God bless you. XXX*

PROLOGUE

Thursday morning

THE REVEREND Pastor Anthony Pious Pratt closed the door of the vestry, or the chaplet as he preferred to call it, and strode through the large empty building jangling a bunch of keys in his right hand. He was sweating and could do with a shower. The morning had been extremely difficult to put it mildly, very hard work, but that wasn't his fault. It absolutely WAS NOT his fault. The Lord had told him to do what had to be done – a soul was at stake – and he had humbly and dutifully carried out divine instruction. As he always did. Obedient unto the end, that's what he was. Well done, thou good and faithful servant. His reward was coming.

Passing through the vestibule, Pastor Pratt furrowed his brow and pursed his lips, as he pondered whether he should have taken her back to the manse after all, like he usually did. But no. He had surely done the right thing in bringing her back to the Sinners Chapel of Mercy. What better place in which to carry out the Lord's will? The Holy Spirit had appreciated the privacy, the mercy seat had been made available to her via his pastoral ministrations, and he would continue to pray for the Lord to bless her and keep showing her the error of her ways. Nevertheless, it had certainly been more of a struggle than previously before she became compliant and obedient. She desperately needed yet another fountain of crimson blood to wash her from every vile sin, however, and then the Good Lord would look favourably upon the Sinners' Chapel, bringing in

1

floods of the unsaved, ready for washing and cleansing and dunking (by Pastor Pratt of course). A further session would be arranged as soon as possible. Perhaps at the Manse was wiser. Warmer there. It was also isolated from any outside listening ears, for the sounds of wickedness were not pleasant. "She won't get the better of me," he mumbled quietly, "the little cow!"

Oh yes, the Lord was undoubtedly satisfied with His humble servant, even if Pastor Pratt had been obeying Him diligently these past two years with no results. In the Lord's time, yes, yes, the timing was His and His alone. It was the Pastor's duty, indeed his pleasure, to continue with the Lord's work in this way. Yes Lord, but do hurry up. At least today's session was over and done with and Pastor Pratt was free to return home and eat lunch for which, in the light of his wife's dodgy culinary skills, he would seek the strength and the stomach to be truly thankful, for every faithful servant has his burden to bear.

Stepping onto the pavement outside the Chapel, Pastor Pratt took a deep breath, sniffed loudly, and quickly wiped his nose with the back of one hand before turning and locking the heavy wooden door behind him. He then faced forward and looked heavenward with thanksgiving and gratitude that so far he had neither fainted nor become weary. While he was doing the Lord's will, the Lord would always renew his strength and he would rise up with wings like eagles as God's mighty angels watched over him. However knackered he felt, help was near. "Lord of the Universe, rend the heavens and come quickly down..." – preferably before the elders and deacons meeting that evening. "Lord, give me Your strength and Your aid that I may face the many challenges that lie ahead this day."

Pastor Pratt then straightened his tie, smoothed down his pinstripe suit jacket, and got into his Smart Car. He slammed the door shut, prayed for protection from speed cameras, and set off for the Manse, stomach rumbling as he belched loudly. "Excuse me, Lord."

The net curtain on the house opposite the Sinners Chapel of Mercy twitched back into position. Well, well. What was going on there? She didn't like the feel of it at all. "I just knew I didn't like that man," she muttered to the empty room. Should she tell somebody what she had seen and heard? For as sure as God made little apples, something was not right. In fact, something was horribly, terribly wrong. She felt it in her water.

PART ONE

February 2005

CHAPTER ONE

PENNY

Thursday afternoon

HAIR STILL WET after her shower, Hayley checked her speed and flicked her lights on as she entered the westbound Greenridge tunnel on her way home from the gym. She'd done her usual stint on the treadmill but hadn't experienced the sought after endorphin rush; in fact, she felt worse if that was at all possible, even after spending so long in the shower that her skin hurt and was still red and hot. Not giving the long tunnel a second thought except for the brief lapse in radio reception which always annoyed her, she hadn't expected what happened next. In fact, what happened next was that she didn't remember what happened next until…

…the policewoman yanked the car door open with one hand while she grabbed her phone with the other, punching in a number to call for backup and an ambulance, annoyed that she was out without her partner, Detective Sergeant Ian Gettum, who was at the dentist having a filling. (How many times had she told him not to crunch Polo mints?) Thankfully there didn't seem to have been any sort of a collision, but a woman alone on the road edge, right outside the tunnel and slumped over the steering wheel, was not good. The tunnels connected the busy town of Truffleton with, among many other places, Sweet Briar village just five miles away through lush green countryside. Penny lived sort of midway between the two.

Detective Inspector Penelope Whistle (Yeh, she knew, it was a stupid name for a police officer) finished her call and gently touched the woman, not sure if she was asleep, unconscious or even dead. Already past the end of her shift she really didn't need lone women having crises, accidents or dying on the roads. What she needed was home, strong coffee, a hot bath and no work for the next few days. Only one late shift tomorrow then – bliss – a weekend off. Sighing, Penny forced herself into professional mode and quickly faced the fact that she'd be home late yet again. Migmos, her wonderful, crazy, long suffering moggy, would not be impressed, but hey ho, this was her job after all. At least for the time being. She wondered if there had been any response yet following her recent interview at the University. She also wondered if the disgruntled Migmos would chuck up a fur ball to mark her displeasure at her owner's tardiness. Oh, the joy of owning a cat! Getting back to the job in hand…

"Hello? Can you tell me your name? Can you hear me?" Feeling the woman's wrist, there was a healthy pulse thumping away so at least there was life in there somewhere. Her chest rose and fell steadily and there was no visible bleeding. She looked to be in her late twenties/early thirties, shoulder length damp hair which promised to be auburn, dressed in old fashioned boho style clothes with brightly coloured beads hanging from her neck. Blimey, she looked as if she had stepped right out of the hippy sixties. The engine had been switched off, the handbrake applied and hazards flashing, which meant she had deliberately pulled over, out of the flow of traffic, before collapsing at the wheel. Well, that's thoughtful at least, especially just past the tunnels. What was wrong though? A heart attack? Stroke? At least she wasn't panting away about to give birth. Penny would have hated that; too many memories. She quickly checked the woman's pockets and bag to see if there was any evidence of a medical condition. Nothing. Neither was there that tell-tale whiff of alcohol you always get when someone has been drinking, or that sweet, pear-drop smell of uncontrolled diabetes. She did find a gym membership card together with sweaty kit and trainers, which might also explain the damp hair if she'd recently exercised and showered. Perhaps she was just knackered after a run?

"I really don't want to be doing this," Penny muttered under her breath. Soon she should hear the wail of a siren, then all she'd have to do was see to the car, fill in the usual reams of forms, get down to A&E… She clenched her jaw, taking in a deep breath, dreading the hours of work which lay ahead. She really, truly didn't want this. Just gone three, the rush hour traffic would be building up soon and here she was, stuck outside a notorious bottleneck on the edge of the Truffleton bypass, right on junction 11. Penny was supposed to have finished at two and was truly, really, genuinely getting to hate her job. Deliberately pushing away a tide of resentment, Penny only just managed to remind herself that it was hardly the woman's fault that this had happened an hour after she should have clocked off. Just get on with it Penny girl…

"Hello? Can you tell me your name love? Can you hear me? Hello?"

The woman's head slowly lifted as if she was reluctantly waking from nothing more significant than a quiet afternoon siesta. So far so good, yet when she turned her head towards Penny, her eyes were unseeing and filled with unfathomable nothingness. It was like looking into two pits of utter despair. At least she was conscious and reacting, but hell, she looked

6

haunted! Penny felt oddly and irritatingly spooked and glanced back at the dark tunnel. Nah. Don't be daft. No ghosts in there, only the dodgy lighting and the fast flow of traffic. Let's see if the lady talks.

"Hello there, I'm Penny. Try not to move. Can you tell me what's happened love? Are you hurt?" Try not to move? This lady hardly had the energy to open her eyes and look, never mind move.

"What's happened love?" Come on, talk, speak to me, let's get going, I want to get home. Come on, come on…

The woman licked her lips and finally spoke, slowly and in a whisper.

"Please help me … I can't take any more." (Neither can I, thought Penny.)

"What? Yes, I'll help you, but come on love, tell me what's wrong." Come on, come on, come on…

Then Penny instantly softened. This was somebody in a spot of bother and for the time being Penny was the only help the poor woman had. She felt guilty for the flood of resentment and irritation and instead switched into gentle mode as she continued to check things out.

At last a body appeared beside Penny. The green uniform of the paramedic was instantly reassuring, added to which it was Dave, and Dave was one of the nice guys. Especially reassuring was that Dave was one of the old school, knew exactly what he was doing, and would have this lady stretchered and on her way to Truffleton General in the blink of an eye. Penny gladly left him and his colleague to their work and got on with what needed to be done from her side of things. As she returned to the police vehicle she could hear Dave speaking to the woman.

"Hiya love! My name's Dave. I'm a paramedic and I'm going to check you over, okay? You're going to be fine, so relax. I'll take good care of you. Can you tell me your name love?"

"Hayley." It was barely more than a whisper. Wonderful, thought Penny, all the negative feelings flooding back, she wouldn't darn well give *me* her name. She felt oddly and intensely miffed by Dave's little success so far. Well, that just proved it. She wasn't cut out to be a damn copper any longer. She'd known that for a while now. Dave chatted on in his easy, reassuring manner.

"Okay then Hayley, that's brilliant. Are you in any pain?" At least she was talking. Always a good sign. Breathing was okay, no blood, no obvious injuries.

"No." Again barely a whisper.

"What's wrong then my lovely?"

"I've got a crazy brain. Can't take any more." Speech slightly slurred.

"Well, join the rest of planet Earth love – we've all got crazy brains, especially in my job. Some days I can't take any more either." Dave laughed out loud, hoping Hayley would do the same. He was usually good at getting a smile from his patients, if not a chuckle. No smile from this one though, so he continued to check her over. BP was raised slightly but pulse, breathing, level of consciousness, all okay.

"You been drinking at all my love?"

"No. Never drink alcohol." Again her speech seemed an effort and vaguely slurred.

"Okay Hayley, you tell me why you're stuck on the hard shoulder with a crazy brain then, okay?"

"Raped. My fault. Now I've got a crazy brain."

"Raped? Okay my love. Don't you worry, we'll sort it. You'll be fine with us." By then Dave's partner, Roger, had the stretcher next to the car and they were gently moving Hayley onto it. Crikey, she was light as a feather and pale as a ghost, immediately turning onto one side and adopting a foetal position. Poor kid.

Meanwhile, sitting in the driver's seat of the police car, Penny was scribbling away and, raising her head, managed to catch Dave's eye and indicate that she was ready to follow the ambulance to A&E. Control were sending out a couple of officers to move the woman's car off the side of the road and as soon as the ambulance pulled out, Penny would move off behind it.

At long last the ambulance doors closed but instead of giving her the thumbs up that they were moving off, Dave came hurrying towards the police car.

"You didn't tell us we had a rape victim. Did you know?"

Penny tilted her head to one side, "What? Oh God! No, she didn't tell me. I'm really not going to get home any time soon am I?" Penny was again unsuccessful in stemming her negative reactions.

"We'll see you in A&E then. We're off now."

Penny spoke briefly to police HQ to make certain a female police surgeon would be at the hospital as soon as possible, and then set off for a long wait in A&E. The weekend couldn't come quickly enough.

CHAPTER TWO

DR EMILY

Friday afternoon

DR EMILY CHATWITH, Consultant Psychiatrist, Psychotherapist, plus a million and one other things, was alone in her office, tapping one of her Van Dahl shoes against the leg of the desk behind which she sat, looking incredibly important but feeling decidedly ghastly. She was puzzling over whether to pick her little dog up from the vet before or after having something to eat. Clinic was finished but it was only 3.50, so she did have time for food first and Doodle should be okay for another hour. But then Doodle would be missing her dreadfully and so she perhaps ought to collect her as soon as possible. The poor love might be a little off colour after her jabs. But then, did it really matter what she did first? Well, it did matter to Doodle, and Dr Emily did need to eat. Maybe she would go to Tesco, then pick up the dog and eat later. Oh dear. Far too many decisions.

Elbow on desk and resting her chin in her hand, Dr Emily wondered at life being so downright complicated and awkward these past months. The day had been a strain, with only half her patients turning up – the other half probably far too unwell to see a doctor – and it had been a waste of time in many respects. Emily hadn't been able to catch up on case notes because her secretary was off sick and the computer was playing up again. The radiator in her office was leaking and cold, and she was wondering why she ever chose psychiatry in the first place. Had it all been worth it?

When, exactly, had Dr Emily become so disenchanted with her work? Thankfully, retirement loomed and couldn't come quickly enough. At least that was what she'd been telling herself. Was that why she was so crotchety, trying to convince herself she was bored of her profession? Gosh, it was awful, simply awful. She felt so useless all of a sudden, as if she was no longer making the difference she had set out to make during those heady medical student days (how many?) decades ago. Let's face it, she was becoming, these past few months, increasingly disillusioned, fed up, and missing any sense of challenge, probably due to the necessary wind down prior to retirement. She, of all people, knew the psychological processes at work, but that didn't help when they were your processes. Dr Emily also knew that nearly all the world was nuts, so how could she hope to continue to make any sort of a difference once she was no longer working? What, she wondered, would the world do without her? Probably carry on just the same? Well... shoot, fiddlesticks and, let's be honest, damn and blast it!

The Van Dahl tapped away as another ten minutes passed. Fingernails, expertly coated with OPI nail polish (purchased from the QVC shopping channel but don't tell anybody) drummed the desk top, keeping time with the foot. Unfortunately, in a bad mood, and let's face it she was in a shockingly bad mood, Dr Emily looked every one of her almost sixty years. The little grey bun at the nape of her neck, reeking of Elnette hairspray, didn't help; neither did the reading glasses hanging from a chain around her neck. Thank goodness the dress was a Windsmoor. She had her standards and at least dressed like the professional she was. But for how much longer? Six months post-retirement would probably find her clothed in polyester trousers and a tunic from Bon Marche. Perish the thought. At that point, she would surely need to be shot!

The phone rang.

"Dr Chatwith here. Hello."

"Dr Emily, it's Penny, Detective Inspector Whistle. Sorry if I'm interrupting a clinic or something but I've got another request from the police surgeon for you if that's okay. Fairly urgent. How are you anyway? Long time no speak." Penny sounded irritatingly chirpy and full of energy, beans and enthusiasm. That made a pleasant change at least. Last time she had spoken to Penny the woman had sounded very down. Perhaps the chirpiness was simply the woman's telephone manner for the day. Yes, that must be it. Or perhaps it was that Friday feeling before a weekend off? That probably explained it. Whatever, Dr Emily was in no mood for chirpiness nor beans.

"No, no, Penny, you're not interrupting anything, I'd tell you if you were. I am terribly busy though, so what's so urgent?" She instantly regretted sounding so abrupt and indulging in a teeny little fiblet. Busy, my foot! There were times when one's shadow side needed to show itself however, and today was indeed one of those shadowy days.

"Charming. Who knocked the sugar off your cake?" Penny laughed briefly. "Seriously Dr Emily, this is a lady in real difficulties and refusing the usual channels of help. We spent most of yesterday evening with her and have tried to question her gently again this morning. The police surgeon's getting nowhere fast and we would value your input." Emily had, for a long time, assisted with rape and sexual abuse cases. "You might find this interesting too. It's a bit of a mystery we're so far stuck with."

"Interesting? Bear in mind I've heard it all over the years, but tell me anyway."

"Right. You got five mins?"

"Yes, yes, fire away." For goodness sake woman, hurry up and get on with it, I'm retiring soon and I'll have all the time in the world. Right now I'm still working, I'm paid to be up to my eyes in the clinically depressed and I think I may be heading that way myself. I'm scared and I'm feeling useless. Emily suddenly squeezed her eyes tight shut, surprised at the sudden tears her brutally honest thoughts had produced. Then, blinking rapidly, she held the phone tight against her ear and listened. She was a professional after all.

"Okay," began Penny, "Name's Hayley Bishford, thirty-three years of age, lives in Truffleton with hubby and two kids. Picked up on the Truffleton bypass, westbound, just outside the Greenridge tunnels 3p.m. yesterday, slumped over the steering wheel. Spoke to the paramedics, eventually told them she had been raped and had a crazy brain. Hasn't spoken a darn word since. We don't know where or when the alleged incident took place but the assumption is that it happened the same day. Discharged from the General this morning. MRI, blah blah, all clear but has slight paralysis left side. She refused the gynae examination but police surgeon found trauma consistent with a recent significant struggle."

"What trauma? Why did she refuse the internal exam?"

"Fought like a tiger apparently, even with a female doc., couldn't get her to consent. Fits in with rape but not exactly helpful. Police surgeon's report records bruising to both legs, lower back, right iliac crest; severe redness and bruising to both wrists consistent with being restrained. Also marked tenderness at the back of the skull. On examination, scalp red, some oedema, obvious bump to the head. Seems she was on her way home from the gym at the Greenridge Hotel from what she told the paramedics before she stopped talking. Found

13

damp kit, trainers and a membership card in the car with her. Query trying to get rid of semen, DNA evidence by showering. She…"

"So it's extremely likely the alleged incident happened that same day. Okay. Is she talking now she's home? Has she written anything down?"

"It's possible. Pass. Don't know. Wrote a short statement refusing to file a complaint but obviously if a rape has taken place then the CPS will…"

"Yes, yes. Of course. Anything else?"

"'fraid so. She could be anorexic, weighs nothing and refuses to eat; self-harms, arms are covered with scars. I've spoken to hubby who's not massively helpful, but tells us she used to be into all this occult stuff, Ouija boards and witches, all that heebie jeebie rubbish. He says that's why she cuts herself. Also says Hayley hears voices in her head but there's no diagnosis of her being schizo, anything like that, and she's never seen a shrink. She and hubby seem very religious and the family goes to that weird church…"

"What weird church is that?"

"That one near the town centre, you know, The Sinners Chapel of Mercy, got a poster outside inviting you to their mercy seat for immediate cleansing, or whatever."

"Never heard of it. Do you have any other evidence apart from the bruising?"

This was sounding rather more complex than the usual cases that were referred to Dr Emily via the police. Was she up to an allegedly raped anorexic who had partial paralysis, heard voices, self-harmed, had some weird spiritual history and refused to speak? Yes. Of course she was. No doubt about it. Dr Emily knew instantly that she was desperately needed on this case and must put her considerable skills to good use as soon as possible. Well, well, how very satisfying. The day's shadows were beginning to scatter.

"No. No further evidence at this moment in time. I've seen Hayley briefly since she's been home, hubby adamant that he'll look after her, they were expecting the GP to call. As per routine we've sent her clothes and fingernail scrapes on to forensics but after she'd showered..." Penny paused. "There *was* something though..."

"What?"

"Well, while she won't or can't tell us when the alleged rape happened, it's obviously possible that the attack took place yesterday morning and even after showering there *was* a significant sample of skin among the fingernail scrapes. Hoping to get a DNA from that. Also, if we could get a description out of her, we now know the perp has a gouge of skin missing, possibly other scratches. Could help with ID. If you could coax any info out of her..."

"Yes, I see," mused Dr Emily. "Interesting."

"Yes," continued Penny, "we really want to know where she was yesterday morning but so far we're drawing a blank on that. We haven't been able to push it as she's in such a fragile state. Something has gone on here, Dr Em, but it's more of a shrink job than a cop job if we want to go any place with this. She did talk in the ambulance to the paramedic who took her to the General but he says it was mostly gobbledegook, garbled and slurred, couldn't make out what she was trying to say but she seemed pretty desperate and screwed up." Shouldn't have used that expression, thought Penny. "Will you see her?"

"You know perfectly well I won't say no, don't you?" It was a statement rather than a question, delivered with the usual abrupt tone but not without a little hint of affection. Dr Emily rather liked DI Penny even though they had only ever spoken by telephone. She seemed a good sort, yet had a way about her lately that seemed completely unsuited to life in the police force in Dr Emily's most humble opinion. Maybe she ought to arrange to meet DI Penny face to face one day, do a little analysing, pass on a little wisdom… "Give me Mrs Bishford's address and telephone number and I'll get in touch with her asap. She has given permission for me to contact her I take it?"

"Yes, yes. She did nod her head slightly when I mentioned you to her so I took that as a yes. Thanks Dr Em. You're a good 'un."

"Yes, I know. I am, aren't I?"

Blimey, thought Penny, she sure doesn't have a problem with self-esteem. Must be the training.

"I guess hubby will answer the phone and speak for his wife," Penny added as an afterthought. "Not sure how they cope with the no talking business, especially with two small kids. That's if she's still not talking."

"I'm sure I shall manage dear. I'm very experienced. I'll let you know how things go. Bear in mind, however, that I'm bound by rules of confidentiality unless Hayley gives me express permission to pass information on." Dr Emily was now sitting up straight, in full professional mode and enjoying every moment of it.

"Yes. I know that. Anything at all would be helpful so I'll leave it in your capable hands for now. I'm reluctant to re-interview her myself just yet as she's so distressed," said Penny. "This one's got to me a bit if I'm honest. Hayley is an intelligent woman, books all over the place when I visited, I liked her, and something has obviously gone on. I'd have liked to have got a lot further by now and it's frustrating when a case seems to be going nowhere, especially if there's some jerk out there who could attack again. I want to see this one through if I'm here long enough."

"You sound as if you might be moving on. Promotion?" Golly, she sure must be a high flier, and yet… there was something about Penny that didn't fit in with career woman cop.

"No, Dr Em, I might be leaving the police force altogether, I've been thinking it over for quite a while now. I've had a few interviews, so I'm just waiting for a yes from somewhere. It's a case of waiting and seeing what happens."

"Really? Will you still be under the police umbrella? In another capacity perhaps?"

"I'm hoping to eventually do something a little bit different, after some studying and training that is. Social work, the homeless, AA, that sort of thing."

"Isn't that part of what you're already doing?"

"Yes, yes, but I want to approach it from a different angle, without the authority my position as a police officer gives me. I want to be more hands on caring, rather than the tough stuff. I need a change."

"How intriguing!" The Van Dhal had ceased tapping and now circled the air slowly while Dr Emily gazed unseeing out of the office window. "Of course, I only know you as a police officer. Perhaps we ought to meet up some time and put faces to names? I'd be so interested to hear about your life and your plans. I really mean that."

"Yes, that sounds good." Not likely, thought Penny, she'd be analysing me. Then again, DI Penny knew she was probably fairly screwed up; maybe she could do with a bit of psychoanalytical input. There were enough people lately telling her she needed to get her head put back on straight. Were they right?

"We'll do that then, Penny dear. Now I must go, I have to see to my Doodle and get myself home. I need to eat and there's so much to do, but I will certainly be in touch again soon. Bye bye now. Yes, bye…"

"Bye…" See to her Doodle? What on earth? Nah, don't even think about it. Very likely true what they said about psychiatrists being more bonkers than their patients. Shaking her head, Penny ended the call, grabbed her coat off the back of her chair and headed homewards. She was starving and planned to cook pasta with mince, lots of mushrooms and onions, and a crusty roll from the Spar. There might be a letter from the Uni waiting for her too. She was looking forward to a quiet evening ahead and found that her conversation with Dr Emily had cheered her up, even if the doctor spoke a bit like an old fashioned school ma'am. Penny wondered if the psychiatrist looked how she sounded, and smiled at the thought.

The Van Dahl was still at last as Dr Emily sat quietly, thinking over her conversation with Penny. She'd be interested to visit Hayley and see what was going on, though that would certainly be a challenge if the woman refused to speak. She'd had some success over the years with elective mutism so her expertise would be invaluable, and that always made her feel good. Hayley certainly needed her. The whole family probably needed support.

She pondered over what might lead a police officer to give up a good career with good pay to go and do something which almost certainly paid less, both financially and in terms of career prospects. Very intriguing, and Dr Emily wanted to know. Not that she was a nosy busybody mind you. Of course she wasn't. She'd recently had an inkling that Penny was in the wrong job and it was just so awfully satisfying when one's hunches were proved correct. Yes. It was indeed.

And another thing, what sort of Church called itself the Sinners Chapel of Mercy for goodness sake? Immediate cleansing? The mind positively boggled! Did they have a bowl of hot, soapy water and a flannel by the door? She'd see if the place had a website. It sounded like Plymouth Brethren and Fundamentalism combined. How absolutely fascinating.

Shoot and darn well screw it! Dr Emily suddenly realised that forty minutes had passed since the phone had rung and she'd be caught up in rush hour traffic, although that hardly mattered now that she had something new to think over. She felt so much better. Her evening was mapped out and promised to be busy as well as interesting. She'd go home, then after eating she'd phone the Bishford household, then check up on the Sinners Chapel of Mercy where instant cleansing was on offer to the great unwashed, and then she'd try and arrange a cuppa and a chat with DI Penny. Not forgetting her little Doodle of course.

Within ten minutes, Dr Emily was settled into the driver's seat of her chunky Volvo. She put on a CD of Vivaldi, The Four Seasons, and began the journey home to Angel's Rest, her small cottage in Sweet Briar village. She really didn't feel like shopping for food on the way home now. Supermarkets were terribly, awfully boring. She'd collect Doodle, her Yorkie cross, from Jim at Vet's Corner, then make do with whatever was lurking in the fridge-freezer. She couldn't wait to make those phone calls, switch on the PC and ... golly, but *should* she go shopping? No, no. There was almost certainly something she could make a quick meal out of. There were two eggs left, that cheese she bought last week, and some salad. Or was there only one egg? Can't make much of an omelette with only one egg. Positive there were two ... she hadn't had one for breakfast because she'd needed Allbran for her bowels, so there must be two left, unless ...

The right Van Dahl, burgundy mock crock with a gold trim, depressed the accelerator and Dr Emily Chatwith was on her way home.

CHAPTER THREE

DAVE

Friday evening. 7.30

"YOU AWAKE, ROG?"

"No."

They were parked up outside McDonald's on Forest Road after refuelling in the nearby Tesco garage. Roger the Dodger was stretched out behind the steering wheel of the ambulance, arms crossed over his chest and with his eyes shut, having actually had time to enjoy a burger and a coffee without interruption. Dave, seated next to him, was carefully peeling stickers from their now empty cups.

"Five stickers Rog. Only need another one for a full card. My turn for the free coffee next time."

"Umm."

"You know what's been bugging me, Rog?"

"No. I don't know what's been bugging you and I don't care. Leave me alone. I've got a wife, three kids and two gerbils. I'm asleep." It wasn't often they got a break this long between calls and Roger the Dodger was making the most of it. At least he was trying to. Dave ignored him, as he nearly always did, and carried on talking while he carefully placed the stickers onto the Mc D's loyalty card.

"That woman we picked up by the Greenridge tunnels yesterday ..."

"The nut job."

"Yeh, the one who yakked non-stop all the way to A&E. You listening, Rog?"

"I haven't got much choice, have I?" Roger turned his head and looked briefly at his partner before facing the front again and closing his eyes.

"I keep, you know, remembering bits of what she was saying. It sounded like a load of gibberish at the time but some of it's coming back to me. Like, when she said she'd been raped I sort of assumed it had happened that morning. Well, you would, wouldn't you, considering where she was, the state she was in, the bruises and scratches …"

"Yeh. I remember her. Hippy clothes and beads. Off her rocker and smelt like shampoo."

"That's because she'd recently washed her hair, you ass bag. Anyway, I keep remembering her saying to me that she'd spent the morning with some people from her church. She said he was Pastor Pitchfork and his wife was a Vulture."

"Very funny," mumbled Roger, eyes still tight shut.

"Then she'd managed to escape from them. Then she went straight to that health and fitness place and had a run before she went nuts." Dave pocketed the loyalty card and stared straight ahead at the traffic on Forest Road, one hand rubbing the back of his neck as he spoke.

"And?" said Roger.

"Well, at first I must have let it go cos it sounded a load of rubbish, but that's definitely the word she used Rog. 'Escape.' Don't you think that's real odd? It's bugging me big time. I mean, why would she use the word 'escape'? If she really went to see her vicar why would she say she had to escape from him? D'you think…"

"I think she was just a nut job. I mean, who gets raped then goes straight out to the gym?"

"Cops reckoned that was to get rid of any evidence, in the showers, you know?" Dave rubbed his chin between the thumb and index finger of his left hand.

"Yeh, I know, but why not go home and take a bath? That's what these women usually do, isn't it? Did she tell the police where she'd been that morning?" Roger still hadn't opened his eyes.

"No. That's my point. She didn't. They spoke to me because they couldn't get a word out of her but I told them I couldn't make out anything she said. Thing is, we were busy at the time, had to get the ambulance cleaned out. You know how it is. I wasn't thinking. I'm wondering now if I should give them a ring and let them know I've remembered something. What d'you think?"

"Yeh. Good idea. You do that. Now shut up and let a man get a nap."

Before he had time to ponder any further, Dave punched the number of Truffleton police station into his mobile and waited. His call was answered surprisingly quickly – they must be having a quiet shift as well.

"Is DI Penny there by any chance?" he asked.

"Who's speaking, please?"

"It's Dave. Dave Wilson, paramedic. I might have some information on the Greenridge tunnel incident."

"Dave! It's Tony! How the devil are you? Penny's here somewhere, she just came in. Hang on and I'll try and put you through to her." Dave was left with a suddenly quiet phone; his right leg started jigging, and he hoped a call-out wouldn't come through within the next couple of minutes.

"Hiya Dave. Penny. What's up?"

"It might be nothing but I've remembered something the Greenridge tunnel woman said on the way to A&E yesterday. You know you said you couldn't discover where she spent yesterday morning?"

22

"Yeees…"

"D'you still want to know? Well yeh, of course you do. Only I remember now that she said she'd been with some people from her church – mentioned them as Pastor Pitchfork and his wife the Vulture."

"You having me on, Dave?"

"Actually, no. Dead serious Penny. And you know, the odd thing was that she was adamant she escaped from them. That's the word she used. Escaped. Kept saying it. I just keep thinking that's a bit odd. Might not be anything but I thought I maybe ought to tell you, just in case."

"Okay Dave, thanks. I'll bear it in mind, although daylight rape by Pastor Pitchfork, aided by a vulture and followed by a great escape to the gym does sound a little far-fetched. I will keep it in mind though. Thanks anyway."

"Okay love. Have a good night."

"You too. Bye now." Penny shook her head slowly but picked up a pen and jotted down, 'H Bishford. Query with Pastor from church prior to incident. Escaped.' She circled the word 'escaped' several times. That church again. The Sinners Chapel of Mercy. She had the sudden desire to pay this Pastor a visit. Yes, she *would* pay him a visit. Ask a few questions. Make a few observations. Take a few notes. Could be interesting.

Dave ended the call, satisfied that he'd passed on the information. Whether or not it was significant was no longer his responsibility and with a bit of luck his mind would now stop churning it over.

"Rog?"

"Hello."

"They're going to bear it in mind. Thanked me for ringing in." Dave started to tidy the cab, screwing up the burger wrappers and shoving them into the stacked coffee cups. He was about to open the door prior to dumping their rubbish in a nearby bin when something caught his eye.

"Rog?"

"Hello." Jeez, Mary and Joseph! Wouldn't this guy leave him alone?

"Quick! There's another one. On the floor by the grass. Over by that red Focus."

"You sure?" Roger the Dodger was instantly awake, sat up and alert, staring through the windscreen. "Where?"

"There, look! See the red car? By the kerb in front of the grass. Your turn, mate. Quick, nobody's looking."

Roger the Dodger slunk out of the driver's door, took a few steps and, after looking both ways to make sure he was unobserved, quickly hunkered down and peeled the sticker off the discarded coffee cup before climbing back into the cab. He was holding his breath in the excitement of the moment: the little transparent sticker bearing the sign of a coffee bean was in pristine condition. What a find!

"Got it!" he exclaimed triumphantly, proudly holding on to the precious little square while Dave reached into his pocket for the current loyalty card. Life could be surprisingly good at times. Even on a late shift when you were knackered.

Then the radio jumped to life and it was time to get those lights flashing and dodge some traffic. They tore out of McDonald's carpark.

"Rog?"

"What."

"You forgot to put that cup in the bin."

Holding onto the steering wheel with one hand, Roger used his other hand to grab a previously blown up latex glove that looked like a cow's udder, throwing it across the cab at Dave.

It missed. They both laughed out loud. They needed to.

Dave and Roger were on their way to a toddler who had stopped breathing.

CHAPTER FOUR

ANGEL'S REST

Friday evening 7.55

DR EMILY had hurriedly made and devoured a cheese and pickle sandwich and knew that unless she then spent a few minutes making a fuss of her Doodle it would be impossible to make those phone calls. Poor Doodle hadn't stopped yipping since they arrived home. It was almost as if Dr Emily was getting a right good telling off for leaving her with the Vet all day. As indeed she was, for Doodle was most certainly a crossed Yorkshire that evening. It did not bode well for the evening ahead if one's Doodle was not in a good mood.

"Poor, darling poochikins… come to Mummy my gorgeous little Doodle… who's been a lovely, brave girl then…" Sensing that undivided fuss and attention was at last available, the contrary little mutt turned her back on Dr Emily, crawled into her basket, curled up and went straight to sleep. Poor love. She must be exhausted after such a trying day. Damn dog!

Dr Emily then quickly settled herself into her favourite chair, pulled her phone out of her enormous handbag and, checking her diary, punched in a number. Her other hand held a pen, ready to write down whatever might need to be written down. Now where on earth was her notepad…

"Hello?" An adult male voice had answered. Good. She appreciated a little male energy.

"Oh, hello. Is that Mr Michael Bishford?"

"Yes."

"Hello Mr Bishford, my name is Dr Emily Chatwith and I've been asked..."

"I know," interrupted the voice on the other end, "you're the shrink that's been asked to see my wife. They said you'd be ringing." He sounded pleasant enough but Dr Emily felt that instant ruffling of her feathers which happened every time she was referred to as a shrink. She was a highly trained professional, not a *shrink*. Swallowing her annoyance and sniffing through her nose, she spoke again.

"Mr Bishford, I'm a consultant psychiatrist and psychotherapist and, as you know, I've been asked to see your wife following the recent incident with the car. I know a little about her from the police surgeon. How is she now if I may ask?"

"They kept her in hospital overnight and she came home this morning. Still hasn't spoken and is very depressed. Won't eat, hardly moves, still hearing voices in her head, but at least she will write things down at times. I don't want her going into any mental hospital, I'm adamant about that, she's absolutely not going into any hospital, so don't..." The man was talking so quickly and loudly all of a sudden. Was he getting defensive? Was he antagonistic towards her? Or maybe simply nervous and upset. She quickly settled on nervous and upset and went with the softly, softly approach. Calm him down before he got even louder.

"I prefer people to stay out of hospital too, Mr Bishford, believe me, so as long as there is support at home your wife will probably be better off in familiar surroundings. She'll feel safer. I understand you were able to have time off work. I hope that wasn't difficult for you to arrange at such short notice."

"No, it wasn't. I've booked some annual leave so I will be home for at least the next two weeks."

"That's good. I'd really like to come and see Hayley as soon as possible if she's agreeable, especially as she's refused any other medical or psychiatric help. Would it be possible for me to call at your home this coming Monday morning do you think?"

"Monday morning? Hang on... Hayley's nodding. Yes, that'll be fine. I have to get the kids to school but I'll be back at about twenty past nine latest."

"Shall I come at 10 o'clock then?"

"Yes. 10 o'clock would be good."

"Splendid. I'll see you both on Monday morn..."

"Dr Chatwith? I have to tell you now that Hayley and I have been told that no psychiatrist will be able to help her, that they wouldn't understand what was wrong. I'm not sure she's going to trust you, but I don't know any more. Hayley has been getting worse and worse and, to be honest, I'm getting desperate. We're both getting desperate. I don't know what to do any more, we don't know who to listen to or who..."

"Mr Bishford. May I call you Michael?"

"Mike."

"Mike it is then. Thank you. Now listen Mike, I don't know who has told you a psychiatrist can't help your wife, but if she's hearing voices, depressed, can't eat or speak, then she needs urgent psychiatric assessment. This is where I *can* help. I'll be with you both after the weekend, we'll talk, I'll assess Hayley's condition and work out a care plan. How does that sound? We'll take things nice and slowly."

"Okay. I'm just at my wits end. I don't know what to do any more, he keeps saying..."

"Who keeps saying?" The poor man sounded really upset.

"The Pastor from church. He's been helping Hayley for a long time now but, you know, we just don't trust him anymore. He doesn't want her seeing anybody else, says he's the only one who can help her, and I don't know who to ask. What am I supposed to do? She's getting worse, my wife is getting worse... the GP came and prescribed antidepressants..." Mike sounded almost in tears.

"It's going to be okay Mike. What you're going to do is get through the weekend. Stay together as a family and try to keep things as normal as possible. Talk to Hayley as much as you can. I'll be with you on Monday and we'll take things from there. Try and keep everything calm and quiet. You'll have my mobile number from this call, so don't hesitate to call me over the weekend if you feel you need to. I mean that now."

"Okay Dr, thanks."

"Who is your Pastor by the way?"

"Anthony Pratt. The Sinners Chapel of Mercy."

"Ah yes. I have heard of it. I'll see you on Monday morning then Mike."

"Okay, thanks. Cheerio then."

"Bye bye, Mike. Bye bye."

Dr Emily ended the call and hung on to her mobile, gently tapping it on the arm of the chair while she furrowed her brow, deep in thought. She looked at the few words she had jotted down during the call. It was easy to conclude that the incident yesterday when Hayley was picked up on the Truffleton bypass was only the tip of an iceberg. She seemed to have been suffering some degree of mental ill health for quite a while so maybe it all came to a head with a psychotic episode as she was making her way home. But what pushed her over the edge? Why the bruising and bang on the head? Both of which pointed to a sustained and aggressive struggle. Rape could certainly account for both of the above. If only the woman would start talking.

Staring at the few words on her notepad, Dr Emily circled 'The Sinners Chapel of Mercy'. Something about the place wasn't sitting right with her even though she'd never been there. Doodle stirred in her basket, sighed deeply, and settled back into doggy dreamland. The hypnotic *tic tic* of a grandmother clock was soothing in the quietness and rather conducive to deep thought. *Tic tic* became more of a muffled *thuck thuck* as Emily's eyelids became heavy. Minutes passed in drowsy contemplation until, suddenly…

Dr Emily nearly jumped out of her skin as Bach's Ode to Joy leapt into full throttle. Grabbing her mobile she pressed the answer key.

"Yes? Hello?"

"Dr Emily, it's Penny again. I'm glad I've got you, you've been engaged for ages." Goodness, Penny sounded almost out of breath.

"Busy evening Penny dear, busy evening. I was actually speaking to Mr Bishford. I've arranged to see Hayley on Monday morning which fits in rather well for me as I don't have a clinic and I did want to visit as soon as possible. She's home from hospital but obviously needs psychiatric help as a matter of urgency. Whatever caused her to pull over on the Truffleton bypass yesterday was only the tip of an iceberg, only the tip, as she has been suffering mental health issues for some time… Anyway, what can I do for you?"

"You've already answered my question. I was going to ask if you'd had a chance to arrange an appointment with Hayley, and I see that you have so that's good, I'm glad, she clearly needs some sort of help."

"Yes, yes. You're quite right. I'm definitely needed on this one." Who was Dr Emily trying to convince? Penny? Or herself? She shook lonely thoughts from her mind as Penny continued.

"I'm also ringing with some information you might well find useful in view of the fact you'll be seeing her soon." Penny took a deep breath. "I had a call from one of the paramedics who picked Hayley up yesterday. Chap called Dave. Seems he's remembered something Hayley said in the ambulance before she stopped talking completely. Sounds very odd, almost made up, but we've decided to act on it anyway."

"What did she say?" Emily sat up straighter in her chair and even Doodle pricked her ears as if she, too, was listening.

"She said that she'd spent yesterday morning with people from her church. Now that's not terrifically odd in itself, but tied in with what the hubby says about the Pastor trying to help Hayley, Hayley getting worse, refusing any medical help... you begin to wonder what sort of help he was giving her. If Hayley *was* with these people, then what the hell happened to freak her out? She referred to him in the ambulance as Pastor Pitchfork and apparently his wife is The Vulture."

"What?" Dr Emily and Penny laughed out loud, which was a welcome relief among all the more serious details. "Doesn't sound as if Hayley likes them too well, does it?" Again the pair laughed. "They sound a little hellish to me." More polite laughter.

"Anyway," continued Penny, "I'm going to pay this Pastor Pitchfork a visit tomorrow morning and have a little chat with our man of the cloth. It'll be overtime but I don't mind. I really want to sort this one."

"I don't blame you, it's certainly intriguing. Where does hubby say his wife was yesterday morning?" The plot seemed to be thickening.

"He's not a hundred per cent certain Dr Em. Says it was arranged for Hayley to go to this Pastor's house, she was due there straight from dropping the kids off at school but she was adamant she wouldn't go. She didn't want to. Hubby assumed she *did* turn up however, as the Pastor would have rung him otherwise to see where she was, and she certainly didn't go straight home. Hubby says he's had no contact with the Pastor whatsoever since Wednesday and Hayley won't even write down whether she was with him or not. Any mention of his name freaks her out and she becomes even more unresponsive.

30

"I'd love to know what sort of help this Pastor Pitchfork was giving her," said Dr Emily.

"Yes, so would we," Penny continued. "Something does not feel right about all this. She was due to see this guy. As far as we know she *did* turn up as arranged. She's found with bruises. Claims she's been raped. This is not sounding good for our preacher man so far."

"You don't think the Pastor..." Emily didn't want to put her thoughts into words.

"That's what we need to find out. If Hayley *was* with this guy, then what the hell happened? Something did."

"Do let me know how the interview with this chap goes tomorrow, will you Penny dear? It'll help me to know what he's been up to before I see Hayley." Besides which, Dr Emily, to her utter delight, was now intimately involved. They needed her expertise and input, so she wanted to be in on everything that was happening. Every little detail. She wasn't nosy, surely not, she just wanted to help Hayley. She needed to know. She simply loved a mystery!

"I will Dr Emily. Have a good night and I'll speak to you again soon."

"Yes, Penny dear, we'll speak again soon. Bye now."

"Bye."

Well, well. Dr Emily wasn't the only one feeling a sense of unease where Hayley's Pastor was concerned. Time to check up on Pastor Pitchfork, she thought.

Going over to the small dining table where her laptop was kept, Dr Emily switched it on and went into the kitchen to make a cup of coffee while it booted up. Doodle, refreshed after her forty winks, trotted in after her and waited patiently next to her empty food bowl. Opening a tin of Caesar, Dr Emily scooped it into the doggy dish while she waited for the kettle to boil. Then, carrying her coffee in one hand and two

31

ginger nut biscuits in the other, she made her way back into the lounge and sat down in front of her laptop.

Google was up and running, waiting for her to type in a request, which she promptly did. In less than four seconds she had thousands of answers but it was easy to find the one she required.

'The Sinners Chapel of Mercy' didn't have a particularly good website in that it didn't give a lot of information other than times of services. There was a grainy picture showing an old church building sandwiched between two terraced houses and opening directly onto the pavement. A large, black board on the wall to the right of a wooden door, next to a frosted glass window, gave information to anyone passing by in bold white lettering.

A big welcome to the lost.
Repent in pleasant surroundings,
Full support during conviction,
Tea served afterwards in the lounge of salvation.
Pastor – the Reverend A Pious Pratt
Come to the mercy seat for instant cleansing, Sundays at 10.30 a.m. and 6.00 p.m.

Goodness! It certainly seemed as if salvation was expected once one had set foot in this place. Dr Emily wondered, could you only get clean on a Sunday? What if one didn't achieve salvation? Did they whip out hot soapy flannels and literally scrub you? As she chuckled softly to herself the ginger nut biscuit she had over-dunked finally disintegrated and sank to the bottom of her mug of coffee. Scrolling down the page she made a mental note of the Chapel's address – Conversion Close, Truffleton – then picked up a teaspoon, carefully retrieved the soggy biscuit and slurped it into her mouth. She scooped out the remaining gloop of soggy biscuit and ate that too. What happened next was a lightbulb moment.

In fact it was more than a lightbulb moment; it was a blinding zing of lightening, promising to illuminate the whole weekend *and* the forthcoming visit to Hayley Bishford. Well, perhaps that was being just a little dramatic, a little over optimistic, but Dr Emily did believe she had come up with a spiffingly good idea.

"Doodle?" The little dog immediately pricked her ears and lifted her head on hearing her name, looking up expectantly at her owner. "I'm going to the morning service at the Sinners Chapel of Mercy this weekend. What do you think about that?" Doodle didn't think much of it at all, closed her eyes, and settled back down in her cosy basket, frankly disappointed. Dr Emily, however, was glad to at least have some sort of weekend to look forward to. Tomorrow she would do the usual weekly shop, take Doodle out, and then there was the call from Penny to look forward to. Sunday would be interesting at the Chapel of Mercy. Monday was her visit to the Bishfords. Yes, it was all going to be just fine.

Having finished her coffee, Dr Emily then moved over to her armchair, sat down heavily and suddenly burst into tears, which quickly descended into loud, shuddering sobs. Instantly alert, Doodle leapt from her basket and hurled herself onto her owner's lap, sensitively quiet, knowing what comfort was needed. A hand stroked the little animal and gradually, as always, the initial overwhelming storm subsided. Dr Emily fished a tissue out of her pocket and blew her nose surprisingly loudly. "Dear dear. Here I go again."

It had been seven long years since Mr Henry Chatwith, orthopaedic surgeon, had died suddenly of a heart attack. When would she start to feel better? When would the terrible, dreadful loneliness ease? She thought she would feel better after moving out of the big house and into the adjoining cottage. Less room to rattle around in on her own. Oh, she was glad she had made the move, no doubt about that. Her daughter and partner loved the big, old house and the three of them were very satisfied with the arrangement, getting together frequently and enjoyably. But once Dr Emily entered her cottage and shut the door that was it, as if she were totally alone in the entire world. She missed her soul mate, that sharing of yourself that only happens within the confines of the most blessed relationships. Alone, she felt cut off for ever from the only person who had ever understood her. Henry's death had been a tortuous severing, hardly eased by the passing of years. A physical ache, a psychic keening.

"Oh Doodle. What would I do without you?" The tears started again and she let them come.

Within half an hour Dr Emily and the little dog slept peacefully together. The grandmother clock ticked on. It began to rain, and the sounds of raindrops against window panes somehow acknowledged the loneliness and desolation of bereavement. Dreams came and went...

CHAPTER FIVE

THE MANSE

Saturday morning

THE TWO POLICE OFFICERS rang the doorbell and waited. So much for a weekend off, thought Penny.

A woman they assumed to be the Vulture answered the door with not a flicker of a smile and Penny could see immediately why Hayley had referred to her as such. Veronica Pratt was possibly only in her fifties but her slender, stooped body unkindly piled on the years, added to which she had a slightly hooked nose, unruly dull, brown hair and a sallow complexion. She wore a tartan skirt with a dark red jumper, over which was a full length old fashioned apron. Her feet were adorned with a pair of pink slippers. She appeared immensely displeased at the disruption to Saturday morning at the manse. As indeed she most certainly was.

"Yes?"

"Are you Mrs Pratt?"

"Yes."

"Hello Mrs Pratt. I'm Detective Inspector Penelope Whistle and this is my colleague Ian Gettum. Is your husband at home?"

"He is."

"We'd like a word with him please. Can we come in?"

"I really don't know." Was the woman serious? And why wasn't she asking why they wanted to speak to her husband?

"What do you mean, you don't know? Is he ill?"

"No, but he is incredibly busy and doesn't like to be disturbed on a Saturday morning. He's in his study writing a homily for the Lord's Day, tomorrow."

"Look," interrupted Ian, "we're here to ask him a few questions and we'd like to come in and do just that. It would be so much easier if your husband would speak to us this morning and I strongly suggest you let him know we're here waiting for him."

Ian was working himself up. Preparing to do the 'bad cop' bit, following on from Penny's 'good cop' introduction. He was tired, fed up, and not in the mood for this sort of crapping about.

"I'll ask him if he's prepared to see you then." The Vulture went to close the door but Ian's foot beat her to it.

"Mrs Pratt, let's put it another way, either we come in now and speak to your husband, or we take him in to the police station for questioning. I know which I'd prefer for starters. Now. May we come in?"

The Vulture scowled before reluctantly showing them in to a dingy lounge overfilled with chairs and small coffee tables. It smelt of stale food and dust.

"Sit down," she pronounced. Blimey, thought Ian. Who rattled her cage this morning? Should have left her in it!

Waving them over to a settee close to the fireplace, the woman quickly left the room and was heard running up the stairs. Penny guessed that must be where the Pastor's study was. Already surprised at the appearance and manner of Mrs Pratt (she was hardly the typical warm, friendly clerical wife), the two officers were further surprised by the sight of her husband when he eventually strode into the lounge. Yet what were they expecting – a pleasant little man in a dog collar? Well, yes, they probably were. At least that's what Ian may have been hoping for. Penny, on the other hand …

Pastor Pratt was an imposing figure, there was no doubt about that. He must have stood a little over six feet, big built, overweight, heavy and stout. Solid. Smartly dressed, he wore a dark grey pinstripe suit with a white shirt and striped grey tie. There was a pristine white handkerchief peeping out of his top jacket pocket. Most striking of all was his hair and beard. Iron grey hair, coarse as a brillo pad, was a stark contrast to his eyebrows and beard which were jet black. Add to that the fact that his beard only covered the lower part of his jaw – there was no upper lip hair – and he appeared sort of Amish from the neck up. His shoes were highly polished, as was his forehead, and he was the most miserable, dour looking man Penny had ever come across. So much for the joy of salvation! She couldn't help feeling that it was the likes of Pastor Pratt who gave Christianity a bad name, even before they had uttered one word.

The two police officers had stood up as the Pastor entered the room but he quickly motioned for them to sit down. The Vulture hovered behind her husband clearly uncomfortable and unsure of what to do. Penny, not wanting to give any measure of control to the Pastor, remained standing and offered her hand, which was refused. This was not going to be easy.

"My name is Detective…"

"My wife has informed me of your respective identities. What can I do for you, officer?" His voice was deep and controlled and Penny noticed he addressed Ian rather than herself. Boy, was that going to annoy her!

"Please," said Ian, "let's all sit down." So they did. Ian and Penny sat side by side on one settee, Pastor and Mrs Pratt sat opposite them on another settee. There was a coffee table between them.

"Would you confirm your name for me please sir?" Penny wanted to get on with this. This guy was annoying her and giving her the creeps, and so was his missus.

"My name is the Reverend Pastor Anthony Pious Pratt." This was addressed to Ian, not to Penny who had asked the question, but before she could jump in, Ian responded in a flash.

"Mr Pratt, please direct your answer to my superior officer." Penny smiled inwardly. Good one, Ian!

"The Lord placed man above woman," the Pastor shot back without a second's hesitation.

"Not in my police station He didn't sir, so please have the courtesy to reply to my senior officer when she asks you a question." Jeez, they hadn't expected this. What was up with this guy? Was this for real?

"Nevertheless…" Pastor Pratt retorted, but this time it was Penny who interrupted him.

"*Mister* Pratt, the apostle Paul wrote that in Christ there is neither male nor female. Galatians three, verse twenty eight. That kind of speaks to me of the equality of the sexes." Penny stared at Pastor Pratt and thoroughly enjoyed the startled look on his face as she quoted from one of the Pauline epistles. Take that mate!

"Where were you last Thursday morning Mr Pratt?" Penny continued, not taking her eyes from his and at the same time giving him one of her sweet smiles that was not really a smile. She was starting to love this.

"It's Pastor, and I was at my Chapel."

"The Sinners Chapel of Mercy, Conversion Close?"

"That's correct."

"Why were you there on that particular morning?" At last he was properly acknowledging her. The creep!

"I pastor the Chapel. I often go there."

"Even on a weekday morning?"

"Yes."

"Was anyone else with you on the morning in question?"

Penny came from a different angle. This was going to be like getting blood out of a stone.

"Yes."

"And who was that?"

"My wife."

"Is that correct Mrs Pratt?" Penny addressed the woman who was sitting on the edge of the settee, hands primly clasped together, a look of pure indignation on her face.

"Yes," she replied.

"Was anyone else there?" Penny again spoke to the Pastor, who paused for so long that she was about to repeat herself just as he spoke.

"Hayley Bishford. She's one of my sinners." Penny shot Ian a glance which conveyed a bucketful of unease and suspicion. Ignoring a rising tide of anger and incredulity she continued.

"Anyone else?"

"No."

"What time was this?"

"My wife and I arrived at the Chapel at approximately 9.30. Hayley arrived late at 9.35."

"Why was Hayley Bishford meeting you at the Chapel?"

"I felt directed to try a different venue."

"A different venue for what?"

"I've been assisting Hayley for some time now and thought she might be more co-operative and amenable in the Chapel building."

"So where did you usually see her?"

"I usually allowed her to come to the manse."

"You *allowed her* to come to the manse." This statement from Ian.

"I did, yes. I very rarely allow members of the church or congregation to enter my home. Apart from the selected elders, that is. I avoid any favouritism that way."

"How have you been helping Hayley Bishford?" Penny seriously didn't like this guy. She didn't trust him as far as she could throw him, which would be no distance at all.

"Hayley has a number of problems. I pray with her and counsel her under the Lord's direction. He tells me how to proceed." Yeh, I bet He does, thought Penny. She nodded at Ian, knowing he was itching to get in on this, thus giving him the go ahead.

"Sir," Ian leaned forward, "how long were you at the Chapel last Thursday morning?"

"About an hour and a half. It was a very quick session."

"Was your wife with you all that time?" Ian noticed that the Pastor glanced quickly at Veronica Pratt, obviously reluctant to answer the question. At last...

"My wife was unwell and so left at just after ten o'clock."

"Is that correct Mrs Pratt?"

"My husband has already told you."

"But I'm asking you, Mrs Pratt. Is that correct?"

"Yes. It is."

Ian turned his attention back to the Pastor.

"So you were alone with Hayley Bishford for about an hour?"

"No."

"No?"

"Hayley became very upset and left suddenly, against my express wishes, at about quarter to eleven."

"Okay," Ian sighed deeply and noisily, "so you were alone with her for approximately forty-five minutes."

"Correct."

"Why was she upset?" This was from Penny now.

"She had been ambivalent towards my help. She became increasingly – um – distressed. Things were very difficult." I bet they were, thought Penny. She seriously did not like this guy. What a pompous, arrogant, obstructive... the guy was a prick.

"Have you had any contact with her since Thursday morning?"

"No."

"Weren't you worried that she'd left suddenly and in a distressed state? Did you not try and find out how she was?"

"That was not my responsibility," replied the Pastor, his voice as cold as ice. Penny, sensing that Ian was about to go in for the kill, held out a hand to stop him. She, too, wanted to take this guy in immediately but knew that they had too little to go on while Hayley wasn't talking and hadn't actually named him as her attacker. She hoped forensics would come up with something they could pin on this creep but it was probably far too soon to be hoping for any definite results. She felt frustrated, but timing was everything in cases like this. Penny continued the questioning.

"How long have you been helping Hayley Bishford?"

"It's been over two years. She's what we would call a hard case."

"Two years? Has she shown any improvement?"

"No. I must point out that that's not my responsibility but the Lord's."

"How convenient. Okay, with regard to last Thursday, were you aware that Hayley Bishford was picked up on the Truffleton bypass and transferred to the General in a distressed state?"

"No. I was not."

"You don't appear to be surprised or concerned."

"As I've already pointed out, that is not my area of responsibility."

"Thank you Mr Pratt. That's all for now." Penny rose to leave and Ian stood up after her. Mrs Pratt remained seated, head bowed, showing no indication of moving. "We'll be in touch again in the very near future."

"There is no need, I assure you," said the Pastor.

"As I said, we'll be in touch again soon." Penny gave him one of her 'don't mess with me' looks. He gave her the Goosebumps big time and she would have loved nothing better than to drag him off to the station stat.

The Pastor led them from the lounge and into the hallway. As he opened the front door Penny noticed a hair on the back of his suit jacket, up towards the collar. Without pausing for thought she very swiftly and gently nipped it off between her thumb and index finger, grateful that the Pastor didn't notice. He held the door open for them and closed it as soon as they had both stepped outside.

"Goodbye to you too!" Ian commented, looking back at the hastily closed door. "That assbag, excuse the expression, is as guilty as sin. I'll get straight on to forensics, see if I can hurry things along. I'm gonna get this one, Penny."

"Yeh, me too, Ian. And guess what? I might just have got us our first piece of concrete evidence."

"Eh? Like what?"

Holding the hair up for inspection, "See this? Just nabbed it off the back of the Pastor's jacket as he was showing us out. About the length of Hayley Bishford's hair, would you say? And auburn? Not that many genuine auburn heads around, you know." The two officers smiled at each other. "How the hell would he have got that on his jacket collar? That sure as eggs points to some rather close physical contact, wouldn't you say?"

"My thoughts exactly. You know Penny? I just happen to have one of those little plastic evidence bags in the glove compartment." Ian retrieved the aforementioned bag and Penny carefully placed the hair inside. "We'll get this confirmed as belonging to Hayley," Ian continued. "Every little helps, as Tesco says. I take it you noticed the scratches on the side of his neck?"

"I certainly did, Detective Sergeant. He also had a plaster on the back of his left hand."

"We sure make a good team, Detective Inspector. Where next?"

"A little office work I think, Detective Sergeant."

Ian started the car and off they went, rather satisfied with the morning's work so far.

"Ian?"

"Yeh?"

"That was extremely odd as well. That guy didn't even ask us why he was being questioned, and showed no concern whatsoever for Hayley. He was colder than ice. Could that be because he's guilty as hell? What d'you think?"

"I guess so. If you know you've done the crime then you maybe forget to act surprised when the cops come calling. Take my word for it boss, that jerk's guilty as hell."

"Exactly. I'm with you there. Weekend or not, I want you to find out as much as you can about our Pastor and his Chapel. What's the set up? Baptist, Methodist, whatever… Where did he train? Is he ordained? What qualifications? Try and get names of the congregation as well. Fancy grabbing a coffee on the way back? I don't fancy instant."

"Mc D's?"

"You bet. My turn for the stickers."

CHAPTER SIX

HAYLEY

Saturday morning

HAYLEY HAD DREAMED the same dream all over again, in glorious Technicolor and full volume surround sound. She dreamed it when she was awake. She dreamed it when she was asleep. It was always the same.

She would be on the floor. He had forced her there, banging her head so hard as he wrestled with her that she actually saw little white bits floating about in her vision. He rammed into her, so hard, as she stared at a damp patch on the ceiling. She never forgot that damp patch. She knew she would see it forever. His weight was too much. Overwhelming. She opened her mouth to scream...

...her screams were terrible. Blood curdling. Pastor Pitchfork grabbed her wrists, hurting her as he tried to hold her still on the floor, but she struggled and managed to get one hand free; tried to hit him across the head but caught her nail on the side of his neck; drew blood and screamed all over again. He was so heavy on top of her but she made another almighty effort, scratching at him like some alley cat, and somehow slipped from under his large frame where he pinned her to the ground.

She gasped, seeing a chance while she had the element of surprise and knowing he was already out of breath. She got up and ran, praying that the door to the Chapel hadn't been locked. Please don't let it be locked. Please, please don't let it be locked...

It wasn't! The Vulture must have forgotten to do that when she left in a hurry earlier on. If she could just get outside, he wouldn't dare do anything in the street, in public. Not that there was likely to be anyone around in the small cul-de-sac. Her car was parked close... if only she could get in it and lock the doors... she was running, running, running. The dream went on and on. Running, running, running... the terror was unbearable, driving her, pushing her. Always running to escape from him. She had to escape to stop it happening, it must never happen again. Never!

Hayley woke, frightened, gasping for breath, sweating, and with those screams still ringing in her ears. Sitting up quickly she took several deep, calming breaths. Overwhelmed with relief at finding herself alone in her pretty bedroom, she put her face in her hands and cried silently for a few minutes while she composed herself and settled into the reality of Saturday morning. Mike was up with the kids, the house was warm and safe. She could hear the welcome sounds of early morning family life, "Come and get it! Breakfast's done!" The cat had already been fed and was curled up on the end of the bed, fast asleep and oblivious to the cruel dreams.

Suddenly, a little face appeared at the door and squealed with pleasure.

"Mummy's awake!"

Mikey and Daisy came running in, each holding a slice of buttered toast. Jumping on the bed and clamouring for a hug, Mikey was the first to ask, "You still got a bad throat Mummy?"

Hayley nodded, not saying a word, managing to smile and gather her children into her arms. A slice of thickly buttered toast stuck itself to the front of her nightdress but she didn't care. She was home with Mike and the kids and at that very minute that was all that mattered.

CHAPTER SEVEN

PENNY

Saturday lunchtime

THEY HAD DRIVEN PAST Tesco, Ian had turned the corner by the Tesco garage, negotiated the drive through, and now the two officers were parked up overlooking Forest Road. Penny had already retrieved the loyalty stickers from their cardboard coffee cups. First things first after all.

"That really, really gets my goat."

"What's that, Pen?" Ian was shaking a second sugar into the delicious smelling brew. They made a decent cuppa did McDonald's.

"Well, look there, right by the kerb. A coffee cup. Sheer laziness! There's a bin not two foot away... how idiotically bone idle can anyone be for goodness sake? Sheer thoughtlessness. I'm surprised these people have the energy to get out of bed and get here, so of course it's too much trouble to put a stupid cup in a stupid bin. Sheer, bone idle, petty thoughtlessness!"

Ian laughed. Loudly.

"So what the hec are you laughing at?" Penny demanded. "What's so blasted funny?" They turned to look at each other.

"You wouldn't complain if the darn cup had a sticker on it, would you? You'd be thanking whoever left it there for you and ordering me out of the car to go and get it."

"That would be different," responded Penny quietly, pouting.

They both smiled and a companionable silence reigned while they took the first few sips of their drinks. It had been quite a morning and a bit of silliness was not out of order. Penny was the first to break the silence.

"Ian, before we get back and dive into the paperwork, I'm going to see if I can get hold of Dr Emily. I said I'd ring her after we'd seen the Pratts. She's going to see Hayley on Monday and I want her to try and get as much useful information out of her as possible. If only we can get Hayley to name the jerk...

"He sure was a jerk of the highest order. How the hell does a guy like that end up running a church with people in it?"

"God knows. Literally. It does make you wonder though, doesn't it? I'd like to know the size of his congregation and what sort of people they are. His name suits him, that's for sure. I'd like to know what his qualifications are as well, apart from a degree in hypocrisy and unpleasantness. Anyway, let's get our Dr Em on the blower."

"Okay Pen. Mind if I nip in and get a cheeseburger while you're doing that? Didn't think I was hungry, but it is lunchtime."

"No probs. You go ahead."

"You want anything boss?"

"No. I'm fine with my coffee. Thanks anyway."

Penny punched Dr Emily's number into her mobile while she watched Ian striding over to the restaurant door. He'd been her partner for all of three months and it had been a good working relationship so far. He was tall and slim built, not bad looking, intelligent, she knew he had a cat, and at forty-six was only two years her junior. She'd discovered that he was surprisingly good company and didn't have a chip on his shoulder about having a female boss. Actually, he was a really nice bloke. She used to think he was married with a couple of kids, but apparently he wasn't. Single and available! Why was she thinking like this? He was a colleague, nothing else, and she was planning to leave the damn force anyway. Penny shook the thoughts out of her head just as Ian disappeared inside McDonald's and Dr Emily answered the call.

"Dr Emily, it's Penny again. How are you today?"

"Hello Penny dear. Yes, I'm fine, although I've had a bit of a busy morning what with trying to get all my shopping done, then having to pick up a parcel from the post office. There was such a queue there but I got talking to this very interesting lady who…"

"I'm calling to fill you in on my visit to the Pratts if that's alright." Penny knew that if she didn't interrupt her, then Dr Emily was likely to regale her of the morning's antics for the next half hour or so.

"Of course Penny, that's fine, you go ahead. What happened?"

"Off the record, they really are a pair of right prats. He came across as a misogynistic creep, women should know their place and all that. He wouldn't even speak to me at first."

"Good heavens!"

"Exactly. Anyway, briefly, he and his wife were at the Chapel on Thursday morning and were joined five minutes after they got there by Hayley Bishford. This would have been just after half past nine. Made a point of complaining that she was five minutes late, believe it or not. Mrs Pratt had to leave because she was unwell, or so she claims, and Mr Pratt was alone in the building with Hayley for at least half an hour. She became distressed during that time and left against his wishes."

"Why was she distressed, did he say?"

"Just said that Hayley had been ambivalent towards him and things had been difficult. He's not an easy man to question. It's like getting blood out of a stone."

"Has he made any contact with Hayley or her husband since Thursday?" Dr Emily wanted to know.

"No. He doesn't know what happened after she left him, where she went, what she did, who she might have been with, and it did strike us as extremely odd that he hadn't bothered to find out. He displayed no concern or compassion towards someone whom he claimed to have been helping for a very long time and who had fled from him in a distressed state. Said it wasn't his responsibility. The guy's as cold as ice."

"That is odd. Sounds like a guilty conscience."

"Yes, Dr Emily, it does, especially as he didn't even ask us why he was being questioned about Thursday morning. Tie that in with Hayley crying rape, having trauma consistent with a struggle, this ain't looking too good for our Mr Pratt."

"Goodness, no, it isn't, Penny, is it. Anything else?"

"Apart from a long auburn hair I managed to nip off the back of his neck without him noticing, he also had a deep scratch to the side of his neck and a plaster on his left hand. Interesting to see what forensics come up with from those fingernail scrapes off Hayley."

"How is the auburn hair significant?"

"Oh, I forget you haven't met her yet. Hayley has shoulder length auburn hair. The genuine variety, not dyed, which is why I guessed it was hers. Coarser than other hair colours."

"Well Penny, *something* happened at the Chapel, that's pretty certain. I take it you want me to see if I can get Hayley to name her attacker, without the use of suggestion, obviously."

"Sure do, Dr Em, you know how to do this sort of thing. We're going back to base now to do the paperwork and try to rush forensics through. I wanted to keep you up to date, as promised."

49

"I appreciate that Penny. Thank you. You have a good weekend now."

"I will. And you."

"Bye now."

"Bye bye."

Penny sat there alone, wanting to know what this Dr Emily looked like. They had spoken so many times on the phone, it really would be good to put a name to the face and the posh voice. Her thoughts then went back over the interview at the manse. That guy was guilty as anything. She knew it. If only they could gather some sound evidence, then they could bring him in. Why did he not seem surprised at being questioned? That spelt guilt in Penny's long experience. And where the heck was Ian? How long does it take to buy a cheeseburger these days for heaven's sake? At last she saw him coming out through the restaurant door and making his way towards the unmarked, carrying a wrapped burger. He slid into the driving seat and slammed the door shut.

"At last! I thought maybe they were churning the milk for the cheese to put on your burger."

"Nah," said Ian, "Saturday lunchtime. Long queue. I knew you'd be a while on the blower with Dr Emily anyway."

"Okay, let's make a move then. You can eat that when we get back."

An hour later, Ian had eaten his burger, caught up with at least some of the paperwork, and was on the phone to the forensics laboratory. He didn't care about their weekend skeleton staff for emergencies only, but they did, and were reluctant to chase up any results appertaining to Hayley's clothes and fingernail scrapings. How exasperating was that? Ian's left leg was jiggling nineteen to the dozen.

"Oh go on, can't you do me one little favour? Anything, absolutely anything would be useful. This is really important."

Ian played with the screwed up burger wrapper before aiming it at the waste paper bin. It missed.

"Yeh," said a bored voice on the other end of the phone, "they're all really important."

"Please? I know how busy you people are, we really do appreciate all the hard work involved in..." Gee, Ian hated being this nice, it really stuck in his throat. Not that he wasn't a nice guy really, mind you, but he preferred to keep his nicest bits for out of hours.

"Look," said the bored voice, "give me an hour, I'll take a quick gander and give you a call back." The bored voice then slammed the phone down and Ian was left staring at his mobile as if the device itself had delivered such abruptness.

"Thanks mate," he muttered, "love you too..."

An hour and a half later, the swine probably kept Ian hanging around deliberately, Bored Voice from forensics was back on the line.

"Anything?" asked Ian straight away.

"It's too soon to run anything through the DNA base but we have got some preliminary findings. The lady was wearing a black cord skirt and one of those bobbly jumpers, both of which easily hold onto hair and fibres. We've got long auburn hairs on the jumper and..."

"She's got long, auburn hair," Ian interrupted.

"... and we have a significant number of short, coarse, iron grey hairs on the front of both the skirt and the jumper. If your suspect is on the DNA base then..."

"He isn't. I've checked. But he does have the type of hair you've just described. Slightly crinkled as well?"

"Yep. Slightly crinkled."

"Yes!" Ian punched the air. "I'm gonna get this jerk sampled. Anything else?"

"Clothes are creased. No underwear unfortunately, 'refused' it says on the form."

"Pity. Damn it! Thanks for this anyway. I owe you." Ian was getting excited now and almost terminated the call.

"Hang on, hang on! The best is yet to come. We've got a significant number of carpet fibres mostly from the back of both garments, worked into the fabrics. Obviously suggests wearer has been supine. The number present, plus the pattern of adhesion to the garments also suggests a long period of contact with a degree a movement. Possibly violent movement."

"How long a period of contact?"

"Pass. But she didn't exactly lie down and get straight back up."

"Colour?"

"Deep red. Non-industry standard, I'd say heavy domestic Axminster, hence easier fibre shedding."

"That's brilliant," said Ian, "thanks for your help. Much appreciated."

"Yeh," replied Bored Voice, "have a good weekend." The call was cut off before Ian could say goodbye. Gee, who *does* want to work a weekend?

The phone at the manse had rung for ages before it was eventually answered by Mrs Pratt.

"This is Detective Sergeant Ian Gettum. Would you answer one very quick question for me please, Mrs Pratt?"

"I'll try."

"Dead easy. Is there any carpet in the Chapel of Mercy?"

"Yes."

"What colour is it?"

"Red with a bit of pattern. Like those old Axminsters."

"Thank you Mrs Pratt. Bye bye now."

Ian terminated the call before Mrs Pratt had time to ask him about his question. Then, standing up, he went and picked the burger wrapper up off the floor and aimed it straight at the bin again. This time it went in. Bingo! Very satisfying.

"Anything?" Penny asked as she came into the office eating a Twix. Ian told her about the hair, the carpet fibre samples and the phone call to the manse. They both punched the air. Yes!

"You want him in tonight for further questioning boss?" Ian was raring to go and stood there rubbing his hands together.

"Umm... I want to time this right," said Penny, slowly, thoughtfully. "Let's hang fire on this until Dr Emily has spoken to Hayley in case she gets her to name him. It'll be easier to get him DNA'd after the weekend so I vote we get off home, sleep on it, recharge the old batteries and go for him Monday morning. What say you?"

"Okay boss, you might have a point and I'll be glad to knock off to be honest. You doing anything tonight?"

"Nah," Penny replied, "Feet up, TV, might get a curry. You?"

"The same," said Ian. "I don't suppose you fancy sharing that curry, do you Pen?"

"You after a date here?" Penny's eyes were wide in surprise. "That's rather bold if I may say so."

"You don't ask, you don't get. You know me. Always ready to take a risk."

"Oh? A risk am I?" Penny now looked decidedly narked and came over all abrupt, which she instantly regretted. She'd truly sounded like the senior officer taking a minion down a step or two. She could have kicked herself. But why? Did she have feelings for Ian already?

"Sorry Ma'am." Ian immediately sensed that he'd crossed the line. "No offence meant. I just thought..."

Penny relaxed her shoulders and her features softened. "Actually, yes please Ian. I'd like that very much." Her smile was warm, her voice now gentle. "I could do with the company."

"Me too," agreed Ian. "Just a couple of colleagues getting together for a curry, eh? We could talk about the Pratts."

Penny laughed. "We could, yes. We could indeed."

CHAPTER EIGHT

THE SINNERS CHAPEL OF MERCY

Sunday morning

DR EMILY had already chided herself for fussing far too long over what to wear, what to eat for breakfast, and how early to leave Angel's Rest for the Chapel of Mercy's morning service. Lord, she needed a dose of mercy. Or maybe it was grace she needed? Eventually settling on an A-line, black, calf length skirt, she teamed it with a rather nice long sleeved purple cashmere jumper which was beautifully set off with a classy string of Honora pearls. A quilted, black winter jacket completed the look and together with warm tights and black ankle boots she was well prepared in case the Chapel was cold. It was an old building after all. She sprayed the old biddy grey bun with Elnette, popped in a pair of tiny pearl earrings and looked approvingly in the mirror. Yes, she looked like the intelligent, well dressed professional woman that indeed she was. Now where was that butter soft leather handbag she had bought the last time she'd been in London? She'd take that one with her. It matched the boots.

Breakfast had eventually been two slices of hot, buttered toast and a mug of strong Nescafe Gold Blend (but it had almost been porridge with Earl Grey tea), after which Doodle had been taken for her morning constitutional. Anticipating that the journey to the Chapel would take no more than twenty minutes, the small town being in close proximity to Sweet Briar village, Dr Emily set out at exactly ten o'clock, giving herself plenty of time to park and get herself to the building. She punched the necessary address details into her Sat Nav – goodness knows how she'd get anywhere unfamiliar without it – and set off in the Volvo.

Dr Emily was very much looking forward to finding out what the Chapel of Mercy was all about, yet also found herself experiencing a certain amount of anxiety which annoyed her intensely. It was a Chapel for goodness' sake! But then, the Pastor was suspected of rape. Good God, how terrible was that? She was about to encounter a churchman who might very well be a rapist and that was disturbing to say the least. However, she knew she must put whatever Penny had said about him right out of her mind and form her own opinion of the man. He could be innocent, but then... Dr Emily simply couldn't wait to see and hear him.

Pastor Pratt was also having a particularly trying morning. His scrambled eggs were most certainly of a standard low enough to make a saint swear, but again the Good Lord had been gracious and merciful, enabling forgiveness to flow in abundant rivers towards his culinary challenged wife. This had undoubtedly been assisted by the fact he had managed to get the offending eggs into the bin, well hidden under an empty bread wrapper, while Veronica was visiting the smallest room. He helped himself to an extra slice of toast and waited impatiently for Veronica to return to the kitchen and pour him another coffee.

The Pastor was NOT in a good mood after yesterday's visit from Starsky and Hutch, or whatever they called themselves. How DARE they come questioning the Lord's servant who had only been about his master's business? May the good Lord forgive them and cleanse them. May the good Lord even direct them unto the Sinners' Chapel of Mercy this very day. Verily,

verily had the Pastor composed his sermon with them in mind. This day there would be rejoicing in the heavenlies over those who were being saved. There would be the increased tinkling of coins and rustling of notes as the grateful saved showed their gratitude. At Pastor Pratt's chapel, of course.

At precisely two minutes after ten o'clock, Veronica Pratt held out her husband's suit jacket, helping him into it before making sure his tie was straight.

"My dear," he said, as he then held her coat for her to put on, "It's time."

The little Smart car backed out of the driveway of the manse and began its journey to the Chapel. They would arrive at, or very near to, ten minutes past ten, giving the Pastor time to pray in his chaplet with the elders and deacons before the service began. Mrs Pratt would discretely mingle and wish good morning to the other members of the congregation. At precisely twenty five minutes after ten o'clock she would take her usual seat at the end of the back row. Both Pratts felt the need to come to the Mercy Seat, as yesterday had been ghastly to put it mildly, but solace was available this very day. Especially to the saints of the Most High.

However, things were not as they should be at the Chapel.

It was twenty-six minutes past ten when Veronica glanced again at the well-dressed woman who was sitting in *her* seat. She didn't recognise her and felt frustrated that one of the greeters had failed to move her to a more convenient place. Convenient for the Pastor's wife, that is. Dr Emily, blissfully unaware that she was in receipt of dagger-like looks from none other than the Pastor's wife, sat gazing around with interest. She was glad to have chosen to wear black, for most of the women were in dark, sombre colours more befitting a funeral than a service of worship. She would not have wanted to stand out and draw attention to herself. The men were, almost without exception, dressed in suits with shirts and ties. It was rather like some sort of quaint social club.

Sat at the end of the back row, Dr Emily noted that the inside of the Chapel was unexpectedly bright and pleasant, although devoid of ecclesiastical adornment. The walls had been painted white and pews had obviously been removed and replaced by seating in the form of rows of chairs. There was a plain wooden pulpit, to the right of which was a large table set with bread and wine for communion. Bibles had been placed in the backs of the chairs and Dr Emily had been given a leaflet and a hymn book on the way in by a miserable looking git wearing round glasses and a blue striped tie.

Interrupting her thoughts, Miserable Git suddenly appeared at the side of Dr Emily, bending to whisper quietly in her ear. Too quietly as it happened.

"I'm awfully sorry, I can't hear what you're saying," she whispered back.

Sighing and in obvious discomfort, the man introduced himself again before repeating his request.

"I'm Mr Crabbe, one of the greeters this morning. I wonder if I could ask you to move along a couple of seats. This one's reserved." Having had to raise his voice a little, several heads turned to see who was being spoken to, looks of disapproval on the already too serious faces.

"There's nothing to say it's reserved," whispered Dr Emily factually, "and I'm quite happy here, thank you. There are plenty of empty seats." She gave Greeter Crabbe one of her steely smiles that was not a smile, folded her arms across her bosom, and made it patently obvious that she had no intention of moving. His request was completely unacceptable and her hackles had risen! She was new to the Chapel, this was her first visit, and they were trying to move her out of her chosen seat because, she guessed, one of the regulars always sat there. No way was that going to happen. What would the Good Lord make of it? He surely would not be pleased. Therefore, Dr Emily would not budge.

By this time the man was becoming quite agitated and Dr Emily almost, but not quite, felt a little sorry for him as he took another frantic look at his pocket watch. It was nigh on ten thirty and any moment now the chaplet door would creak open and out would come Pastor Pratt followed by his little entourage of elders and deacons. Mrs Pratt had yet to sit in her seat and was hovering nervously behind the back row. What was he to do?

Matters became even worse as a man, who looked to be around the same age as Dr Emily, came in wearing – wait for it – jeans and a leather jacket. He was very obviously not a regular either and he took a quick look around before sitting in the seat right next to Emily. There was plenty of room between the rows and so she barely needed to move to allow him access to the next seat along. Greeter Crabbe was almost apoplectic and literally hissed at the two newcomers. The truth came tumbling from his dripping lips.

"This is where the Pastor's wife always sits! So she can see everybody. Could I ask you two new people to move along?" The little man went to turn around in order to signal to Mrs Pratt that her seat was being vacated, then remembered something else and spoke again, "Welcome," he said. "Welcome."

"Thank you, and no worries, my good man," said Mr Jeans and Leather Jacket, "the rest of the row is empty; plenty of room, she'll get a good view." He grinned, obviously amused by both the request and the poor man's obvious discomfort.

"Well said," whispered Dr Emily. This time the smile was genuine.

A sudden stillness announced that the chaplet door had opened and the Pastor was about to appear. The whole congregation stood, heads bowed, except for Dr Emily and Mr

Leather Jacket who, unfamiliar with the order of service, were watching every move. They both watched Pastor Pratt slowly climb the few steps into the pulpit. While a small stream of suited men followed him and then quickly found their seats, the Pastor scanned his congregation, eyes resting momentarily on the newcomers in the back row. He noticed his wife was sitting a few seats away from them and he hoped Veronica still had a clear view of everyone who needed to be watched throughout the service. He knew she would not like sitting in a seat which was not hers. The trials of the truly faithful were many and varied. He took a deep breath and began.

"Let us pray. Almighty Living God, we thank you that you have brought each and every one of us here today to seek thy mercy seat and beg forgiveness for our many transgressions this week. Help me, thy humble and obedient servant, to gather back to thee the backslidden and the lost who are on their way to that great lake of fire and brimstone. Everlasting punishment awaits those who reject Thee O Lord. Wash us. Cleanse us in the thick, viscous, crimson blood which flowed from those blessed veins at Calvary. Convict and cleanse and save those who are new to us. Thank you for bringing us those dirty sinners. May they leave this building clean and fresh. Amen."

Dr Emily's eyes were open wider than cathedral organ stops. She turned to look at Mr Leather Jacket just as he turned to look at her, the same wide eyed expression of incredulity on his face. They both turned again towards the pulpit as the Pastor carried on...

"We will now bring our woefully inadequate worship unto the Lord as we attempt to sing hymn number forty-seven. 'Oppressed with sin and woe, a burdened heart I bear.' May the Lord bless us in our wretchedness as we make noise unto him."

Goodness, gracious me, thought Dr Emily, what a thoroughly miserable start, and what a miserable tune to sing a hymn to. As the congregation stood, there must have been about thirty of them, she took the opportunity to study the Pastor as he bellowed from the pulpit. Although immaculately dressed he looked vaguely odd. She thought that was due to the beard, jet black and only covering the lower half of his face, contrasting with grey hair which was thick and reasonably well groomed. Put him in a track suit and he could look like a cult leader.

Dr Emily wasn't the only one having a good look round while the hymn was being sung. Veronica Pratt was leaning forward over her hymn book, very obviously watching Dr Emily very obviously watching her husband. Dr Emily spotted the Pastor's wife looking in her direction and lowered her eyes to her hymn book. What shook her most of all was the icy cold feeling she'd felt whilst watching the Pastor. She didn't think she had ever seen such a dour, serious, miserable looking man, and goodness knows she'd seen plenty of odd people in her line of work. There was something about him and his wife didn't look any happier. As for the diminutive Mr Crabbe, that was some welcome he'd given her before scuttling away down the aisle and sidling into a seat next to an equally anxious, serious looking woman. So far, what a joyless, miserable place full of joyless, miserable people! Some advert for the Good News this lot were. Dr Emily would have her work cut out if Hayley was deeply into all this; enough to make anyone depressed. She suddenly wished she had stayed at Angel's Rest.

CHAPTER NINE

PENNY

Sunday morning

PENNY STRETCHED, turned over, and curled back up again, reluctant to get out of a warm bed on a cold February morning. It was Sunday after all and she was entitled to a lie in on a Sunday. She could feel Migmos curled up next to her feet. Darn cat had woken her up twice during the night – once for food and to be let out, then howling at the bedroom window until she was let back in – but at least she was as good as a hot water bottle for keeping Penny's toes warm.

Last night had been an eye opener for her and Ian, for although they'd known each other for many years they definitely knew very little *about* each other. She'd always assumed that Ian was a typical family man with a wife, a couple of kids, nice house, nice car. It had surprised her that they'd been partners for three months and she hadn't found out that Ian was, like her, single and shared a small house with a cat who sounded as crazy as Migmos. What a coincidence. There had, however, been a few girlfriends who, according to Ian, eventually broke up with him because of his job. Couldn't cope with the shifts. Was that true? Plenty of cops had wives or girlfriends. Penny wondered if it was because Ian was no good at relationships, and if so, why? Anyway, what did it matter? She wasn't after any sort of relationship. Was she? Nah! It was just good to have company on a Saturday evening. She'd enjoyed it.

Ian had arrived just after seven o'clock, laden with a carrier bag out of which wafted warm, delicious smells. There were two types of curry, rice, poppadoms and a large bottle of diet Coke. "I remembered you didn't drink," he said as he let her lead the way into a cosy lounge. Penny fetched plates, cutlery and glasses and they sat down, one each end of the settee, coffee table in front of them. Conversation flowed easily and comfortably.

"So tell me about yourself Ian. What makes you tick?" Penny poured two Cokes and Ian, busy unwrapping the food, began telling her.

He told her that he had always wanted to be a policeman and lived for his job. He'd joined the force at twenty-one and had never regretted a day of it. Even through the hard times and when he'd worked with some right... The only thing he regretted was the lack of a partner to share his life with. He spoke sadly about broken romances, confiding that the longest girlfriend had lasted seven years. He'd been gutted when they split up and she'd moved out of his semi-detached house on the outskirts of Truffleton.

"No kids then?" Penny had asked.

"No, thankfully. I suppose that is something to be thankful for. I wouldn't have wanted kids involved in my mess of a life. Seems I'm not good at being with anybody, kids need stability and commitment. Guess I'd have made a lousy Dad."

"Oh, I don't know," said Penny, "don't be so hard on yourself, you've got a soft side to you. Caring. Maybe you just haven't met the right woman yet."

"Huh! How long is that supposed to take? How many tries do I have? Yet maybe you're right. Perhaps I haven't." Ian suddenly lapsed into silence and Penny sensed it was time to change the subject.

"One thing I've been meaning to ask you," she continued, "why haven't you gone for Inspector? You love the job, you're dedicated, a hard worker, intelligent, all that stuff. You'd get it easily. You're perfectly capable Ian."

"Well, thanks for the compliments." They laughed.

Ian had then gone on to tell her why he'd never gone for further promotion. Two reasons. The first was that he genuinely didn't want the extra responsibility and was happy where he was. Penny could sort of understand that. The second reason completely took the wind out of her sails. She would never, in a month of Sundays, have believed that Ian was a...

"Pen. Please keep this between us. Please? I know there's nothing wrong with it, but I've had a bit of ribbing, you understand?"

"Sure," Penny replied, holding eye contact with Ian, "You can trust me on this. Believe it or not, I understand more than you think I could, but cannot see *that* as a reason not to go for promotion."

"Um. Anyway, tell me about you instead. Probably far more interesting."

"I'm not sure about me being far more interesting," Penny had laughed, "but if I tell you about myself, then you have to promise to keep *that* between the two of us as well. Deal?"

Ian smiled, obviously relieved.

"Deal!"

Penny had gone on to confide in Ian, as he had in her, both surprised at the evening's revelations and at how relieving it had been to speak to each other of long held secrets and desires. Who'd have thought it about Penny Whistle? You could have knocked Ian down with a feather. Well, well, well. Both of them! Although Ian had been subjected to far more teasing over it than had Penny.

The food eaten, Coke bottle half empty, hours had passed quickly as they talked. It was almost midnight when a silence eventually descended on the warm, cosy room. An extremely realistic gas log fire flickered away in shadowy lamplight and the easy quietness wrapped itself around them, creating a bond of friendship that promised to endure, whatever happened. Penny then got up to make cocoa and when they both held their drinks Ian had spoken again.

"I'll be off after this Pen, but talking shop for a minute, are we still going for Pratt after the weekend?"

"Oh yes! I'm applying for an arrest warrant first thing Monday morning, it should be straightforward enough. The policewoman side of me is looking forward to questioning our man again."

"Yeh, me too."

The two police officers had lapsed into silence again while they finished their drinks. Totally comfortable with each other.

"Right! I'm off then." Ian had placed his mug on the coffee table and stood up, rubbing his hands together. "Thanks for this evening Penny. It's meant a lot to me. I mean that."

"It's meant a lot to me as well, I'll see you on Monday bright and early. Well, at least early! We'll keep our social side completely separate from work. Both of us want that, and that's how it'll be."

"Thanks Penny. I appreciate that."

Ian had gone home. Penny had cleared up and gone straight to bed, knowing that she had a friend she would always feel safe with. What an extraordinary evening.

Now it was Sunday morning. Migmos stirred and walked up the bed, nudging Penny's face and emitting the sort of meow that means 'feed me or else I will become a pain in the ass'. Penny always said that you would never win against a toddler or a cat and so, glancing at the clock and deciding it was about time she was up anyway, she slipped out of bed. Putting on her dressing gown, she padded down the stairs, Migmos ahead of her, tail held high. In the tiny kitchen Penny fed the little tabby before popping two slices of wholemeal bread into the toaster and switching the kettle on. It was eight minutes past eleven o'clock but boy, she'd enjoyed the lie in. Soon she was curled up in front of the artificial flames, enjoying breakfast and engrossed in a book. Migmos had gone out to do her business and the TV was on simply for company, the news channel giving out its usual grim tidings. Penny heard not a word as she read and ate and sipped coffee. She turned a page and continued reading the Apostle Paul's letter to the Romans... "For we know that all things work together for good..." She raised her eyes from the page before lowering them again and reading the rest of the verse. "...for those who love God, who are called according to his purpose."

CHAPTER TEN

THE SINNERS CHAPEL OF MERCY

Sunday morning

DR EMILY glanced at her watch. It was ten minutes past eleven o'clock. After the first miserable hymn, she had sat through a Bible reading, another miserably sung hymn, and now 'your ten per cent unto the work of the Lord and the feeding of the Pastor' was being collected while the aforementioned sat in his pulpit in an attitude of prayer. The plates of money were duly escorted to the front of the Chapel and placed on the floor in front of the pulpit. Pastor Pratt then stood up. You could have heard a pin drop. He clasped his hands together and, closing his eyes, face raised heavenwards, he began to pray.

"Lord, as I deliver the sermon you have instructed me to deliver, I pray that lives will be changed. Rend the heavens and come down, split open those skies and gather the washed into thy bosom. Have mercy on the unwashed, the wretched, the dirty, those on their way to eternal damnation. Won't you bring them to this Chapel, O Lord?"

Yes, thought Dr Emily. Bring 'em here with their ten per cent for the coffers... that'll keep the Pastor fed, although he looks well fed enough... plenty of junk on his trunk, as the saying goes.

"Bring in those vile sinners!" bellowed the Pastor. "Save our souls!"

A few muffled 'Amens' broke the silence. Mr Leather Jacket fidgeted and coughed. Dr Emily stole a sideways glance at him and realised that he was not suffering any pulmonary or laryngeal discomfort but was desperately trying to stifle a laugh. Smiling broadly into her lap she found herself relishing this somewhat entertaining morning. She would take time later on to analyse the goings on. How utterly fascinating. Then she literally jumped as Pastor Pratt boomed out...

"There is therefore now no condemnation to those who are in Christ Jesus. Who will bring any charge against those whom God has chosen? I tell you now, how DARE anyone bring a charge against we who are washed, we who are cleansed, we who are saved, we who are the very elect, we who are stained with the blood, we who are doing the will of the Living God, we who are following divine instructions... WHATEVER... (pause for effect here)... those instructions might be."

Trembling now, the Pastor continued, "Those of us who are covered and smothered and saturated in that crimson tide are beyond reproach! I tell you now, we shall NOT be questioned, we shall not be condemned, we shall be LIFTED UP. And heaven help those who come against us to accuse us and mock us as we seek to do HIS will. (Another pause for effect.) Let us support each other and defend any brethren whom the world would put asunder, for we are not ignorant of the wiles of the devil and of this evil, wicked world. O that the Lord would indeed rend the heavens this very day and come quickly, and gather us up before the storm comes... come and get us Lord... we are waiting... take us home..."

Blimey! However, Pastor Pratt had only just started. He took a noisy swig from a glass of water and continued.

"We know what awaits those who do not belong to the Living God. HELL! DAMNATION! Eternal, everlasting pain and torment in the furnaces of Hades where the worm never dies and screams of unending agony are forever heard. Ooooh, it's a terrible, terrible place. Your sins will be MAGNIFIED! They will haunt you, torment you and cause you more pain than you can ever imagine. AND... it will go on for eternity. Burning, burning, agonising torment.

"Do you want to go there, my friend? If so, then do nothing. The devil will keep a place for you. If you do NOT want to go to hell, the answer is here, today, at the mercy seat. It's not difficult. You must cry out to God, who will convict you of your rottenness and utter depravity. Then you must confess every single dirty, foul, evil sin you've ever committed, even the ones you enjoyed. You must repent in sackcloth and ashes, being sorry to the point of clinical depression. Then you must receive his forgiveness, pray for assurance of that forgiveness, believe on the Lord, become justified, then sanctified, receive his salvation, ask for the indwelling of the Holy Spirit and accept cleansing in the precious blood. It's that simple my friend, it's that simple...

"Then, as a trophy of his grace..."

Dr Emily had had enough. She had never heard such miserable and utter drivel in all her life, at least not from a pulpit even though she had attended church regularly at times. Anglican, of course. What was this man trying to do? Frighten people into God's Kingdom? Wasn't God a God of love and compassion? She genuinely feared for the mental well-being of those in the congregation. Why did people go to listen to such rubbish? My word, how long had Hayley been under this religious nut's fire and brimstone teaching? No wonder the poor woman had cracked up. The psychology of all this was both frightening and fascinating and all of a sudden it was time to stand and sing another ghastly hymn about sin and human wretchedness. At least the sermon, if you could call it that, was finally over. Religious mania, that's what he had. The man could even be bi-polar. Golly, she could do with a cuppa. Where was this lounge of salvation that served the tea?

But alas, more hellfire and brimstone, intolerant religiosity, legalism, fundamentalism and hypocrisy were to come…

The Pastor continued relentlessly. "We now gather around the Lord's table to obey his command to remember him as we partake of the bread and the wine. At least, those of us who have been born again and truly know the Lord may gather and take part. I would respectfully ask those who are not yet saved to leave quietly, else stay sitting in prayerful contemplation of your unwashed state as the servers pass you by. If you feel you have truly been born again during the service, then please refrain from taking communion until you have spoken to either myself or my wife. We have a useful ten point list which will help us decide if you are truly saved and washed in the blood. Thank you."

Greeter Crabbe scuttled from his seat and stood watchfully behind the back row, while Mrs Pratt moved a seat closer to Mr Leather Jacket. It was all a little bit threatening.

"Are you saved?" whispered the Pastor's wife rather frantically, her face up close to Mr Leather Jacket.

"Probably not," he whispered back, adding, "are you?"

Too indignant to make any response, Mrs Pratt then leaned over towards Dr Emily.

"Are you saved? We're waiting to gather around the table. For those who are born again. If you are unwashed then…"

Well, enough was enough. Dr Emily's feathers were more than ruffled, her hackles well risen, her flabber well and truly gasted, her response wonderfully immediate…

"My dear," she said, "saved or unsaved, I am going to the pub for a double whisky and some rather more pleasant company than is available in this establishment." Mrs Pratt's face was already a picture even before Dr Emily had finished speaking. "I will be warmly welcomed, I won't be asked to vacate an altogether more comfortable seat, and I might even pick up a bloke!" With that, Dr Emily swiftly made her exit, only slightly annoyed over her little outburst, for she had so enjoyed seeing the shock on that woman's face. Crazy, frumpy religious nut! Who wouldn't be, married to him? She ought to feel sorry for the poor woman but, at that moment, she didn't. As for that Pastor, he was mentally ill, he had to be...

As the leather boots squiffed rapidly towards the Volvo, Dr Emily heard a voice calling out to her.

"Hello? Excuse me..." It was Mr Leather Jacket, also hurrying from the Chapel door, presumably not clean enough to stay for communion. She didn't know if she was pleased or not to have him call out to her but what the heck, he might be interesting. She stopped and waited for him to catch up with her. He held out his hand and she took it, noticing that his grip was firm and confident. She liked that.

"Richard Preston. Hello again. I couldn't help but notice that you seemed to be one of the great unwashed, according to the gospel of A. Pious Pratt, that is." He was smiling and spoke with a deep, rounded, educated voice. Dr Emily laughed and relaxed a little. She had thought him younger because of the attire, but close up his face was – what? – pleasantly weathered, that's what. Rugged, lived in, very masculine, yet also warm and friendly. She was surprised to find herself taking an instant liking to this man.

"Emily Chatwith," she responded. "Unwashed indeed! I take it you are a fellow dirty sinner on the path to everlasting torment in the bowels of Hades." They both laughed again.

"No," he said. "I'm on the path to a little hedonistic pleasure in the Black Swan Inn. I couldn't help hearing what you said to the Pastor's wife. Care to join me for a drink?"

"Well," grinned Dr Emily, "I truly wasn't serious about the double whisky, or the bloke, but yes. Why not? Is it far? Walking distance?"

"End of the cul-de-sac, just round the corner. Less than a minute I assure you."

They smiled again at each other and began walking. On reaching the Black Swan Inn, the man opened the door for Dr Emily to enter before him, which she did, well impressed by such gentlemanly manners.

"Welcome," he announced dramatically, "to the lounge of salvation!"

CHAPTER ELEVEN

HAYLEY

Sunday evening

HAYLEY ABSOLUTELY DETESTED Sundays and didn't know how she had managed to get through this one. At least the Pastor hadn't rung, as he usually did on a Sunday, to arrange another session. God, how she feared and hated those sessions, yet fearing the lack of them even more. That failed to make sense to her as she never wanted to see the Pastor again for as long as she lived. Especially after that last session in the Chapel where he had…

The kids safe and warm in bed, Hayley swallowed another couple of Co-codamol, hoping that the codeine would ease her headache and help her get some sleep. Mike had been brilliant with the kids that day, had even taken them to the park for a few hours to give her a break, but she knew he was tired and stressed out. She wrote 'I'm sorry' on the pad she kept at the side of her chair. Mike read the words and ran his hand down the back of his head. How many times had she written those words? How many more times would she write them before she spoke them? When would she start talking again? When was this whole, crazy nightmare going to end?

"Yeh, I know," Mike spoke quietly, "so you keep telling me. But 'sorry' ain't much help to me when I'm running around like a lunatic, seeing to the kids, trying to keep things normal for them, trying to get some help for my stupid, crazy, blasted wife!" His voice was rising. "I'm telling you now, H, I'll get you damn well sectioned if you carry on like this, not talking, not eating, not anything..." Mike suddenly sat down heavily on the settee opposite his wife, put his head in his hands, and wept. "God, H, I'm sorry. I'm tired. Tired of it all. If I'd known the Pastor was going to... well, I'd never have let him near you, you know that. He sounded so plausible, we both believed him. Now look at us. We're barely holding things together."

Hayley went to pick the pen up.

"No!" Mike barked. "Please don't. Don't write anything else down for now, I don't think I can cope with it. I love you more than ever but... I don't know what to do anymore." Mike rose and quietly left the room, closing the door softly behind him.

Hayley sat, feet curled up on the chair, silent, scared. So very scared. She felt herself dropping back into that other world of voices, smells, feelings, terror, pain...

...he was on top of her again, heavy weight, so much screaming, pain, shout, shout, shouting, then running, running... She had run out of the Chapel. She knew that if only she could make it to the car...

Hayley didn't sleep too well that night.

Too much running.

Too much screaming.

CHAPTER TWELVE

ANGEL'S REST

Sunday evening

DR EMILY always washed and trimmed little Doodle on Sunday evenings. As she towel dried the docile and delighted creature, for what little Doodle *doesn't* enjoy a bit of fuss and undivided attention, her mind again went over the awfully pleasant time she had spent with Richard Preston that day in the Black Swan Inn. My word, it had been an extraordinarily interesting couple of hours. Straight from church and into the Pub! How terribly Anglican. Exactly what she and Henry used to do once Isobel had grown up and become independent.

The Black Swan Inn had been warm and inviting, not at all like the Sinners Chapel of Mercy, and much goodwill to all men was going on if the jovial chatter and clinking of glasses was anything to go by. Or else perhaps a few sorrows were being eased or drowned by the supping of various beverages. Dr Emily had sat in a cosy window seat, the sort with two padded high back bench seats and a table in between. The little window had leaded glass and was pleasantly framed by red velvet drapes. They had both chosen to have coffee and Richard Preston soon returned, placing a tray on the table then taking the drinks off the tray and placing a small jug of cream in the middle. The coffee proved hot and delicious, just what was needed after the cold Chapel. Cold in so many ways.

"Tell me, Mr Preston, are you a regular at that Chapel? You don't look like one if I may be so bold." Dr Emily sipped at her coffee as he clinked his cup into his saucer and replied.

"It's Dr Preston, but please do call me Richard, and no, I'm most certainly not a regular at any place of worship. First and last visit. You?" He picked his cup up again.

"Definitely first and last visit for me, too," Dr Emily replied. "Are you a doctor of medicine?"

"No, no. I lecture at Truffleton University. Do you work at all Mrs Chatwith?"

"It's Dr Chatwith, but you must call me Emily..."

"You're joking! We're both doctors? What a coincidence. Medicine? Or are you a real doctor?" They both laughed easily together and the conversation had continued very pleasantly until another cup of coffee was needed, this time accompanied by a sandwich and a bag of crisps each.

Dr Emily's mind drifted back to the present. "What d'you think, Doodle? Don't you think Richard is a really nice man?" The little dog sat patiently on her lap, wrapped in a warm, dry towel while a pair of doggy grooming scissors snipped away at some long hairs threatening to cover her eyes. "Now that I've told you all about him, would you like to meet him? Not that I'm giving you much of a choice as he's coming to see us this Wednesday afternoon. What do you think of that?" Doodle said nothing, and by doing so gave Dr Emily the approval she needed for the aforementioned gentleman to call on her.

He really was a nice man, was Dr Richard Preston. Dr Emily had been surprised to learn that he lectured in Theology, although why that should be a surprise she wasn't quite sure, perhaps because he had been so adamant that he was not a regular worshipper anywhere. He had been just as surprised to find out that she was a psychiatrist.

"I'd always assumed that theologians were Reverends or at least serious Christians," she'd commented by way of explaining her raised eyebrows, "but I stand corrected."

"Aha!" had come his immediate response, "just because I don't come to church, does that mean I am not a Christian, dear lady?"

"Of course it doesn't," Dr Emily had laughed, "so are you? And why Theology may I ask?"

"You may indeed ask. My late father was a vicar. I was brought up in the Anglican church, pushed towards the priesthood, knew it wasn't for me, but was fascinated with all things religious and theological. Decided to teach religious studies instead, which was a bitter disappointment to my father but I did rather fancy myself as a teacher. However, I got to university and loved academia so much that I stayed there." He'd gone on to tell her how he had met his wife, an English student whom he married after they had both graduated. There followed two much loved kids, life was looking good, then along came the other man...

"I'm so sorry." Dr Emily had said, softly.

"No need to be. Long time ago, we've been divorced twenty years, kids are adults now and thank God doing okay in spite of the break up. I don't see much of them as they emigrated with my ex to Australia. She already had family out there. Speak on the phone often, that's about it. Threw myself into my work and haven't looked at another woman since. Never wanted to. Still don't."

"Why's that?" Dr Emily had felt a little jolt at Richard Preston's admission of never wanting another woman, even though, as a psychiatrist, the reasons were patently clear. So why should that bother her? She never wanted another man after Henry. Maybe it got to her because he'd been there with her, in a cosy pub, sharing lunch, talking the hind legs off a herd of donkeys, so at ease, conversation flowing so naturally... She had thoroughly enjoyed herself and it was obvious that he had too.

"Oh, I don't know," Richard Preston had answered, "too afraid of being hurt again. Of being dumped and told I'm a lousy lover, lousy husband, lousy dad... afraid of screwing somebody else's life up along with my own. Lots of reasons I suppose. Looking back, I was way too selfish, I see that now it's too late. Maybe I'm still like that."

Dr Emily had gone on to tell him about Henry, how proud she had been of him, how wonderful they had been together, how there could never be another man to take his place, how he had really, truly understood her and kept her sane. Richard Preston had laughed at that.

"You're a psychiatrist and you needed someone to keep *you* sane? Maybe not looking too good for the rest of us then!"

"Look at it this way," Dr Emily had retorted, "If you were a top surgeon with appendicitis, you'd need another surgeon to carry out the operation. That saying, 'doctor heal thyself', doesn't work, let me tell you."

"No. I suppose not. It must have been shattering to lose your husband."

"Yes, but I have to choose to be thankful for the happy years we had. Not everyone has a happy marriage as you know only too well. And the thing is, I know that Henry didn't *choose* to leave me. He's not in the next town having run off with another woman. I don't know how I would have coped with that."

There had been a few moments of silence in which Dr Emily wondered if she'd said the wrong thing. They both sat staring into their coffee cups. Richard Preston eventually broke the quietness.

"Why psychiatry, Emily?"

"Hmm. My parents were both doctors, mother a GP, father a surgeon, so it was expected that my sister and I would follow in their medical footsteps. My sister did, she's a GP, but I just didn't quite make it. Oh, I sailed through medical school, qualified, did my hospital stint, but still wasn't particularly interested in which side of the body the appendix lay..." Again they both laughed, so comfortable with each other. "I simply didn't enjoy the physical contact with people if I can put it like that, yet still felt drawn to a healing profession. Psychiatry seemed an obvious progression and I've loved it and never regretted my decision. It's been quite a career, I can tell you."

"I bet it has. You must tell me more someday."

"Yes," Dr Emily had said, "I'd like that."

Again there had been moments of silence as they both sipped their coffees.

"So getting back to this morning," Dr Emily put her cup back down and wiped her fingers on the serviette that had arrived with the sandwiches and crisps, "what made you go to the Sinners Chapel of Mercy?"

"Research. I'm doing a post-doctoral paper on psychological issues in fundamentalist religion. I'm particularly interested in the non-conformist, independent church or chapel side of things. What makes their leaders tick, why do people follow them, why do they break off from any recognisable line of authority? How do they get people to believe what they purport to believe? How does the psycho/socio-economic/educational make-up influence choice in religion, faith and belief for both leaders and followers? That sort of thing. Absolutely fascinating. There's a lot of stuff out there about known cults, but I'm interested in the sub-cult, if that makes sense."

"Perfect sense. Sounds interesting too. I gather this morning was no more than a field trip then?"

"Exactly." Richard Preston took another few sips of coffee and appeared deep in thought before continuing. "To be honest, the weekends can seem endless when you're on your own so it's been fascinating to visit a number of places of worship and check out the people and the theology behind the set-up. I've met some wonderful people and I get to feel when it's okay to stay behind and ask questions. I certainly didn't get that feeling today!" He laughed, looking Dr Emily straight in the eyes. "So why were you there? Sussing out what, or who, might be responsible for the mental demise of a section of the local community?"

"Ha! Now you just might have hit the nail on the head there. Obviously I can't divulge any details, but a patient of mine comes here, or came here, not sure which at the moment. I felt it would be useful to check the place out, see what goes on."

"Trouble?"

"You could say that." Dr Emily was bursting to tell him more and it was obvious the man was interested, but of course she couldn't. Drat it! She was a stickler for the confidentiality part of her profession, as she should be, and already felt she might have said too much. Henry had always been safe to tell and she desperately missed confiding in somebody other than a colleague. She changed direction. "Do you adhere to any particular faith, Richard?"

"Phew. Tough question. I'm not altogether sure. As I said, my late father was a vicar and after years of listening to him preaching, watching as he celebrated the Eucharist, then coming home and being a sullen, argumentative bully, it kind of puts you off. Ha! He used to take a belt to me until one day, when I was about fourteen, I hit him back. He never did it again. Of course I know he wasn't exactly an example of a Christian, but..."

"He was your Dad," put in Emily, "he claimed to be a Christian, and these things go deep into the psyche and stay there."

"Yes, they do. Nevertheless, despite what he was like, I've always found a profound comfort in the Christian message and I must admit I like a set of rules to live by. Trouble is, those who claim to live by them usually don't, but since my divorce the offer of forgiveness, redemption, a new start, well… it does sound pretty good. I guess it's 'church' that's my stumbling block. I often think that if we could move all the churches, chapels, cults, whatever, out of the way, then we might all just get a clearer view of that Greater Intelligence. Are you a believer Emily?"

"Now, I suppose I might describe myself as a non-practicing believer in that I was brought up in the Anglican tradition, went to church regularly – all terribly middle class – but stopped in medical school. Besides not having time to attend any church it was there that I questioned the whole concept of a loving God in the light of what I was seeing on the wards. Yet when I studied anatomy I was so awestruck by the complexity of the human body that it seemed impossible and beyond reason to deny the existence of an Intelligent Creator. I'm afraid I'm Christmas, Easter, hatches, matches and dispatches now, although my husband and I did go regularly to an Anglican church for a number of years."

"Any children?"

"Sadly only the one. I have a daughter, Isobel, grown up and living with her partner in what was mine and Henry's house. I've got the lovely, little adjoining cottage. Much easier for me. I don't want a big house to look after on my own."

"Sounds sensible."

The conversation had continued before they parted with a handshake and an arrangement for the following Wednesday afternoon. Richard would collect Emily from Angel's Rest and take her to a lovely garden centre he knew of that served the most wonderful cream teas. They would then carry on talking where they left off. Emily felt wonderfully, ridiculously excited, like a teenager being asked for a date, and was left wondering if Richard Preston had held on to her hand just a little bit longer than necessary. She found herself hoping that he had.

"So there we are, Doodle. You must behave yourself when our guest is here, although I don't even know if he will be coming into the cottage. He's going to pick me up and take me out for a cream tea. That will be such a treat. Now you go and curl up in your basket. I need to get myself some supper." That said, she gently lifted Doodle, placing her in her basket before making her way into the kitchen to decide what to eat for supper.

"One thing's certain," she mused out loud whilst thinking back over her visit to the sinners Chapel, "I'm experienced enough to recognise that Pastor Pratt is most certainly unbalanced and definitely not neuro-typical. Goodness, he's almost a pantomime version of a hellfire and brimstone preacher. Too over the top. Hyperbolic. Manic. He'll come crashing down. The question is, how many people will he drag with him on the way?"

Underneath are the Everlasting Arms...

CHAPTER THIRTEEN

THE MANSE

Sunday evening

IT WAS LATE, very late, and Pastor Pratt was sat up in bed in his purple jim jams. The ones from Marks and Spencer. Next to him sat Mrs Pratt in a flannelette nightie, also from Marks and Spencer, with a high neckline, long sleeves, and ankle length hemline. Modesty at all times was not only becoming to the wife of a man of God, but also essential if she was not to tempt the Pastor to fornicate. It was not the first of the month after all. There was a time and a place for everything. Tonight they were certainly in the right place but thanks to the date she would not need to cry out for her wifely duty to be over as quickly as possible. Unless the Pastor was in one of his moods when he would…

"Has Matthew phoned this week?" Pastor Pratt only ever asked this question on a Sunday evening. As usual he received the same reply.

"No. He hasn't. You know how it is, you need to contact him first this time."

"What? You know how it is as well, Veronica. Me contact him? He is choosing to indulge in sin. He is wilfully, deliberately unwashed and unsaved. Heaven alone knows what he gets up to in his heathen life with that slut of his. And you want me to make the first move? Again?"

"But he's our son, Anthony!"

"So you keep telling me Veronica, but let's not go there. Okay, we brought him up as our child but he's not yet a child of God."

"Maybe he chooses not to become God's child *because* of how you brought him up. Have you thought about that? How you may have turned him against the Lord? None of us is without sin, Anthony. Let him who is cast the first stone. You know the scriptures well enough."

"Don't start that again Veronica, I've got more than enough on my plate at the moment without..."

"Having to apologise to Matthew?"

"Apologise?" Pastor Pratt turned to glare at his wife, his face almost the same colour as his night wear. "You want me to apologise for calling him what he is? A..."

"Don't say it Anthony. Just don't!" Veronica clenched her fists, so angry she could scream.

"He should honour and obey us as his parents Veronica, you are quite well aware of the Lord's words concerning how offspring should behave."

"Yes, I am, but Holy Scripture also warns fathers not to provoke their children to wrath, does it not?"

Pastor Pratt caught hold of Veronica's arm and shook it. "Don't you dare use the Word of the Lord to try and win an argument with me woman. It won't work."

"An argument? I was not aware this was an argument Anthony. And please take your hand off me."

Ignoring her plea, the Pastor continued to squeeze his wife's upper arm, now bringing his face close to hers. "I know you go to see him, you think I don't, but I do. You don't deceive me Veronica but the Lord will judge you for trying, be sure of that." He then let go of her arm and turned his face forwards again.

"Judge not, Anthony, lest you be judged yourself." She could hardly believe she had dared to say that to him. Now they sat in silence. Bolt upright. Arms crossed. Enjoying a little sinful seething.

The Pastor was the first to break the silence. "Did you see those new sinners in the back row? That man came in wearing jeans and a leather jacket, are there no standards at all in this dark world of iniquity?"

"Yes, of course I saw them, the lady sat in my seat, how could I not have noticed them? Mr Crabbe did try to move her but she had the audacity to refuse. In fact, both of them refused to move when asked but at least they left before communion. They seemed to grasp that they were not able to take part."

"Indeed. Do you think they'll come back?"

"You know as well as I do that if the Lord wants them saved they'll be back, but they *were* seen going into the Black Swan together after the service."

Veronica hated it when she sounded as judgemental and condemnatory as her spouse, knowing that she did it only to keep the peace. Truth be told, she was becoming more and more disturbed by his behaviour lately. He was too much of the hellfire, too intolerant, too legalistic. She didn't know what to do about it. What *could* she do about it? The Pastor interrupted her thoughts…

"That den of iniquity? Gambling machines, the demon drink, the devil's own fluid! It's a long, hard fight with these unregenerate people. May the Lord strike them with the rod of correction and pour His wrath upon them."

"Yes, dear. Apparently they even looked as if they were enjoying themselves."

"God help them, for no-one else can."

"I often wonder at that you know," Veronica stared straight ahead as she spoke, "how the people in the Black Swan always sound as if they're having a good time while we in chapel are so miserable and serious."

"Veronica! What's the matter with you now, woman? We have life after death to look forward to."

A little life *before* death might be nice though, she thought as she pulled the blankets up around her shoulders, shivering in the sudden chill that had crept into the bedroom. How much more of him could she put up with? But then, what choice did she have...?

"We must pray for them to be convicted of their evil wickedness and for the Lord to tell them what utterly wretched, depraved sinners they are in their unwashed state. Filthy sinners!" The Pastor also then pulled at the blankets, suddenly cold.

There was another silence. This time Veronica broke it.

"What happened to Hayley Bishford?"

"The Lord told me to have no further contact with Hayley Bishford, I'm to hand her over to Satan now in order that she might come to her senses. It's not up for discussion."

"But it was the Lord who kept telling you never to give up on her. At least you *said* it was the Lord's instruction." Veronica again turned to face her husband. "You even *promised* her, many times, that you'd never give up on her, telling her that you were the only one who could help her. Were you wrong about that?"

"Don't be ridiculous woman, of course I wasn't wrong."

"But?"

"But nothing. She has persistently failed to do as I say, 'Obey those that have the rule over you', and has refused to co-operate, you know that." The Pastor's voice was rising, which meant he was dangerously cross. Veronica, however, was ignoring the signs and carried on...

"God also tells us in Holy Scripture that we are not to lord it over anyone else and we are to forgive seventy times seven.

You can't just leave her after all this time, surely? We must care for His lambs."

"She's hardly a lamb! She is evil and unregenerate and takes wickedness to herself, spreading it everywhere she goes. God alone knows I've been patient. How many times have I seen her and done exactly what the Lord has told me to do? How many times have I allowed her to come here? God help us, we even made her a cup of tea when she was here last month."

"You mean I did."

"That's because I needed to be alone with her, the Lord told me. When you were in the kitchen I..."

"You what? What *did* you do when you were alone with her? And you were alone with her again on Thursday morning when she ran from the chapel, then the police call asking questions. What happened Anthony? Something did. Tell me!"

Veronica could hardly believe she had spoken so boldly and it was obvious the Pastor had had enough.

"In Jesus' name keep quiet! A woman is to remain silent and learn from the man. I have done only the Lord's will, only what He told me to do, and I won't be questioned about it by you or by anyone else. Understand? Have I made myself clear?"

"I hear you, but if the police come back you won't have much choice but to answer their questions."

"If the Lord commands my silence, and I'm sure He will, then I shall obey Him and not any so called earthly authority. Now shut up woman!" With that, the Pastor reached over and switched off the bedside light. The two of them then lay down, facing away from each other.

"Goodnight Anthony. God bless."

"Thank you."

"You're welcome."

"Veronica?"

"Yes Anthony?"

"Did you iron that shirt I want for tomorrow? The one left out for you?"

"No! I did not. I shall not. I won't. Iron your own shirts. I'm tired and I've had enough."

"The Lord rebuke you!"

"I'm sure He will if you ask Him to." She could hardly believe her courage at answering him back. About time she did, too.

"I'll speak to you in the morning," the Pastor grumbled, too tired to stay awake any longer. It was then only a matter of minutes until his heavy breathing promised that a deep sleep was on its way.

Veronica could not sleep and lay ill at ease, fretting over what had happened to Hayley Bishford. Should she speak out about their ministry to her? *Could* she? But what about the times Anthony had been alone with Hayley? What had gone on then? Did she trust Anthony that whatever it was had been within the will of God? Besides which, confidentiality required and demanded her silence so was she to break that now that the police were involved? Plus, she was bound by Holy Scripture to be a support and a help to her husband and had always promised to obey him. Why, now, was her mother's warning ringing loudly in her ears – 'If you marry a Pratt you'll become one'. She'd known what her mother meant by the play on words, how could she not? Both her parents had taken an instant dislike to the young man she had met while he was handing out religious leaflets in town, not that Veronica had then been much concerned about what they thought. 'Pratt by name, prat by nature', they would tell her. Trouble was, at nineteen she thought she knew it all. Home life was wretched, she couldn't wait to leave, and by the time she came to her senses she and Anthony had gone through a marriage ceremony as members of the Community of Saintly Followers.

To be honest, their twenty-five years of so-called marriage had not been happy, except for the birth of Matthew, her only child following several miscarriages. "Oh Matthew...," she sighed softly. She forced her thoughts away from this son, the person she loved most in the whole world, and allowed herself to dwell on what had happened to Hayley, the young mother Anthony had been seeing on a regular basis.

Hayley had been sitting quietly in the chapel when Veronica left the building last Thursday, so what had then happened to make her flee like she did? She'd never done that before. Then why were the police asking questions? Anthony had not spent *much* time alone with Hayley, she'd seen to that. Something did not feel right and Veronica felt there was precious little she could do about that. "Oh Anthony," she sighed almost silently, "what have you done now?"

The manse was deathly, unnaturally cold that night. A thick blanket of frost was settling and the world, inside and outside, was raw and harsh. Pastor Pratt muttered between snores. The world was awash with evil and wickedness and he must do his part to cleanse the masses. He'd made a start...

CHAPTER FOURTEEN

THE YELLOW HOUSE

Monday morning

THE EVIL, wicked and totally unregenerate Hayley had been up since seven o'clock helping Mike get the kids off to school. Despite a slight limp and not having full use of one arm she had managed to spread their uniforms out in front of a cheerful gas fire before setting cereals, dishes and milk on the dining table. Two slices of toast popped just as Mikey and Daisy came down the stairs, bleary eyed, Daisy still rubbing her eyes. Hayley hugged and kissed them and soon the four of them were seated together for breakfast, Hayley sipping slowly from a mug of black, unsweetened coffee.

It was quarter to nine when Hayley once again hugged and kissed her beautiful children and waved from the gate as Mike set off with them to the local school. Hayley then cleared away the breakfast things, set the room straight, and curled up in her usual chair. She was so nervous and not at all looking forward to meeting this Dr Chatwith. At least it was a lady doctor, which she reckoned was something to be thankful for. Hayley placed her notepad in her lap and picked up her pen, twiddling it between the fingers of her good hand, her right hand. It wasn't long before she heard Mike's key in the door.

"Only me, H, kids in school, no probs." Mike shut the front door and came into the living-room rubbing his hands together. "Blimey it's a cold one. Shall I make us another cuppa or shall we wait and have one with this shrink?"

Hayley wrote 'wait' on her notepad before closing her eyes, her signal that she was opting out of any further communication. Mike noted the time, twenty past nine, and decided he'd pop upstairs, make the beds and tidy the bathroom. Truth was, he couldn't bear to sit in the room with Hayley when she shut him out like this. It was getting harder and harder and he honestly didn't know how much longer he could cope. But of course he would cope! What choice did he have? He loved the crazy mare, besides which the kids needed him and that mattered big time.

At four minutes to ten o'clock the chunky Volvo pulled up just past the Yellow House. The Sat Nav had not let her down and Dr Emily noted that the house was, as its name suggested, yellow. Instantly annoyed with herself, she huffed. Well, what colour had she expected it to be for goodness' sake? She decided to wait in the car for a few more minutes and used the time to flick through the sparse notes she had made concerning Hayley Bishford. Home visits were rare, but Dr Emily sensed that it had to be this way or no way, for if the woman had resisted the usual NHS channels of help then it was probably useless to give her a hospital appointment. Anyway, it would make a change to see a patient in their home environment. Only two more days and she'd be seeing Richard again. She was so looking forward to that. Perhaps she could invite him to tea over the next weekend? She hadn't yet contacted Penny about meeting up for coffee and a chat either. She must remember that when she updated her on Hayley this afternoon. So much to do all of a sudden. Wonderful!

Bringing her thoughts back to the present, Dr Emily took a deep breath, got out of her car, pressed 'lock' on the remote, then walked the few yards to the Bishford house. She rang the bell and waited, noticing that the little yellow house was well maintained. There was a pot full of bright artificial flowers by the front door which added a friendly splash of colour to a dull and chilly morning. The door was opened by a tall man, fortyish, wearing jeans and a baggy, navy sweater. This must be the husband, she thought.

"Mike? Hello. Emily Chatwith."

"Hi there. Yes, I'm Mike. Come in." They shook hands briefly and Mike held the door open as Dr Emily stepped inside a small porch where she waited for Mike to close the door before following him into the house. He went before her into the living-room, going straight across to where a small woman was curled up in a chair by the side of the chimney breast. "This is my wife Hayley." He turned to glance quickly at Dr Emily before turning back to address the woman in the chair. "Hayley? It's Dr Chatwith to see you."

"Hello Hayley." Dr Emily offered the woman her hand, which she took. "May I sit here?" She pointed to the settee opposite to where Hayley was sitting. Hayley nodded and Dr Emily and Mike sat at opposite ends of the settee. "Okay then, let's get straight on with it, shall we?" She smiled at Hayley before continuing. "I'm a consultant psychiatrist and psychotherapist, and as you both know, I've been asked by the police to come and talk to you, Hayley, with a view to offering you any help that I can give. Now the first thing I want you to be absolutely certain of is that, unless you give me express permission, I will NOT divulge anything you tell me to the police, or indeed anyone, unless I feel there is a danger to you or anyone else if I don't. How does that sound?"

"Okay by me," said Mike.

Hayley scribbled on her pad, "You can tell police anything. Don't care."

On reading those words, Dr Emily immediately rustled away in her large bag, produced the necessary consent form, and asked Hayley to sign it, which she did. Things would be so much easier if she could tell Penny anything Hayley came out with. That done, Dr Emily settled back, lacing her fingers together on her lap and crossing one leg over the other. Hayley watched, fascinated, as one foot, clad in a patent green court shoe, slowly circled the air. Hayley wondered where the shoes came from, surprised to find herself even mildly interested in what psychiatrists put on their feet.

"Would you like a cup of tea or coffee?" Mike asked, leaning forward.

"That's very kind of you Mike, coffee would be lovely. Milk. One sugar. Thank you." They both smiled briefly as Mike got up and went out into the kitchen to make the coffee.

"So, Haley. As you are sitting there now, this very moment in time, can you tell me how you feel?" Good. The woman was writing something down. This was going to be a long session, but so what? While Hayley wrote, Dr Emily had a quick look around the room, mindful of how much information you could pick up about a person by seeing them in their home environment. The room was neat and cosy. It was a through lounge with windows at either end, seating and TV at one end, dining table and chairs at the other. Several bookcases lined one wall, filled with books she would love to scan the titles of. Children's toys and books were stacked tidily in a large box and Dr Emily particularly noticed the number of clocks. They seemed to be everywhere, all types, many with pendulums swinging away, the ticking almost hypnotic. Now what was that about? Was it simply a collection of clocks? Or was there a deeper significance? The analyst in her was hard at work.

Eventually Hayley passed her writing pad across the coffee table to Dr Emily, just as Mike returned with three steaming mugs and a plate of biscuits on a tray. He placed a mug of coffee in front of each one of them, putting the plate of biscuits in the middle of the coffee table before resuming his seat. Dr Emily would rather have spoken to Hayley alone but felt it was right for Mike to be present at least during the first session while they were both getting to know her. He seemed more than happy to sit there quietly anyway. She quickly read through what Hayley had written.

Feel very depressed. Black. Don't want to talk, feel like I can't. Never get better. Wish I could be dead.

"Can you tell me what it is that makes you feel this way?"

Had problems as a kid, sexually abused by family friend, think it all stems from that. Got worse after kids were born. Even worse after going to church. Pastor trying to help but it all went wrong.

"How did your Pastor try to help you, Hayley?" Dr Emily again passed the pad back to Hayley before picking up her drink and taking a sip, noting that the plate held a number of chocolate digestives. She helped herself to one and, in complete denial and abandonment of social etiquette, dunked it into her coffee. Bliss! As usual she left it in too long and, as was to be expected in such circumstances, the biscuit broke. She then reached over to the tray, picked up a teaspoon, fished the chocolate digestive out from the bottom of the mug and ate the soggy mess from the spoon with obvious delight. Ecstasy! The process was repeated until she was sure no more lurked at the bottom of the mug. Mike and Hayley watched this little performance, transfixed by the sight of this awfully well dressed, terribly well-spoken professional lady enjoying the spoils of an overlong dunk with no thought as to who might be observing her engagement in such quirky pleasure. They looked across at each other, eyes wide, and shared a half smile which said, 'is she really doing that?' Mike was thrilled to see a genuine smile on his wife's face and Hayley returned to her writing, totally amazed to find herself rather liking the eccentric Dr Emily. After scribbling a few sentences she passed the pad back across the table. Dr Emily put her mug down and took it from her.

Then something unexpected and quite extraordinary happened. Hayley spoke, but not in the adult Hayley voice. Mike quickly whispered to Dr Emily, "That's not Hayley's usual voice. It happens sometimes."

"Me too?" a quiet, childlike voice said as Hayley reached out for a chocolate digestive which she then plopped, whole, into her coffee. Reaching for the same teaspoon Dr Emily had used she then proceeded to scoop out the soggy biscuit, bit by bit, and eat it. Mike, gobsmacked to see Hayley eating anything at all, was about to say something further but Dr Emily managed to shush him. They both watched with bated breath until Hayley had finished her tiny meal.

"Was that nice, Hayley?" Dr Emily asked.

"Hayley not allowed to eat," said the same childlike voice, "but I'm hungry." Another biscuit was then dropped into the coffee, scooped out and enjoyed. "Nice!" exclaimed the same voice. "Hayley don't eat."

"So who are you then? Who is hungry?" asked Dr Emily, almost holding her breath, afraid of saying the wrong thing, asking the wrong question.

"Please don't hurt me, I know he won't," pointing to Mike, "but I'm so hungry and the silly cow never eats enough. Please, help us…"

"Yes, I'll help you. I'd like to help you. You imply you're not Hayley. Do you have a name?"

"Lizzy."

"Hello Lizzy. That's a very nice name. My name is Emily and I promise I won't hurt you." With that, 'Lizzy' burst into gut wrenching sobs, trying to talk at the same time but making no sense through a deluge of snot and tears. Dr Emily went and sat on the arm of the chair, gave her a tissue and simply let her cry. She indicated for Mike to sit still and say nothing. This was certainly not what she had expected to happen. Was this an alter ego? A personality created by Hayley's subconscious to enable her to deal with severe trauma? Easy does it in that case, she needed to be careful.

'Lizzy' cried wretchedly for almost ten minutes until the torrent eased and she was able to take some deep, calming breaths. Dr Emily waited a few more minutes, staying where she was and placing a hand on 'Lizzy's' forearm.

"Tell me how I can help you Lizzy. What can I do for you and for Hayley?"

"Please, you have to keep him away from us, he hates us, he..."

"Who hates you Lizzy? Tell me who I have to keep you safe from."

"Pastor Pitchfork! Please don't let him near us again, please... Make him stay away, don't make us see him, don't, please don't..."

"Now then Lizzy, I want you to blow your nose and listen carefully." Dr Emily handed over another tissue into which 'Lizzy' blew loudly and wetly. "I want to help you to get better, therefore I don't want you to see anyone you don't want to see, because that would make you feel bad. I want to keep you safe and I'm going to try my very best to make sure Pastor Pitchfork doesn't come anywhere near you. Okay? Are you in agreement with that Mike?" Dr Emily turned to Mike, nodding her head up and down, hoping to God he was about to go along with her on this.

"Yes," said Mike, "I promise you Lizzy, and Hayley and Little Lizzy, that if I have anything to do with it you'll never see him again as long as you live."

Dr Emily swallowed. *Little* Lizzy? She was thinking fast, asking God, anyone, to guide her on how to proceed. What the bally heck was she supposed to do or say? Two alter egos so far. How old were they? Was Hayley aware of what was happening? Could she hear the conversation? Did she even know about Lizzy and Little Lizzy? What about Mike? He didn't seem at all surprised by his wife's sudden dissociative state. What could he tell her about Hayley's mental status?

"How old are you Lizzy?"

"I'm fifteen."

"And Little Lizzy?"

"She's three and she's driving us nuts, crying all the time, we can't stand any more of it, please keep him away from us, he hates us, everyone hates us and wants us dead. The scissor man is always coming! There's always a damp patch…"

"Try and calm down. Take some deep breaths. I don't hate you and neither does Mike. We want what's best for you, to help you and make you feel much, much better."

"I want another biscuit. Can I have the last one?" As 'Lizzy' reached forward and helped herself to the one remaining biscuit, Dr Emily noticed that there was no evidence whatsoever of any unilateral, slight paralysis as displayed by Hayley. Obviously she was dealing with some sort of conversion disorder – a physical infirmity with psychological issues as its root cause. If 'Lizzy' was a true alter ego then she wasn't anorexic. She had admitted to hunger, but was denied food when Hayley was in control. Dr Emily sat back on the settee and continued to talk to 'Lizzy', gently probing, easing her into opening up and speaking freely. All was going pretty darn well, then suddenly…

The clock on the wall above 'Lizzy's' chair threw open two little doors, a plastic sheep shot out and uttered the loudest 'Baaaa!' Dr Emily had heard in a long while. This was followed by sounds of galloping before a horse, just as plastic, emerged from another clock and whinnied loudly. Then a cat shot out of another timepiece, squealed a ridiculous 'meow' and shot back in. This was followed by various tunes and 'cuckoos' which seemed to be coming from everywhere, synchronised to perform one after the other. It had to be Little Lizzy, the three year old, who clapped her hands delightedly. Mike apologised, saying that he should have warned the unsuspecting visitor, while 'Lizzy' acted as if nothing out of the ordinary was going on, as indeed it wasn't if you were used to it. Dr Emily sat, startled, thanking the Lord for Tena Lady and waiting for her pulse rate to slow down. By jingo, that had made her jump.

Fifteen minutes later Dr Emily sensed that she should bring the session to an end as it wasn't good for any of them if she tried to do too much too soon. This sort of psychotherapy could be exhausting for the patient, besides which, much progress had been made so far and Dr Emily was rather pleased that she'd had privileged access to Hayley's world via the two Lizzies.

"Lizzy," she said, "I have to go soon so I'd like to speak to Hayley before I leave. Is that okay with you? Then when I come again on Wednesday we can talk again if you want to. How do you feel about that?"

"Okay. Will I have more biscuits?"

"I'm sure we can find some biscuits for you. Thank-you for everything you've told me today, that's been really helpful. I want you to know that I mean to do everything I can to keep you safe from Pastor Pitchfork." Dr Emily then mentally crossed her fingers before asking one last question. "Lizzy, before I go, can you tell me any more about last Thursday morning? When Hayley was at the chapel?"

"What about it?"

"You've already told me that Hayley didn't want to go, and the Pastor was reading to her and talking to her, then he was very angry and Hayley ran away because she was so frightened and upset. What was it that frightened her so much? What happened? Can you tell me what happened after the Vulture went home?"

"Will I be in trouble? Will someone be dead if I say it?"

"No, no. You won't be in any trouble, I promise, and no one will be dead if you say it."

"Promise?"

"Yes, Lizzy, I promise."

"Okay, I'll tell you then. He raped her."

"He *raped* her?"

"Yes. He raped her again."

CHAPTER FIFTEEN

DR EMILY

Monday lunchtime

IT HAD BEEN QUITE A MORNING and Dr Emily decided she would pop home and have lunch before her afternoon clinic. For once she was grateful for the winding down of her duties prior to retirement, which meant fewer clinics with fewer patients. It would give her more time to mull over her work with Hayley, and of course there was Richard Preston to think about as well. For once she didn't bother to switch on the car stereo, preferring instead to drive quietly, which was proving conducive to her thought processes. She was glad Mike had her mobile number and would ring her if she was needed, yet she would probably give him a call herself later that day to see how Hayley was after their session.

Dr Emily had managed to speak to Hayley before she left, discovering that Hayley was well aware of her 'little selves' as she called them. She experienced Lizzy and Little Lizzy as voices in her head, sometimes as feelings of fear or distress, and often there were gaps in the day after which she would 'come round' to find that Little Lizzy had been playing with the kids' toys, or Lizzy had made the beds. However, since the Pastor had been counselling Hayley there had been trouble between the three of them. The little one cried pitifully most of the time which was exasperating to the other two. Lizzy and Hayley were barely civil, arguing and harming one another – Hayley by refusing food, Lizzy by suddenly lashing out with a knife or a pair of scissors. The promise of peace between them existed only if Hayley stopped seeing Pastor Pratt, which she was now more than willing to comply with. What, in the name of God, had this man been up to? Hayley and her little selves were terrified of him and Mike never wanted to see the man again as long as he lived. Pratt the Pitchfork had hardly been the Lord's reconciler or peacemaker as far as Hayley Bishford was concerned, in fact quite the opposite. What an extraordinary, bizarre, unholy mess!

"How's my lovely Doodle then?" The small dog, overjoyed to see her owner coming through the door unexpectedly early, was yipping away and demanding to be fussed and picked up. "I've come home for lunch today, now that makes a change for a Monday, doesn't it?" Dr Emily tucked her furry companion under one arm, marched through into the kitchen, and began to prepare cheese on toast, all the while chatting away to her little Doodle. She also made herself the usual mug of Nescafe Gold Blend and was soon on the settee watching the news and enjoying her lunch. Doodle was grappling with a chew on the rug in front of the fire.

Soon there was an empty plate and half a mug of coffee left when Dr Emily exclaimed aloud, "What the heck! Why shouldn't I?" before marching back into the kitchen. She returned holding one ginger nut biscuit, sat down, over-dunked it until the greater part broke off into the hot liquid, then scooped it out with a teaspoon. For the part of a minute it took to indulge in such sogginess she felt as if a portion of heaven itself had descended upon Angel's Rest. Kicking off the patent green shoes (another pair of Van Dhal's) she leaned back and sighed with pleasure. "Life's too short not to dunk. What do you say, Doodle?" Doodle said nothing. She was in her own portion of heaven thanks to a helping of 'Chewy Delights for Discerning Dogs'.

It had just gone half past twelve when Dr Emily picked up the phone. Wanting to update DI Penny on this morning's visit to Hayley, she punched in the number and was eventually put through to Penny's office.

"Hello Dr Emily. Good to hear from you. Anything you can tell us?"

"Yes, indeed. Well, very briefly, Hayley Bishford is a victim of child sexual abuse, don't know when or where, but that could explain why she accepted help from her church for depression, anorexia etc., although the wrong sort of help has greatly exacerbated her condition in my opinion. Anyway, she presented to me as what we could call an alter ego, a part of her personality she calls Lizzy. As Lizzy, Hayley has no weakness in her limbs and is able to eat. Absolutely fascinating. Most helpful of all as far as you are concerned is that, as Lizzy, Hayley told me that on the Thursday morning in question she was raped by the Pastor. Not only raped but, quote, 'he raped her again', unquote. Now while I was there..."

"Hang on Dr Em", Penny interrupted, "are you saying that Hayley said Pastor Pratt raped her on Thursday morning?"

"Right, now what I'm saying is that Hayley has DID, Dissociative Identity Disorder..."

"Explain that to me please."

"Okay. Hayley is displaying two distinct personality states, apart from her own, which can take control of Hayley's actions with or without her knowledge or consent. These other personalities are, it is thought, a psychological creation at the time of extreme abuse, like a self-defence mechanism. For example, when something terrible was happening to Hayley as a child, something she could not understand or cope with, she dissociated, or went into a trance if you like, and her mind created this other 'person' for it to be happening to. Therefore,

101

as this terrible thing happened to somebody else, Hayley's psyche was rendered capable enough to carry on with everyday life."

"So Hayley has three personalities, is that what you're saying?" Penny was frowning as she tried to get her head around all this.

"Simply put, yes, but of course Lizzy and Little Lizzy, as she calls them, are still Hayley; her mind has partitioned them off with their own memories and characteristics in order to preserve a functioning Hayley. Does that make any sense?"

"Yes, yes. I'm with you. A bit like that film, the Three Faces of Eve?"

"Exactly. Although take out the drama. My problem is that DID is rare, or maybe rarely diagnosed, mostly occurring in child abuse victims who dissociate at the time of abuse, BUT… it can also be iatrogenic, that is, induced by a therapist via suggestion, during hypnosis, or simply through lousy counselling. I'm seriously considering whether Hayley's present dissociating might have been made worse by whatever was going on between her and Pastor Pratt."

"Do you think the Pastor may have *caused* the condition?"

"No, no. The husband tells me that Hayley has always displayed characteristics of what she calls her 'little selves', and has been hearing voices for many years."

"I'm with you so far, Dr Em. At least I think I am. So it was a dissociating part of Hayley, called Lizzy, who claimed that Pastor Pratt had raped her on Thursday morning?"

"Not quite. Lizzy refers to Pastor Pratt as Pastor Pitchfork…"

"Now that's interesting," Penny interrupted once more, "that's what Hayley called him in the ambulance on the way to the General. Remember I mentioned it when we spoke at the weekend?"

"Yes, I do remember. Lizzy is absolutely terrified of him and made me promise she'd never have to see him again. Not wanting to make an 'ass' out of 'u' and 'me', I have nevertheless found myself wanting to assume that Lizzy was telling me that Pastor Pratt raped Hayley at the chapel last Thursday morning and it wasn't the first time either. When she said 'he raped her', I asked 'he raped her?', and she replied, 'yes. He raped her again'."

"Right," said Penny, "so it *appears* as if part of Hayley's mind, called Lizzy, is *claiming* that Pastor Pratt raped Hayley, but this Lizzy doesn't claim to *be* Hayley, and doesn't *literally* name Pastor Pratt as the rapist. Is that it?" Oh boy! This was going to be complicated.

"That's correct," Dr Emily confirmed, smiling to herself, well pleased with her involvement so far.

"Gee Dr Em, this is going to be an awkward one. Looks like we're going to have to rely on forensics for the time being, but we've got more than enough to bring him in for questioning. Judge Thomas has granted the warrant for his arrest so we'll probably get to the manse this afternoon and bring him in. Dr Fuss-Artist from…"

"Who?" Dr Emily chuckled.

"Oops! Sorry Dr Em, we always call him that. Dr Fuseley from forensics. Thankfully he *is* a fusspot where work is concerned and he managed to get somebody out to the chapel this morning for a sample of carpet fibres. Pastor was NOT happy about it, one wonders why, but in light of a search warrant there was not a lot he could do to stop them. Fuseley's going to give me a bell as soon as he's made a comparison with fibres found on Hayley's clothing. Fuss-Artist has also got hold of the suit Pastor Pratt was wearing that Thursday morning. Did you speak to Hayley's husband at all? Mike? Is that his name?"

"Yes, Mike. Briefly, he didn't say anything that you don't already know. He's obviously concerned for his wife. Says she's lost over two stone in weight since the Pastor's so called help. Six and a half stone is nowhere near good enough for five foot four."

"Gosh. Why the hell did they carry on going there?"

"Very reasonable question, Penny, the answer to which lies within the whole complicated, perplexing psychology of abuse. It's a typical pattern, where adults who were abused as children subconsciously put themselves in situations where the abuse is repeated. Hubby tells me they are now breaking away from the chapel and any further contact with the Pratts, thank God. He's still adamant his wife should have nothing to do with the police however, and she still doesn't want to make a statement. I'm going to ring him later, ask how Hayley is, and I've arranged to see her again on Wednesday morning."

"As soon as that? Well, actually, I guess that's not a bad idea."

"She needs the support at the moment, Penny, and I'm free on Wednesday anyway."

"Brilliant. Okey dokey then, thanks for calling Dr Em. Stay in touch."

"I will Penny dear. Let me know how things go and if I can be of any further assistance."

"I will indeed. Bye now."

"Bye bye." Dr Emily ended the call, pushed her feet back into the green shoes, picked up her coat and made for the door. How she'd love to be a fly on the wall when they questioned Pastor Pitchfork. Good name for him. Dr Fuss-Artist? She liked that as well. 'I wonder what they call me?' she mused out loud to herself.

"Bye Doodle, I won't be long." She closed the door behind her and set off for her afternoon clinic, wondering if she should have told Penny about her visit to the Pastor's chapel yesterday. But then it surely wasn't important to the case against him and besides which, she didn't want Penny thinking she was a nosy old biddy, which, of course, she most certainly wasn't. Oh dear, there again, perhaps it was important that she pass on her concerns about the Pastor's mental health. He might well have been putting on a good performance of hellfire preaching, yet it was still too over the top, and if he was mentally unbalanced he needed help. Quickly. She decided to think over what she should do about that as it would be easy enough to contact Penny later on.

Dr Emily experienced yet another moment of near heavenly bliss as she entered her office that afternoon. It was warm! The radiator had finally been fixed, her computer was already switched on, and behind it sat her secretary, Jill, hammering away at the keyboard.

"Welcome back Jill, are you feeling better?"

"Oh, hello. Yes thanks Dr Em, it was only a cold but I felt absolutely lousy with it. Sorry about that. I've just been updating a few things here, finished now though so I'll go and make us a cuppa, shall I?"

"Thank you Jill, that sounds splendid." Dr Emily was so very blessed to have a secretary who shared her own deep appreciation of liquid refreshments with regard to the intensely important part they played in the life of the NHS. Keeping one's consultant adequately hydrated dramatically increased the possibility of a smoothly run clinic, and well timed liquid refreshments also ensured a happier life for one's secretary. There were benefits to all.

"Jill?" Dr Emily called through to the adjoining office where Jill was popping tea bags into mugs. "How did you get on with my replacement this morning?"

"He's okay actually," Jill shot back. "It's going to feel strange for a few months but I dare say I'll soon get used to him. He's settling in really quickly, so that makes things a lot easier. Really nice guy."

"Oh." Dr Emily sounded disappointed.

"Not that anyone can replace you," Jill added quickly, mindful not to sound overenthusiastic about the doctor who was to take over from Dr Emily. "I'm going to miss you."

"Aw, bless you, that's nice to hear. We've worked well together, haven't we?"

"Yes, we have. You'll be back on locum anyway, so it's not as if you're totally disappearing. Right, here comes the tea."

"Any chance of a biscuit, Jill?"

CHAPTER SIXTEEN

PENNY AND IAN

Monday lunchtime

THE PHONE RANG in Penny's office and she snatched up the receiver. She'd been hoping for five minutes to gather her thoughts together but that obviously wasn't going to happen. "Yes?" she barked, frowning.

"Is that the inspector?" enquired an oldish, female voice. "The lady who put me through told me I needed to speak to the inspector. It's about that man at the chapel opposite where I live. She said you would want to know."

Penny was instantly alert and attentive. "Yes, I'm Inspector Whistle. Which chapel are we talking about?" As if she didn't know, but all information needed to come from the informer in cases like this.

"The Sinners Chapel of Mercy," the lady replied. "My husband goes there. I don't because I was brought up Pentecostal. Went a few times but it was too serious for me."

"And what would you like to tell me?" Penny was all ears now.

"Well, it was last Thursday morning. I was watching TV, the Wright Stuff, I sit where I can see out, watch the road. I'm in my seventies, you see. Anyway, I saw Pastor Pratt and his

107

wife going into the chapel, which was unusual for a Thursday morning, and then a lady arrived and went in as well."

"Could you describe the lady for me Mrs…?"

"It's Mrs Crabbe. I don't remember what she was wearing but I do know it was Hayley Bishford. My husband knows of the Bishford family as there's been some trouble at the chapel concerning Mrs Bishford."

"What sort of trouble?" This was interesting, thought Penny.

"Well, she was taken off the membership and banned from taking communion. There was an awful lot of disgruntlement over that, I can tell you," Mrs Crabbe continued.

"Do you know why Hayley was treated that way?"

"Because Pastor Pratt decided she wasn't a Christian, although what gives him the right to…"

"Going back to Thursday morning Mrs Crabbe, can you tell me what happened after the three of them entered the chapel?"

"Yes. It was about half an hour later when Mrs Pratt came rushing out on her own. She seemed upset and walked very fast down the road. I guessed she was walking back to the manse as it's not far. She didn't take their car. They've got one of those peculiar looking Smart Cars, looks as if they've been chopped in half. Then about half an hour after that… or it could have been longer, I can't be certain now, I'm not very good at times, I thought I could hear someone screaming so I opened the window. It was definitely screaming, as if something utterly dreadful was happening. Shrill and loud, you know? A woman screaming. Definitely a woman."

"Go on," Penny prompted.

"This seemed to be going on for a while – I was starting to think about dialling 999 – but then the chapel door was flung open and Hayley ran out, sobbing, and didn't close the door after her. She got straight into her car and drove off. It wasn't long after that when the Pastor came out. He locked the door, looked up, fiddled with his tie and jacket, then got in his car and drove off."

"Anything else?"

"No. I think that's about it. Was I right to call and let you know?"

"Yes Mrs Crabbe, you've done the right thing. Thank you for letting us know and will you get back to me straight away if you remember anything else?"

"Yes. I will. Bye bye. And it's very nice to talk to a lady inspector. I was expecting you to be a man."

Penny chuckled. "Bye Mrs Crabbe, and thanks again."

"Excellent!" DI Penny slammed the phone down and startled as it rang again immediately. "Blimey, this is like the city editor's desk," she mumbled as she put the receiver to her ear once again. Five minutes later she ended that call with a smile on her face. "Splendid! Ian? You there?" she called, "We've got a witness and a preliminary report from Fuss-Artist. Are you listening to me or am I talking to the walls again?"

"I'm on my way boss," Ian called out as he strode into Penny's office carrying a ham salad baguette in one hand and a coffee in the other, courtesy of Greggs around the corner. Placing his lunch on Penny's desk, he sat in the chair opposite, the desk being between them. "What have we got then? Good news?"

"Very good news for us," said Penny, "but not very good news for the Pastor. The carpet fibres from the chapel match those found on Hayley's clothes, Fuss-Artist will fax over the written report as soon as it's ready. Also, the hair I retrieved from the back of Pratt's jacket is a match with one found on Hayley Bishford's jumper, which also matches a similar length hair found on the chapel floor. PLUS, there are carpet fibres on the Pastor's suit, concentrated in the areas of knees and arms. EXTRA plus, we have a witness who saw the three of them going into the chapel, leaving separately, and this lady also heard screaming. How about that then?" Penny sat back with a satisfied grin and crossed her arms as she awaited Ian's response.

"Yes!" Ian punched the air. "I knew it. If that jerk's not guilty then I'm no cop. We've got enough to go for him this afternoon as planned then." It was a statement rather than a question.

"Yes Ian, we certainly have, and as if all that wasn't enough, I've had a call from our Dr Em and Hayley *might* have claimed that the Pastor raped her. All in all, we've got some strong evidence so far."

"*Might* have? Surely the woman knows if he raped her for goodness sake." Ian spoke through a mouthful of food. Unwrapping her own lunch, a cheese and pickle sandwich also courtesy of Greggs around the corner, Penny took a large bite. "What d'you mean by *might* have?" Ian repeated.

"Hang on, I'm chomping and it's complicated." Penny kept Ian in suspense until she'd swallowed her first mouthful. "Right. Well. Dr Em says Hayley is terrified of the Pastor and pleading never to have to see him again, which figures if the jerk has raped her. Normal so far. However, she also appears to be suffering from DID, a Dissociative Identity Disorder which means that…" Penny went on to tell Ian what Dr Emily had found out, trying to explain it as simply as she could. Ian listened intently as he continued to demolish his baguette as if he'd not seen food in the last six months. He paused briefly to retrieve a slice of tomato that had fallen onto his left trouser leg. Throwing his head back, mouth wide open, he daintily dropped the tomato slice into his mouth and chewed quickly before speaking.

"Blimey," he said, "so there's another Hayley called Lizzy, who has said that *he,* whom we guess could be the Pastor, raped *her*, who we take to be Hayley, on Thursday morning at the chapel. Is that about right?" He pushed another piece of crusty roll into his mouth then followed it with a long swallow of coffee.

"That's about it as far as I understand." Penny took another bite of her sandwich and they both ate silently for a few moments. "It's obviously not straightforward," Penny continued, "and only the Good Lord knows what a jury would make of it, but it's early days yet so let's get going with what we've got so far. I really need to question Hayley again myself if she'll let me but I'll get back to Dr Em on that later. Anyway, I vote we finish lunch, get up to the manse and bring our man in for questioning. What say you?"

"With you all the way boss."

"I can't wait to hear what he has to say for himself. Should be *very* interesting."

They ate in silence for a few more minutes.

"Ian?"

"Yes boss?"

"Do you *have* to make so much mess when you eat?"

"Can't help it boss. Crusty baguette. You try eating this without dropping crumbs."

Penny's brows furrowed. "Why don't you spread the wrapper out over your lap and then catch the crumbs in it? That way they don't make it onto the floor and mess my whole office carpet up."

"Because if I did that boss, when the crumbs hit the wrapper they'd make a sort of noise, like a *pwhuff*, whereas when they drop on your carpet they don't, the sound is muffled and not discernible to the human ear. Therefore I'm able to multitask. That is, I can eat my lunch, listen to you and concentrate all at the same time without being disturbed by the sounds of crumbs dropping onto…"

"Ian?"

"Yes boss?"

"Shut up!"

"Okay boss. What d'you think of the coffee?"

"Not the same as Mc D's. No stickers. Now shut up."

The two officers finished their food and coffees, screwing up wrappers and stuffing them inside paper cups before depositing all the rubbish in the bin at the side of Penny's desk.

"Right. Let's go. Did you sort out interrogation room B for us?" Penny asked as she shrugged herself into her jacket.

"Sure did," Ian replied, "tape machine's set up ready to go and I've told them down there to keep it vacant for us."

"Got some keys to a car?"

"Yes boss."

"Fab. Look out Pastor Pratt, here we come!"

It was less than ten minutes later when Penny and Ian pulled up outside the manse. They spotted the Pastor's Smart car parked in the driveway so he was almost definitely at home. Good. They got out of the car, crunched across the gravel, rang the doorbell and waited. It was seven minutes before two o'clock. The door was eventually opened by Mrs Pratt, again in a pinny, again not at all pleased to see the visitors on her doorstep. She really did resemble a vulture, and a particularly miserable one at that.

"Mrs Pratt? Detective Inspector Penelope Whistle and Detective Sergeant Ian Gettum."

"Yes, I know, I remember you."

"We're here to see your husband? We'd like to come in. Is he at home?"

"Yes, he's home. Come in. He won't be pleased to see you though. He's extremely busy."

I bet he won't be pleased to see us, thought Penny. Ian was thinking much the same. They were shown into the same dreary lounge but this time declined the offer to sit down while they waited for Pastor Pratt to appear. As before, Mrs Pratt scurried up the stairs and in no time at all the Pastor appeared in the lounge dressed, as usual, in a suit and tie. His face looked thunderous, not exactly oozing Christian hospitality, never mind the love of the Lord he professed to follow.

"Pleasure to see you too," Ian muttered under his breath, only to receive a stern look from Penny.

CHAPTER SEVENTEEN

THE ARREST OF PASTOR PRATT

Monday afternoon

PASTOR PRATT stood before them, seeming to be stretching himself up and puffing himself out, as if physical stature indicated superiority over one's visiting police detectives.

Idiot, thought Ian.

Plonker, thought Penny.

Following an impatient sniff, the Pastor spoke. "What can I do for you detectives? I'm extremely busy this afternoon and have an important meeting later on but I can give you a few minutes." He widened his mouth, not exactly a smile, and raised his jet black eyebrows, his whole demeanour challenging and arrogant. Boy, was Ian raring to go, barely managing to hold his tongue. He hated men who raped. He hated arrogant jerks like this one. He hated having to take his time and keep his cool.

"We need to question you about what took place at the Sinners Chapel of Mercy last Thursday morning," said Penny. "There's a lot more you can tell us."

"Fire away then. Like what?" The Pastor stood there, not moving, making it plain they were wasting his precious time and interrupting his incredibly busy day.

"We'd prefer to question you at police HQ," Penny informed him. "We'll take you there. You might want to put on a coat. It's cold."

"What?!" Pastor Pratt went nigh on purple with outrage. "Are you serious?"

"Deadly serious sir," said Ian.

"The Lord requires me to be here, doing his work. I must obey him before all earthly requests. Surely you understand that? Besides which, I have done only his will, which cannot possibly be wrong."

"Then it is your *interpretation* of his will which we hold in question Mr Pratt." Penny was struggling not to get more annoyed than she already was. "Please fetch a coat and accompany us to the station."

"And if I refuse?"

"Then I have a warrant for your arrest sir. I'm sure you'd much rather we did this the easier way." How she'd enjoyed uttering those words. At the same time, Ian had produced a pair of handcuffs from his jacket pocket, jangling them as much as possible. Mrs Pratt stood there, hands to her face, and groaned out loud. The Pastor took in a long, slow, deep breath, finally realising he had little choice but to do as he was asked.

"The Lord rebuke you!" he uttered, trembling with rage.

"I beg your pardon?" Penny could hardly believe he'd said that and held eye contact with him. The Pastor was the first to look away.

"You won't need those," he said, glancing at the handcuffs. "I'll get my coat. You'll regret this, you mark my words, vengeance is mine sayeth the Lord, I will repay. This is utterly outrageous. Utterly, utterly outrageous!" With that he stormed out of the room and stomped upstairs. Wearing an overcoat he stomped back downstairs less than a minute later.

"Stay here," he growled to his trembling wife, "I won't be long. Don't tell anyone where I am. I'll have that smoked haddock for tea. With crusty bread rolls. Butter, not margarine. Tea instead of coffee." His instructions were fired at the poor woman like bullets as she stood there looking as if her whole world had imploded.

"Yes, dear," she replied meekly.

"He ain't gonna be back in time for any loaves and fishes," Ian whispered to Penny as they waited for him to finish buttoning up his coat. Penny smiled grimly before turning to speak to Mrs Pratt.

"Would you like to come with us now? There's a waiting area and we'll need to speak to you at some point anyway."

"No. She wouldn't like to come with us," interrupted the Pastor.

"Mrs Pratt?" Ignoring her pig of a husband, Penny indicated that she would like Mrs Pratt to speak for herself.

"I'd rather not come if that's okay, I'll stay here." The woman was as pale as porcelain.

"Sure you'll be okay? Is there someone who could come and be with you?" Penny felt some degree of pity and concern for the woman.

"I'll be fine, honestly."

"Okay then Mrs Pratt," said Penny, "we'll be in touch as soon as possible and let you know what's happening and when we'd like to speak to you." With that, Penny and Ian left the manse with the Pastor and made their way straight back to HQ.

Interrogation room B was warm and contained a table and three chairs. On the table was a tape recorder, paper and pens, a box of tissues, and a tray on which was a jug of water and several plastic beakers. Pastor Pratt had already gone through the preliminaries of form filling and advice about contacting a solicitor. He was now seated at the table. Penny sat opposite him, Ian sitting next to her, and a uniformed officer stood by the closed door. Penny was speaking.

"Are you absolutely certain you don't want to contact a lawyer?"

"Yes. Quite certain. Why would I need one?"

Ignoring his question, Penny continued, "Do you want us to contact one for you?"

"No. I do not."

Breathing deeply through her nose, Penny then turned on the tape recorder, stated the time and names of those present, then began the interview by asking the Pastor to confirm where he was last Thursday morning and who he was with.

Sitting back in her chair and keeping eye contact with the Pastor, Penny proceeded...

"Why did you and Mrs Pratt arrange to meet Hayley Bishford at the chapel?"

"We usually saw her at the manse but thought a change of surrounding might prove more conducive to a spirit of co-operation. We've been seeing Hayley for around two years."

"Why have you been seeing her?"

"She has a number of problems."

"Such as?"

"That would be a breach of confidentiality. I'm not able to tell you."

"How frequently do you see her?"

"Usually weekly. Sometimes more frequently if the Lord leads us to."

"You spent a lot of time with her," Penny gave him one of her surprised looks. "Was your wife always with you?"

"Most of the time, yes, but she left early on Thursday as she had a migraine."

"So you were alone with Mrs Bishford?"

"Yes."

"Since you've been seeing Hayley Bishford, have her problems improved?" Penny leaned over the desk and put her head slightly to one side as she awaited the Pastor's reply. He sat in silence, looking at the wall opposite, sucking his lips into a straight line.

"Please answer the question. Since you've been seeing Hayley Bishford, have her problems improved?"

"No."

"So did you at any time suggest that she see her GP?"

"No. I did not."

"So to get this straight, you'd been seeing her for two years during which time you saw no improvement in her condition, in fact she was getting worse, yet you did not suggest or seek any other form of help."

"No," the Pastor sighed deeply, "I did not."

"Why not?"

"Because I was working under the Lord's direction. Things often get much worse before they get better. We were looking to Jesus to heal Hayley." He took a neatly folded cotton handkerchief out of his trouser pocket, shook it and wiped his perspiring forehead.

"So Jesus makes people worse before he makes them better, is that what you're saying?"

"In this case, yes."

Penny was fighting now to control the anger she was feeling. Raising her voice slightly, "So you expected Hayley to become more depressed, near suicidal, cutting herself regularly and losing over two stone in weight as part of being helped by you? She was being healed?"

"It's in the Bible that..."

Penny interrupted, "I have great difficulty with your interpretation of the Bible Mr Pratt. Let's keep to the facts. If you were helping Hayley then why was she becoming worse?"

"She was uncooperative."

"In what way?"

"She would not do as I instructed even under rebuke from the Lord when..."

"Mr Pratt," Penny felt as if she was in the presence of some sin-shifting fundamentalist from the dark ages, "why was Hayley Bishford lying on the floor of the chapel?" Penny was eager to hear how he would answer *that* one. The sudden change of direction had rendered him temporarily silent and he stared first at Penny, then at Ian.

"I'm not sure I know what you mean." He licked his lips.

"The question is quite straightforward," said Penny, "why was she lying on the floor of the chapel?"

Staring down at the table in obvious discomfort, the Pastor was most satisfyingly flummoxed. Come on you creep, thought Penny, get out of that if you can. He eventually spoke, lifting his head to look at Penny with undisguised contempt.

"What do you mean by 'lying' on the chapel floor? What makes you think she was lying on the floor of my chapel?"

"Okay," put in Ian, following a nod from Penny that it was his turn, "this is what we've got thanks to our wonderful forensics laboratory. The back of the clothes Hayley Bishford was wearing Thursday morning have on them a significant number of carpet fibres which match those from your chapel. The suit *you* wore that morning also has the very same carpet fibres in significant numbers, especially on the trouser legs and jacket forearms. A hair from the back of that same suit jacket perfectly matches a hair collected from the chapel floor. Both hairs are from Hayley Bishford's head." He paused here for effect, and because he was enjoying himself. "Adhesion and distribution of said carpet fibres on Hayley Bishford's clothes indicate she was supine for a period of time and also suggest movement, possible violence. I believe that's more than enough evidence for us to draw the conclusion that Hayley was lying on the floor, don't you agree? Now. Please answer the question. Why was Hayley Bishford lying on the floor of your chapel?"

"No comment."

"That's fine Mr Pratt but it won't help your case. What are your qualifications for church leadership?" Again the sudden change of direction caught the Pastor off guard and he became flustered. Good.

"It's Pastor, not Mr," was his only rather pathetic response.

"Shall I prompt your memory *Mr* Pratt?" Ian was really hotting up the interrogation. "You don't *have* any qualifications for church leadership, do you? You have undergone no training in church ministry whatsoever, you have no academic qualifications, you are not ordained, you have never set foot in any theological training establishment, neither have you any qualifications in counselling. The titles 'Reverend' and 'Pastor' have been given to you by none other than yourself. Am I correct?"

"This is outrageous. I..."

"Furthermore, you lied and claimed qualifications you did not possess in order to take over the former Baptist chapel in Conversion Close, did you not?"

"I am called and ordained by God himself and have no need of human recognition of those facts. I take my instruction and teaching from him alone. He told me to say those things... the Bible says..."

"The Bible says 'thou shalt not bear false witness', Exodus chapter twenty." Penny interrupted. "You lied about your qualifications! To claim that God told you to lie is complete and utter rubbish."

"God qualifies the called rather than calls the qualified. He has ordained and qualified me."

"How?" Penny shot back.

"How? I'll tell you how. I live by the book, by the inerrancy of scripture. I've shown myself faithful in obedience to him; when he speaks to me I check it out in his infallible word."

"And find the verses that suit you? Where is the verse that tells you to lie?"

"Don't be ridiculous."

"So what happens," continued Penny, "if your interpretation of what God is saying to you happens to be wrong? What happens if your interpretation of scripture is incorrect? In other words, what line of accountability is there if you get something wrong because, let me drum it in to you, you got something seriously wrong concerning Hayley Bishford. Didn't you?"

"She was unco-operative, I've told you that. That's not my responsibility. I did what God told me to do."

"So what do you claim God told you to do to Hayley Bishford on Thursday morning?"

"I will not breach confidentiality."

"You mean you are refusing to tell me the truth? What if I produced a signed consent from Hayley giving you permission to tell us everything that went on between you?" Penny crossed her fingers under the table. She had no signed consent from Hayley but the Pastor wasn't to know that.

"You wouldn't understand..."

"Try me!" demanded Penny, getting annoyed as it was obvious the Pastor didn't want to open up. "Shall I tell you something Mr Pratt? The book which you hold as infallible and inerrant says, quote, 'the truth shall set you free', unquote. But let me assure you, when we get to the truth about what happened between you and Hayley Bishford, and believe me we will, you're going to be anything *but* free. Do I make myself clear?"

"The Lord demands my silence." Pastor Pratt again sucked his lips into a straight line.

"Does he really?" Penny shot back, "I doubt that. What caused the bruising to various parts of Hayley's body?"

"I don't know."

"You *do* know, Mr Pratt. It would be in your own interests to come clean and start telling us what's been going on." This came from Ian who had jumped in, sensing that Penny was starting to lose it. He continued, "How did you get those scratches to your neck and hand Mr Pratt?"

"I don't know."

"I believe you *do* know. Please answer the question."

"Hayley Bishford lashed out at me."

"Why?" (Come on, you complete and utter plonker, land yourself in it.)

"She became distressed and would not co-operate."

"Would not co-operate with what?"

"With what the Lord was telling me to do."

"We're going round in circles," said Penny, "you mean she was not co-operating with what *you thought* you were being told to do. Human interpretation of divine revelation is surely subjective Mr Pratt." The Pastor looked at her with a mixture of confusion and barely hidden contempt. Penny needed to be careful with the wording of her next question. She nodded ever so slightly to Ian to let him know she was going in for the kill at this point.

"I want to make you aware, Mr Pratt, that words spoken from Hayley Bishford's mouth claim that she was raped. On Thursday morning. When she was with you."

"What?"

"Why was she screaming in the chapel on Thursday morning before she ran away?"

"How do you know she was screaming?" The Pastor had admitted the truth about that without realising it, caught out by the rapid fire questioning.

"We have a witness."

"Who? Tell me!"

Ignoring his demand Penny shot out, "Did you rape Hayley Bishford?"

"How dare you! I was... it wasn't me... this is utterly ridiculous. I don't understand what you are asking or why..."

"DID YOU RAPE HAYLEY BISHFORD?" Was that loud and clear enough for him? The arrogant, pig ignorant ass wipe...

"Oh no. She's not pinning that one on me. I'll tell you, she was raped all right, it was her own fault, I saw it happening, I tried to... What I was attempting was far more serious, extremely dangerous, let me tell you. And she knows it." His voice had deepened to a guttural tremble that was menacing and threatening, even unbalanced and disturbing. Penny felt suddenly cold.

"Did you rape Hayley Mr Pratt?"

"No. I did not."

"Were you alone in the chapel with her when the alleged rape took place?"

"Yes. I was."

"Then who raped her?"

"Don't ask. You don't want to know."

Penny had had enough. "Anthony Pious Pratt, you are under arrest on suspicion of the rape of Hayley Bishford. You do not have to say anything. However, it might harm your defence if you do not mention when questioned something which you later rely on in court. Anything you do say may be given in evidence."

"This is outrageous! I did not..."

"You've told us you were alone with Hayley when she was raped! What does that mean?"

"No comment."

"Fine!" With that, Penny got up to leave the room, barking out orders as she did so. "Get him processed. Inform the wife and get her in for questioning. Interview finished. Turn the tape off." She was followed by Ian as she quickly exited the interrogation room.

123

"Penny, stop…" he caught her by the arm as she went to march off down the corridor, "don't let him get to you, just take a chill pill, okay?"

"I want that wife of his in for questioning. Stat. I'll be in my office, call me when she's here. It goes without saying they're to have no contact whatsoever with each other. God help me Ian, I hate that man."

"This isn't like you Pen…" but Penny was gone and so Ian returned to the interrogation room to begin the necessary processing that followed an arrest.

"I didn't rape her." The Pastor looked up and spoke as soon as Ian was back in the room.

"What happened then? She has some pretty nasty bruising."

"I had to hold her down…"

"Go on. So you held her down? Then what?"

"She was struggling, I had to grapple with her, I had no choice, I was trying to save her from being raped, you don't understand…"

"No, I don't mate. You said you were alone with her. So who raped her if you didn't?"

"Incubus."

"What?"

"She was being raped by a demonic entity."

"Yeh, okay, and my name's Elvis Presley. I'll tell you what though, that's got to be one of the best excuses I've heard for a while…"

"But…"

"Save it for later chum. We'll be questioning you again soon."

The phone was ringing on Penny's desk as she approached her office. Hurrying in, she snatched up the receiver. "Yes?" Her eyes closed in annoyance. She'd desperately wanted five minutes peace and quiet to gather her thoughts together.

CHAPTER EIGHTEEN

VERONICA PRATT

Monday afternoon

VERONICA PRATT was beside herself. After witnessing her husband of twenty-five miserable years taken away by the police, scales at last began to fall from her eyes, as if she was being relieved of a dark presence. For so many years she had put up with his overbearing fanaticism, his unreasonableness, his lack of compassion. Oh yes, he could find a bible verse to justify his every word and action, but his was a harsh, unyielding theology where everything was either black or white. Life, as she had discovered, simply wasn't like that. Over the years she had silently questioned this man as he dragged her and their son from town to town, setting up yet another religious group, or a chapel, or a church. It was never his fault that these groups never survived, of course it could never be his fault, and once again they would shake the dust from their sandals and move on, away from those Godless people who refused Pastor Pratt's particular form of salvation. Now it was happening all over again, but this time it was worryingly worse. He was becoming more severe and uncompromising; what he had been subjecting Hayley Bishford to could not possibly be right. Now, finally, she had

had enough. She wanted no further part in any of it. But what if he spoke of the thing *she* had done?

Unaware that there was a car on the way to pick her up and take her to Police HQ, Veronica Pratt scribbled a note to her husband before hastily packing a small suitcase. She then collected her handbag and some cash out of a drawer before leaving the manse. She did not have a clue what to do but one thing was certain, she never wanted to return to that dowdy, sad house or the miserable religious nutcase she was married to. Even accepting that she may well be making herself homeless, she had never felt so free, so light, or so optimistic, even though he knew something about her that nobody else did. Would he say something after all these years? Would he really spill the beans if she disobeyed him? Did she care anymore...?

Veronica thought that maybe she could stay a few days with Matthew while she sorted herself out. He'd begged her often enough to leave his father. Only last Wednesday, the last time she'd sneaked out to see him, he had questioned her all over again about why she stayed with him.

"Because I promised before God, for better or worse. I would be breaking my vow to the Lord if I walked out on him."

"But Mum," Matthew had replied, ""Dad has been breaking his vows to you for the last twenty-five years! He's supposed to reverence you and love you as Jesus loves the church. There's no blasted evidence of that. Is there? He's the most callous, hypocritical human being I've ever come across. Does God really expect you to carry on being a doormat, because that's what you've been for..."

"Matthew, please don't..."

"No, Mum, don't shush me up like you usually do. Dad's fond of quoting scripture, but doesn't the Bible say that Jesus died that you might have life in abundance? Abundance! Look at you! Old before your time. Where are your friends? Where are your family? Driven away by him! You even have to sneak out to see me. Mum, this is not right. When was the last time you had a new dress, or went to the hairdresser or..."

"I know it's not right Matthew, and don't think I haven't wanted to up and off many times over the years. I'm weak, and that would take guts and courage I'm not sure I've got. He knows something about me."

"Like what? Nothing can be bad enough to make you stay with him, surely? Think seriously about it Mum. He's killing you. I don't care what he knows about you, it isn't worth living your life like this."

"I will think about it, I promise. I love you Matthew."

"I love you too, Mum, but I hate seeing you so unhappy all the time. Something's got to be done."

After walking for fifteen minutes, Veronica stilled her thoughts, placed her suitcase on the pavement and rang a doorbell. She was shaking like a leaf, not knowing what sort of a reception she would receive now that she had finally left the Pastor. A light went on in the hallway, it was already getting dusky, and the door was opened by a tall man in jeans and a white t-shirt.

"Mum?"

"I've finally left him." As Veronica burst into tears, Matthew pulled her into the hallway. "Please can I stay here, with you, only for a few days until I can make some arrangements? I can't take any more of him."

"Mum? How did you know?" It was only then that Veronica noticed how pale and drawn Matthew was.

"How did I know what? Is Tracey okay?" Tracey was the girl that Matthew had set up home with almost two years ago.

"Tracey's inside, come on through, it's..." Matthew led Veronica into their small but neat living-room where Veronica saw immediately that Tracey was pale, her eyes puffy and red rimmed, still brimming with tears. There were several vases of flowers on a small dining table and a number of cards.

"Where's the little one? Matthew? Tracey? What's happened?" It was Tracey who answered.

"Why the hell would you be interested? We couldn't even let you know because of that vile excuse for a human being you're married to! Don't EVER bring him anywhere near me for I swear I'll kill him, d'you hear me? I'll kill him, I'll kill him with my bare hands…" With that, Tracey burst into sobs and collapsed into the corner of the settee clutching a pillow to her abdomen, sobbing as if her heart was breaking, which indeed it was.

"Matthew?" Veronica looked from one to the other, startled and genuinely puzzled.

"It's Chloe Mum …"

"What about Chloe? Where is she? Is she unwell?" Chloe was the little girl Tracey had given birth to fifteen months ago and who Veronica had seen so little of, thanks to you know who. She knew she had failed as a mother and grandmother, and if she hadn't been called on to help now that Chloe was ill, because of Anthony, she'd never forgive herself. Matthew's next words, however, knocked any thoughts out of her head and pierced her heart and soul like an icicle.

"Chloe's dead Mum. She's *dead*." Matthew covered his face with both hands, his shoulders shaking, his tears utterly dreadful. He stood there, overwhelmed with far too much pain…

"*Dead*?" Veronica paled visibly and, shocked, sunk down onto the settee next to Tracey. "Why? How? She can't be. I saw her on Wednesday and she was fine."

"Mum," somehow managing to compose himself, Matthew knelt on the floor in front of Veronica and took both of his hands in hers. "Chloe wasn't well on Thursday. We thought it was the start of another cold but she took a turn for the worst on Friday and stopped breathing." Matthew caught a sob in his throat, struggling to carry on. "She was dead by the time the ambulance got here; there was nothing anyone could have done. They think it was meningitis." Matthew then buried his head into the lap of this woman he loved dearly and wept loudly. Tracey sat up, flinging her arms around Veronica. The three of them clung to each other and wept aloud for the little soul who had entered their lives unexpectedly, at first not even wanted, but who had gone on to bring so much joy and love. During those awful moments, each one of them felt as if the sun should never again dare to shine, such was their exquisite agony.

"Tracey," wept Veronica, "my poor, poor love." For how would a mother ever get over the death of a loved child? The answer was very simple and straightforward. She wouldn't.

As the early evening gradually became colder, the three people continued to express a raw agony only those who have lost a child can begin to comprehend. It was a pain that would last forever as they would wonder, as the years passed, just how Chloe would have grown and laughed and smiled and made her way through life. Pretty, giggling Chloe with those arms that hugged so readily. Those beautiful, trusting eyes. That cute little pink beaker she insisted on drinking her milk out of. The 'blankie' that she dragged around everywhere with her. Her smile. Her beautiful, innocent smile. Oh, Chloe, Chloe … The house was filled with Chloe, yet Chloe was not there.

And they say that God is good…

CHAPTER NINETEEN

POLICE HQ

Tuesday morning

BRRR! IT WAS A COLD MORNING and Penny shivered again even though her office was warm, smelling comfortingly of coffee. It wasn't the temperature that was making her shiver, however. Things had progressed somewhat crookedly with the Pratt situation last night. Nobody could possibly have guessed at how things would unfold. Mrs Pratt was not at the manse when the officers had arrived to collect her. Patrol had then returned to HQ to enquire of the Pastor where she might be. He'd hit the roof because his wife was not where he'd told her to remain and then he'd refused to hand over the key to his front door. God, that man was hard work.

"We need to get into the house to see if your wife is alright," Ian had told him when they'd asked for the key. Surely that was obvious unless you were a thickhead.

"Why wouldn't she be alright?" the Pastor argued. "I don't want everyone nosing around my house. It is my own personal, private domain. Nobody should have the right..."

"Look," Ian had his hands on his hips as he addressed this increasingly obstructive, unpleasant individual. "You tell us your wife should be at home this evening, we get to your place, there are no lights on and there's no answer when we ring the bell. Seeing as her husband is being questioned by the police, your wife is likely to be upset. We need to check inside the house, see how she is, make sure she's okay. And while I'm at it, with regard to 'everyone nosing around' your house, two of us aren't 'everyone' and we have a search warrant anyway. You can't stop us. If you don't provide a key then we break in. Simple as that." So stuff that into your one wilting, shrivelling brain cell, you dickheaded cowpat…

So Patrol had returned to the manse with the front door key, made a quick search of the place and found the letter from Mrs Pratt on the kitchen table. Blimey! She'd upped and gone, just like that. The note said she'd gone to Matthew's house. Who was Matthew? A call to HQ had informed them that Matthew was the Pratt's only child and his address wasn't very far from the manse. They then went from the manse to Matthew Pratt's home where they discovered the grief-stricken trio. Finding themselves in the midst of heart-breaking tragedy they'd sent for Penny. She rang the bell on arrival no more than twenty minutes later and the door was answered speedily.

"Penny?" Matthew had been surprised to recognise her.

"Matthew? I'm actually looking for a Mrs Veronica Pratt. I guess she's your Mum? Is she still here? She left a note saying…"

"Yes, she's left Dad and the officers here have told me about Dad being arrested but won't tell me what it's about. I don't want to know, I can't…"

"It's okay Matthew," Penny laid a hand on his arm, "don't worry about that right now." Penny's thoughts were whirling. She knew Matthew who was with Tracey. They had a little toddler. She knew of him from the Salvation Army citadel she'd been attending for about two years. She knew Tracey even better. She was shocked to the core to realise that he was Pastor Pratt's son, but then she'd not known Matthew's surname, he looked nothing like his stern father, so why would she have made any connection? Without another second's thought she gave Matthew a quick hug before demanding to see Tracey. Matthew led her straight into the living room.

"Tracey?" Penny held out her arms and the woman flew into them and resumed her heart wrenching sobs while Matthew explained about Chloe. "Have the Captain and his wife been?"

"Yes," Tracey managed to get out, "they call every evening and should be here soon. They come about eight o'clock and stay as long as we need them to. Gloria stayed with us all weekend. I don't know what we would have done without her."

Veronica had sat silently watching the exchange, brows furrowed. Who was this Captain and his wife, Gloria? How did Matthew and Tracey come to know the Detective Inspector?

The small living room suddenly felt too crowded and so Penny took control, sending the two patrol officers on their way and asking Veronica if she would make them all a hot drink. That would give the woman something useful to do. Penny then sat with the bereaved couple and they filled her in with all the details of what had happened. She pulled a tissue out of the box on the coffee table. This was heart-breaking stuff and, despite her rank, she was not embarrassed to shed a tear.

"They are going to take a sample from Chloe's spine," explained Matthew, "and if that's positive for meningitis then she won't have a full post mortem. I couldn't bear the thought of them cutting … doing that to her."

"Yes," Penny responded, "that's reasonable." She'd managed to stem any further tears, knowing that they needed her to be the strong one. Veronica returned with a tray of hot drinks and some biscuits. "I found some cocoa, is that alright for everyone? I think we could all do with it."

Nobody seemed to care what they were drinking, simply going through the motions robotically because that's what you did when somebody died. You kept making hot drinks. It was something to do. They each took a drink and sipped in silence. The biscuits remained untouched. Veronica was the next to speak and addressed Penny.

"May I ask how you come to know my son and Tracey?"

"Of course," said Penny, "the three of us attend the same church. However, I had no idea Matthew was your son when I came to the manse as I'd never known his surname. Just knew him as Tracey's boyfriend. Of course I knew little Chloe as well."

"You go to *church* Matthew?" Veronica turned to her son, a look of shock and confusion written all over her face. "I didn't know. I mean, I thought after your father... I thought he'd well and truly put you off."

"Mum, you know next to nothing about those first few months after I had no choice but to leave. I'll tell you something though, being homeless was far better than living with Dad. God, what a perfect hypocrite! But I didn't suddenly land as if by magic in this little house."

"Then tell me now that happened Matthew. Please. I know I've never asked, probably I felt too guilty and responsible, I didn't want to hear about it, but it's time I knew."

"Yes, Mum, I think it is. To cut a long story short, after about two weeks of sleeping rough..."

"Oh, dear Lord, I'm never going to forgive myself for..."

"Mum, please, just listen. It was me who brought things to a head with Dad, demanding he gave me a house key, stopped opening my mail, started speaking to me as if I was part of the human race... Anyway. I slept rough but was able to sign myself into a Sally Ann hostel where..."

"Sally Ann? Who's Sally Ann?"

"For crying out loud Mum, it's short for Salvation Army. That's where I met Tracey, homeless and desperate like me. Another of life's rejects. Then when Tracey became pregnant..."

"Which she shouldn't have done! The Bible says…"

"Veronica! Please!" Penny swiftly interrupted, seeing the shock and anger on Matthew's face. She managed to lay a hand on Tracey's arm to stop her getting up and, presumably, leaving the room. "That's a totally inappropriate thing to say, so hurtful…"

"I'm sorry, I'm truly sorry… but…" Veronica clasped her hands together.

"No 'buts'! Leave it there Veronica. Okay," said Penny, taking a deep breath. "Go on Matthew."

"As I was saying," continued Matthew, "when Tracey found out she was pregnant and Dad didn't want to know, the Sally Ann found us this place, helped me get work, have supported us ever since."

"Yes," said Veronica, "I remember the two of you coming to the manse for help and your father turned you away. Yes, I remember that, you were both kept standing on the doorstep. I argued with him, pleaded, but…"

"You damn well sided with him! The two of you wanted nothing to do with 'the unfruitful works of darkness' as the Bible puts it. I can't begin to tell you how angry that made me and to be honest, I'm not sure I'll ever forgive you. But I have come to realise that you are more a pathetic victim of Dad than anyone else has ever been. If that's even possible. He really had you trapped and controlled. Anyway, looking back, it wouldn't have worked, us living at the manse with Dad the way he is. How did I ever think he might help? It was stupid of me to hope that he might have changed but we were scared stiff and utterly desperate."

"Matthew, Tracey, I'm so, so sorry. Please forgive me…" Veronica wrung her hands and furrowed her brow.

"Well at least we've been happy enough here until…" Matthew stopped speaking as Veronica, having recovered from her pleas for forgiveness, interrupted him.

"You didn't tell me you and Tracey went to any church. Why didn't you tell me? And this church is still helping you even though you're not married?"

"Mum..." Matthew heard the words but couldn't tell if his mother was genuinely puzzled or being deliberately judgemental.

"Mrs Pratt, Veronica," interrupted Penny, "the Christianity we adhere to worships a God of unconditional love. What, Biblically, is marriage if not a long-term, committed, faithful relationship between a man and a woman? Is this not what Matthew and Tracey believe they have embarked upon? I understand they are planning to get married this summer anyway. Please don't judge them on this; we all fall short according to God's standards – that's why He sent Jesus. He understands, He loves, He welcomes. He does not judge them and neither should we." Penny had spoken quietly and earnestly and Veronica couldn't have been more surprised by a Detective Inspector spouting God.

"But ... You're a policewoman. How can you also be a Christian?"

"Mum, for God's sake..."

"You mean Jesus didn't die for police officers? Perhaps," said Penny, amazed to find herself actually warming to the confused woman, "the police force is in more need of salvation than most." With that, the four of them laughed. Not that it was particularly funny, but it was enough to stir up an emotion other than raw, primal grief, therefore momentarily relieving the cold, unforgiving evening.

"So, you *are* a Christian?"

"Yes, Mrs Pratt, I'm a Christian, but don't tell my colleagues that." Penny smiled.

"But... Why not?"

"Look at it this way, I'm a senior officer in a male dominated environment, can you imagine what they would

135

make of their boss being in the Sally Ann? Obviously some of them know, but I don't broadcast it."

"Then how can you spread the Good News? We are commanded to go forth and..."

"By living it. My colleagues know me as fair, hardworking, caring and honest. The few who do know about my faith respect me for it because they see it in action. You don't need to speak a word about Jesus in many of life's situations; you simply need to *be* Jesus for that person at that point in time."

"Anthony is the opposite," Veronica commented softly and thoughtfully. "He shouted it out loud enough but he didn't live it. I've left him you know. Arrived here not long ago and found out about Chloe. I'll never go back to him now, not after this."

"I'm so very sorry." Penny laid a hand on the other woman's arm, wanting to comfort her but sensing that no comfort was possible this soon after so great a tragedy."

"I'll never forgive him. I'll never forgive myself either. Never ever ever!"

"Veronica," said Penny, "let time pass. Support Matthew and Tracey, be here for them. Tracey hasn't any family she can go to. They need you."

"Well of course I'll be here as long as they want me, and not only because I've got nowhere else to go. I need to make up for so much lost time. With both of them."

"You seem to have 'seen the light' in some ways..." Penny smiled just a little.

"I suppose I've been glimpsing chinks of it for years," Veronica explained, "I just didn't have the courage to do anything about it. It's taken something as serious as this to confirm to me I never want to waste another moment of my life. My husband doesn't believe in divorce..."

"Jesus did," Penny said.

"Yes, He did, didn't He?" Veronica was thoughtful for a few moments. "But we weren't properly... nobody knows..."

Penny put her right index finger to her lips and whispered, "Leave it there for now Veronica. Look!"

They both looked over to where Tracy was snuggled into Matthew on the settee. She looked as if she was sleeping and Matthew, too, had his eyes closed. Was it too much to hope that, just for a short while, they rested from their grief?

Matthew's eyes flickered when there was a soft tapping at the door. "It's okay Matthew, I'll go," Penny whispered as she got up to answer the door. Standing there were the two officers from the Salvation Army, Captain Tim and his wife Major Gloria. The room was once again pretty crowded as Penny introduced the visitors to Veronica before explaining that Matthew's father had been taken to police HQ and was under arrest. She didn't say what for, and they didn't ask, for which she was grateful. Now was not the time to discuss it.

"Veronica...?" Penny turned to the woman who was then busying herself collecting mugs onto a tray.

"Yes, I know, it's time for me to come with you for questioning. I've been expecting it." Veronica's face was etched with pain as she looked from Penny, to Matthew, and back to Penny.

"No, Veronica," Penny replied, "you've had one hell of a nasty shock, I want you to stay here, it'll do you more good than coming with me this evening. I can't put it off for long, however, so I'll pick you up around ten o'clock tomorrow morning."

"My husband?"

"I won't tell him yet what's happened, we'll leave that till the morning as well." Penny paused here. "Do you want to tell him yourself?"

"Yes! Yes, I do. I'll tell him I've left him, and about Chloe, but only if there's somebody with me. I have to have somebody with me. I can't be alone with him, I couldn't face that at the moment. I can't..."

"That's fine," replied Penny, "we wouldn't leave you alone with him anyway." Penny looked to the floor to hide her thoughts.

"Penny for them? If you'll excuse the pun." Ian rattled into her office and jolted Penny out of her thoughts about yesterday evening.

"Hi! Sorry. I was thinking over last night. Didn't get much sleep afterwards and I'm not looking forward to the conversation with the Pratts this morning. Probably end up more like a scripture-chucking slanging match if I know the Pastor."

"You've really changed your mind about her, the Vulture, haven't you?"

"Yes, I have Ian. Judge not and all that! As I said to you on the phone last night, at first I thought she was pretty much in the same league as her husband. You know, legalistic, hypocritical, judgemental, a dangerous religious fruitcake with less love for mankind than the devil himself. But she's just another one of his victims, Ian. Like Matthew, like Hayley, like who knows how many others. I'm only surprised that she's not as totally under his control as he thought she was and still thinks she is. I can't begin to imagine how he will react this morning."

"Yeh," said Ian, "how *will* he react? He's gonna get the double whammy all right. Hey, a *triple* whammy! His wife's left him, his granddaughter is dead, and we've arrested him for rape. What a start to the day!"

"…and this is the day that the Lord has made. We shall rejoice and be glad in it," Penny whispered, almost under her breath.

"Eh?" Ian put his head to one side, not quite sure if he had heard correctly.

"How was he last night?" Penny was instantly back into professional mode.

"Huh!" Ian nodded to himself. "Predictably outraged at being kept in a cell, demanding to know what the unforeseen circumstances were, demanding a Bible. Then he slept like a log, ate a full English breakfast and said the cooking was better than his wife's!"

"Good heavens," Penny exclaimed, "I didn't think anyone's cooking could be that bad!" They both laughed. Not genuinely, but enough to relieve the tension they were both feeling.

"What's the plan then boss?"

"We'll arrange for Mrs Pratt to see her husband as soon as she gets here. She can fill him in on what's happening with her, and let him know about little Chloe. I want both of us in the room so that they don't discuss anything to do with Hayley Bishford."

CHAPTER TWENTY

BATTLE OF THE PRATTS

Tuesday morning

"**V**ERONICA, I'm told you have something to tell me." The Pastor was seated in interrogation room B and had spoken as soon as Veronica had appeared, wanting to be in control as always. "However, first of all, I won't have you discussing me, or Hayley Bishford, with anyone. I absolutely forbid it. Is that clear? The Lord spoke to me in the night and..."

"Oh shut up!" Veronica snapped.

"What?" His head jerked up and his eyes looked straight into hers. Wide. Staring. Challenging.

"You heard me. Shut up!"

"How dare you! You stupid..."

"Mr Pratt, I would strongly advise you to keep quiet and listen to what your wife has to say." Penny spoke quietly but firmly from where she stood against the closed door, next to Ian. Gee, this guy was unreal. Was he mad or bad? It was hard to tell but, boy oh boy, was it good to hear Veronica standing up to him!

"Anthony, our son Matthew is going through the worst tragedy that can befall any parent. As is Tracey."

"You mean they've realised they're living in sin and bound for hell? I'd hardly call that a tragedy. That's a wakeup call and not before time. Maybe there's a chance after all."

"Anthony, will you please just listen for once? Will you? It's terrible, terrible news. Our little grand-daughter, Chloe, died suddenly last Friday, probably from meningitis." Veronica caught a sob in her throat as she spoke but failed to stop the tears streaming down her cheeks. Anthony sneered and glared at her.

"The wages of sin is death! What do you expect? How can anything good possibly come out of such a wicked, rebellious, utterly depraved lifestyle?"

"Don't quote scripture at me Anthony, just don't go there, and don't you dare, dare judge. I'm warning you!" Veronica shook, her voice low, as she pointed an index finger at the Pastor. Her rage was profound.

"That child was born in sin," the Pastor continued, "the result of wilful fornication. It was not God's will that the child should even exist and the three of them belong in hell. This death is God's punishment!"

Penny, who had been standing, open mouthed, at last found the voice to but in, so appalled was she at such depth of nonsense, callousness and cruelty. The Pastor spouted wicked, utter rubbish. "*Mr* Pratt," she said, deliberately stressing the 'Mr', for no way on God's earth should this despicable man be referred to as a Christian Pastor, "Chloe was born because two people loved each other and she has been nothing but a blessing to everyone who knew her. How dare you have the audacity to question the existence of a human being created in God's image? How dare you!"

"That child was the product of sin! Her parents had not entered any form of wedlock. What do *you* know about it?" His sneer chilled Penny to the bone, Veronica was now openly sobbing, Ian had his fists clenched, fighting the urge to lash out at this excuse for a man.

"Any form of wedlock?" Penny shot back immediately, "How quaint you are, although your meaning here is obscure. What is not obscure is that God created humanity and *every* human being is made in His image, precious and special to Him. Do you worship a lower case god Mr Pratt?"

"How dare you, woman!"

"Don't you 'woman' me Mr Pratt, or you'll be in even more of a hell than the one you speak of!"

Veronica spoke next, incandescent with rage, "May God forgive you for what you've said Anthony, for I never will. I've held that child in my arms and known nothing but joy in God's creative giving of another human life. I thanked Him for the gift of Chloe, thanked him from the bottom of my heart. Jesus said 'suffer the little children to come unto me'. He meant *every* child."

"Don't be ridiculous woman. She was the product of a sinful liaison. Lust! Born out of wedlock."

"I understand that Jesus Himself was not born to married parents. Mary was an unmarried, teenage mother." Penny was about to really lose it.

"D'you know something?" Veronica butted in, her voice actually becoming stronger and more confident, "maybe God spared Chloe from the pains of this world. Spared her from growing up and finding out she had a callous hypocrite for a grandfather. Maybe she was too good to ever meet *you*. Too gentle and beautiful to risk the stain of *you* in her life, to discover the horror of how cruel and evil you can be. Maybe God has spared her from *you*! You are colder than ice, d'you know that? There is more compassion in half a brain cell of a retarded cockroach than there is in the whole of you. God forgive me for speaking ill of a cockroach. And while we're talking about wedlock, you lousy, rotten hypocrite…"

"I'm warning you Veronica. Don't!"

"Let your wife speak Mr Pratt. I'm interested in your version of wedlock myself." Penny and Ian, though utterly appalled, were also morbidly fascinated at this point. It would be good for Veronica to sound off anyway. Get things off her chest.

"Don't what? What are you warning me not to do? Come on then? Say something?" Pastor Pratt appeared too angry to utter another word and so Veronica continued. "You don't want me to tell these officers that *we* are not married in the eyes of the law, is that it? Because we're not, are we Anthony? We were 'married' in that crazy community you got us involved in, but that was never a real marriage. Both of us have acted as if it was ever since though, haven't we? We almost convinced ourselves. Our particular 'wedlock' does not exist in the eyes of the law. We are not married Anthony, are we! So what does that make Matthew? He's a…"

"Be quiet! I demand silence in the name of…"

"That makes our son a bastard if you want to use the good, old fashioned word. The product of sin. The result of our fornication Anthony. Or was it *your* fornication, for I was not exactly willing was I?"

"You've gone far enough Veronica. I command you to be silent!"

"Well, well. Anthony Pratt the fornicator. We *fornicated*. Isn't that right according to your interpretation of God's Word? You love that word 'fornication' don't you? Love applying it to others. Well take a long, hard look in a mirror because there you will see a fornicator who produced a bastard son…"

"Don't put yourself through this Veronica." Penny realised that this exchange had gone far enough and laid a restraining hand on Veronica's shoulder. Veronica, however, would not be stopped until she'd had her say and brushed the hand away.

"Matthew is the product of a sinful liaison, *your* bastard child, my son whom I love with all my heart and who happens to be the best, maybe the only good thing, you've produced in the whole of your miserable life. You wretched, arrogant, judgemental hypocrite! You're nothing but a pile of stinking dung even the flies want to avoid!"

"And what are *you* Veronica? What have *I* kept silent about all these years concerning your own dear self? Don't you dare accuse me of..."

"Sit down! Now!" Ian had leapt across the room as the Pastor rose from his seat and attempted to reach across the table and grab Veronica, who rose to fight him off. "Calm down, both of you. Now!" The two Pratts had then sat back down, facing each other, the hard breathing of their rage the only sounds in the room as they stared at each other with raw hatred. Seconds passed...

"Mr Pratt," Penny spoke slowly, as if to an uncomprehending child, "Your little grand-daughter has died. That's what your... Veronica wanted to tell you. The funeral date will be announced hopefully later this week. You are entitled to seek permission to attend although in the circumstances I will personally see that you don't. I understand Veronica has something else to say to you as well. Go on, Veronica. Calmly. Try and keep it calm, for your own sake." He's not worth it, thought Penny.

"Yes," Veronica took a deep breath before continuing, "I do have something else you need to hear. I'm leaving you Anthony. In fact I've already left you." She looked him straight in the eye. "I won't even need a divorce, will I?" Veronica then stood up and turned to Penny. "I can't do any more. I have to get out of here. Please!" Ian went to unlock the door and Veronica turned back to look at her husband before she left. "You are the most hateful pig of a man I've ever met and I'm sorry I've wasted so much of my life putting up with you. I'm not going to waste any more of it. And by the way, even if you get to heaven, which is doubtful, you won't see Chloe – she'll be too close to the throne, too close to Jesus. Yes, and tell the whole world about me for all I care. I might well spend the rest of my life in prison but I'll still count myself freer than I've ever been during the miserable, wretched years I've spent with you. I hate you Anthony. I absolutely hate and detest everything about you." With that, Veronica left the room.

Penny followed her into the corridor and held her while she sobbed. "Come on, you and I need a hot cup of something. Let's go back to my office and have a chat. We won't be disturbed and we can both take a deep breath and calm down a little, for that was positively ghastly for you." She handed the weeping woman a tissue and led her along the corridor and up a flight of stairs.

Over mugs of steaming coffee, the two women talked.

"Veronica," said Penny, "I've got to ask, has he always been this way? If so, and the two of you weren't really married, then why did you stick with him for so long? He's unbalanced to put it mildly." Penny sat, holding her mug with both hands, hoping the warmth would disperse the lingering chill she always felt when she was with the Pastor.

"Phew! How do I answer that? Lots of reasons I suppose. I was always weak, low self-esteem, no confidence. At first I thought I could change him. Being with him was like being an only child kicking back at lousy, no good parents, except this time I would win. I couldn't change my parents, but I would change Anthony. I wasn't happy growing up." Veronica then fell silent, her head dropping and her fingers locked in a knuckle whitening grip. Penny allowed the quietness to prompt her to continue, which she did. "He was blackmailing me."

"Blackmailing you?"

"Yes."

"For twenty-five years?" Extraordinary! What had the man held against this poor woman for so long?

"Almost twenty-five years," said Veronica, "It was terrible. Something so terrible. Just after we were... I was going to say married... it was about three years after we had gone through a wedlock ceremony at the Community of Saintly Followers... I'd just found out I was expecting Matthew." Veronica lapsed into silence, watching the steam swirling up from her coffee.

"Tell me about it Veronica." Penny placed her own mug back on the table and pushed a box of tissues across to the now quietly weeping woman, waiting for her to continue.

Ian and the duty constable had escorted Pastor Pratt back to a holding cell. The man had not uttered another word and so they left him sitting on the small, utilitarian bed.

"It's almost lunchtime," Ian explained, "you'll be brought something to eat and drink shortly. Anything you want before we go?" By way of reply the Pastor looked at Ian, shook his head slowly, then looked away. Ian started to close the door...

"There is something."

"Yes?"

"Could I have a pen and some writing paper?"

"It'll have to be a pencil, but yes, okay."

Ian soon returned, leaving a pencil and a small writing pad with the Pastor before clanging shut the cell door and locking it. A few minutes later he looked in to see the man seated on the bed, pad on lap, scribbling away. Ian wondered what he was writing.

Back in Penny's office, Veronica was finding it hard to speak and Penny felt a wave of compassion for her. Whatever beans she needed to spill, surely they could stay in the tin until after lunch. It had been one hell of a morning and they could both do with a break.

"Veronica, it's nearly lunchtime. Why don't we both take a break, get some food, have a walk, chill out, whatever. Then perhaps we could meet back here at about two? I'll show you the canteen and rest rooms. Have an hour, then we'll continue."

"I'd appreciate that. I couldn't eat anything but I'll get another drink and sit quietly somewhere. Calm myself down a bit hopefully."

"Tell you what," said Penny, "I'll come and get you from the rest room at two-ish. Is that okay?"

"That sounds good. Thanks." Truth be told, Veronica didn't know if she'd be able to unburden herself here, in a police station, however kind Penny was being. Yet this is where she'd belong as soon as she explained what had happened all those years ago, what she had done, why Anthony was blackmailing her. She'd be arrested. Taken to court. Sent to prison. Did she even care anymore? She'd thought she didn't. Now she wasn't so sure.

CHAPTER TWENTY-ONE

THE TIME OF DAY

Tuesday lunchtime

DR EMILY returned to Angel's Rest after her morning clinic and, after playing with her little Doodle, was cogitating over which biscuits to choose for the pleasure that lay ahead. Ginger Nuts were particularly good for dunking as they retained a degree of inner 'bite', providing one judged the temperature of one's brew and carefully timed the actual dunk. Emily thought she might also add a Cadbury's chocolate finger, a special treat requiring two dunks – one to part melt the chocolate which one then licked off slowly, another to soften the inner biscuit. Decision made, she carefully placed one Ginger Nut and one Cadbury's chocolate finger on the arm of her chair, fetched her Nescafe Gold Blend cuppa, and entered heaven as she watched the news and enjoyed her biscuits. As the grandmother clock chimed one, Dr Emily leaned her head back and closed her eyes. She began thinking about Hayley and what had happened at the Yellow House yesterday. Penny had rung later that morning to say that the Pastor had been arrested on suspicion of rape and Dr Emily wondered how she would tell Hayley tomorrow and what the woman's reaction might be. Glad? Distraught? She couldn't hazard a guess. Traumatic, that's for sure, but she would have to be told. *Tic tic, tic tic…*

Oh, she was so comfortable, finding herself drifting off into what promised to be a most pleasant afternoon nap...

Suddenly, inexplicably, Dr Emily jolted awake, felt a freezing cold sense of dread, and thought immediately of Hayley. Such was the strangeness of the feeling, one she had never before experienced concerning a patient, that she straight away grabbed her coat and decided to call at the Yellow House and see how things were. It might be nothing at all, but something connected to Hayley felt terribly, terribly strange. Not *wrong* exactly, just strange, odd. She didn't even consider phoning and speaking to Mike, such was this depth of feeling which had chilled her to her core. Anyway, it wouldn't hurt to turn up, say she was passing by and decided to stop.

As Dr Emily put her car into gear and released the handbrake, she glanced at the digital clock on the dashboard. 13:23. She was on her way.

At the Yellow House, Mike was at his wits' end again. He'd managed to get Daisy and Mikey off to school but Hayley had started crying as soon as he'd returned from the school run and had hardly stopped since. He made lunch for himself and sat eating it while Hayley curled up in her usual chair, wrapped in a throw, cuddling a hot water bottle. Every few minutes she would bang the side of her head with a fist, as if she were trying to get rid of something. Which she probably was. Her one-sided paralysis had seemed particularly bad that morning, she was really dragging that one leg, and Mike was expecting a complete breakdown plus another hospital trip.

"I'm sorry," she wrote.

"You always are," Mike replied, not too unkindly.

"I can't get warm, I'm so cold," Hayley scribbled.

"I know," Mike agreed, "the house is warm enough according to the thermostat on the boiler, but I feel a chill as well. Very odd." He was finishing off his cheese on toast. "Hayley, please love, if you don't stop this crying and head

149

banging I'm going to ring Dr Chatwith." Mike then stood up, turned the TV on, and filled the room with News at One. They both sat, not really watching or listening to the television, but simply glad of the distraction from each other. Minutes passed...

Suddenly, completely out of the blue, Hayley discarded the throw, dropped the hot water bottle, and walked out of the living-room. Mike, startled, got up to follow her. He glanced at the time on the news channel. 13:23.

"You okay, Hayley?" What the hell was she up to now? God alive, he really couldn't take much more of this.

"I'm hungry Mike, I'm going to make myself some toast."

"You spoke!" Mike caught hold of her arm, turning her to face him. "Hayley, you spoke! Say that again love, please say it again!"

Hayley smiled, she actually smiled. "I can't explain it, I feel suddenly different, like a switch has flicked and I'm allowed to eat and talk again. I know it doesn't make sense, it's like some dark hold over me has been released, and I'm hungry. I'd love some toast with a cheese triangle."

"Oh Hayley, thank God, I've been so worried. I can't tell you what this means to me, to all of us. D'you think this is the start of you getting really better?"

"I hope so Mike. It's only a piece of toast, but I do hope so." She continued into the kitchen as Mike looked on in amazement, hardly daring to hope that this was for real, for there was no evidence of any one-sided weakness. No limp. No stiff arm. They even chatted as Hayley popped a piece of bread into the toaster and soon they were sitting together on the settee, catching up with so many conversations while Hayley ate her toast. Whatever had happened, however abruptly, it was good and they weren't about to knock it. Mike felt ridiculously happy as he watched Hayley eat, and listened to her voice.

Hayley was so surprised she could hardly stop smiling. Lord, that toast tasted good! Please, please, let this be real...

Then the doorbell rang...

Over on Forest Road, McDonald's was busy as usual for lunch. Dave and Roger the Dodger were parked up in their usual place drinking their usual coffees. They had already peeled the stickers from the cardboard mugs and stuck them onto the current loyalty card.

"I can't get that out of my mind."

"What's that, Dave?"

"Last Friday. That toddler. Fifteen months old. It's nothing, is it?"

"I know what you mean, it's got to me as well. The parents were only a couple of kids – shouldn't have to be coping with that."

"Rog, I know this sounds crazy but I've got this cold as ice feeling about those parents. It's chilling me to the bone, even the blasted coffee ain't warming me. I think I'm just worried about them. You fancy calling by the house on the way back to base?"

"Yeh, why not, we could do. We'll just stop by and ask how things are. Check on them, so to speak."

It was almost 13:25 when Dave and Roger pulled out onto the main road, heading for Matthew Pratt's house...

...where Matthew and Tracey had been alone so far that day, waiting to be told when little Chloe's body would be released for the funeral. But that hardly mattered because she would still be gone, funeral or no funeral. She was dead. Their Chloe was dead. They were sat cross-legged on the floor, coffee table between them upon which was a jug and two glasses. They had almost finished sharing out the pile of tablets they'd collected together. There were mostly painkillers, plus some sedatives and sleeping tablets prescribed by their GP on the day Chloe had died. They had each written a suicide note, explaining why they had made their deadly pact (not that an explanation would be necessary in the circumstances) and apologising to whoever found them. It was the most sensible thing to do as they simply could not face life without Chloe.

"Ready? You still sure about this?" Matthew asked, making eye contact.

"I'm ready," Tracey replied, "and quite sure I want to do this."

"It's twenty-two minutes past one," Matthew said, before looking at his devastated partner. "Tim and Gloria won't be here until this evening, it'll be over by then." They locked eyes, eyes that were bloodshot and puffy from crying, red rimmed from lack of sleep, glassy pools of despair and desolation. They were beyond grief.

The time on the digital clock clicked over into the next minute. 13:23.

Suddenly, violently, Tracey swept her arm across the coffee table, scattering the pills over the floor. "No!" she yelled, panting now, "Chloe wouldn't want us to do this, we can't do it, we mustn't..." Gabbling, she reached over the table and took both Matthew's hands in hers. "Matthew, we can't! We won't forget her or ever stop missing her, but we shouldn't add to all the bad in the world by killing ourselves. I suddenly feel that would be so wrong. We can't change the fact of Chloe's death, but we can change the way we react to it. She was a blessing, Matthew, a blessing. That's what Gloria said, and maybe we have to get through this in order to help somebody else. This *has* to mean something or else Chloe's life was in vain and I won't ever believe that. I won't. Somehow the world is better because she passed through it. I have to believe that, we have to get through this..."

152

"Huh!" Matthew almost sneered at her. "Do you really think that? Or have you chickened out."

"No. I haven't chickened out. It takes more courage to live like this. Killing ourselves would be easier, but it wouldn't be right. If you stop and think it through right now, you'll see that as well. Please, Matthew, let's not give up. It'll be the hardest thing we've ever done, but it has to be the right thing too. Remember what Gloria said? That Chloe won't ever be ill again, she'll never hurt, or be bullied at school, or poor, or out of work, or homeless, or in trouble... She's safer where she is."

"Okay, I hear what you're saying, Miss Perfect Christian, but tell me about us. How do we get through this? That little kid was our world!" Matthew withdrew his hands and covered his face, sobbing loudly. "I can't do it, I can't! I loved her so much. I can't bear it..." He began to scrabble around on the floor, frantic, desperately trying to gather up the tablets Tracey had scattered. Sobbing herself, Tracey tried to stop him...

"Matthew, no! Please don't. Please! What about me? This isn't all about you for God's sake, this has happened to me as well. I carried her, I gave birth to her, I fed her..." She tried to hold on to him but he shook her off. "No!..." She let out a primitive wail of excruciating, unimaginable pain...

There had been a knock on the door which neither of them heard. Matthew continued to grab at the tablets, pushing them into his mouth, whilst Tracey was powerless to restrain him. She shouted at him again and again as they struggled on the floor.

"I can hear yelling and crying," said Dave, knocking harder.

"So can I. Try the handle and give the door a shove. Quick! Something ain't right." The front door was locked. "Damn it!"

"Quick! There must be a back lane to these houses." They hurtled up the road, turning the corner four houses along and racing down the narrow lane behind the terraced houses.

153

Reaching what had to be Matthew and Tracey's home, they barged through a broken wooden gate and ran up the garden path to the back door. Locked! But they could still hear Tracey screaming and crying.

"I'm going for it. Stand back!" Roger, the bigger of the two men, braced himself before throwing his shoulder at the door. It took several attempts before the wood splintered and the bolt gave way. Minimal damage, not that that mattered right then.

"Hello! We're coming in! Paramedics. Dave and Roger. Hello?" They hurried through the kitchen. On entering the living-room both men saw what was going on and immediately took control of the situation, their professional calmness exactly what was needed.

"Thank God we came," whispered Dave.

"Yes," said Roger, "thank God."

Veronica had bought coffee and a small packet of digestive biscuits in the police canteen and was now sitting in one of the rest rooms.

"Sure you'll be alright?" Penny had asked.

"Yes, thanks, I'll be fine. It'll be good to sit quietly and have a think." It was warm and she appreciated being alone with her thoughts. Yet what *were* her thoughts? Did she truly want to be alone with them? They were dark and threatening, almost pushing her over the edge, nudging her onto some path of destruction. What did she have to live for? Chloe was dead. Anthony had been arrested for rape. Is that really what he had done to Hayley that caused her to flee? She was surprised to find herself feeling that it was a possibility, for she hardly knew this man she had lived with for so long. Veronica had no doubt whatsoever that she, too, would be arrested and sent to prison once she confessed to Penny. Both of them in prison! That would get the gossip going. Would probably get into the papers as well. Matthew and Tracey briefly nudged their way

154

into her thoughts but were dismissed with a chilling callousness she would have thought herself incapable of. What was happening to her? What was she being pushed to do? Her life instantly appeared so out of control, so wicked, so crazy, that she knew she could not stop the rollercoaster of events that were unfolding. A malevolent whispering in her head assured her that she must take the only way out available to her... and she must take it NOW!

So having finished her coffee, Veronica left the small packet of biscuits unopened on the table and made her way to the ladies cloakroom adjacent to the restroom. An almost tangible, freezing cold heaviness gripped her and pushed her towards the sink. She was powerless to resist as, without a second's hesitation she took the small, sharp nail scissors out of her handbag and began to cut her wrists. The clock showed 13:23.

Penny threw the biro she had been chewing down onto her desk. She couldn't concentrate at all and realised she would have been better off taking a proper break for lunch instead of eating at her desk and trying to catch up on paperwork. She was worried about Veronica and would be glad to get back to her at two o'clock. What on earth did the woman have to tell her that was so terrible? And should she have left her in the restroom at all? True, there were other people about, but what if Veronica had left the building and scarpered? She felt it was unlikely, but stranger things had happened and one thing this job had taught her was that folk were unpredictable, especially under stress, and Veronica was certainly stressed to the limit. Blow it! She really shouldn't have left her, so she'd pop down now, poke her head around the restroom door, and see if Veronica was okay. If she was still there...

"Darn and blast it!" Penny found the restroom empty and was immediately cross with herself. Why had she trusted the woman? She should have known better. Wait a minute though, stop and think! Veronica might not have legged it after all. She might simply be in the loo. What time was it anyway? She glanced at her watch. 13:23. Penny strode the short distance across the restroom floor and opened the door of the ladies toilets…

"Oh my Lord! Veronica, no!"

Down in the basement of police headquarters all was quiet. The prisoners had been served their lunch and the duty officers were on their way to collect the trays from each cell. Ian was still behind the duty desk looking through some of the paperwork relating to Pastor Pratt. That had been some conversation between that man and Mrs Pratt. Phew! Ian had never heard anything like it. The Pastor had still been scribbling away when they'd taken his food to him. Looked like he was compiling a shopping list.

"What the …?" Ian jumped, startled, as the alarm suddenly rang out, indicating there was a problem in one of the cells and assistance was needed immediately. That Neanderthal plank of wood in cell B had probably thrown his tray at the door again, though why two officers needed help with that was beyond him. Ian looked back down at what he was reading.

"Sarge! Quick!" The young PC (John, was it?) came hurrying towards the desk, flushed and out of breath. "It's the Pastor. Quick!"

Ian glanced at the clock on the wall – 13:23 – before quickly following the PC to the open cell door, outside of which WPC Jane Williams stood, hands covering the lower half of her face, wide eyes staring straight ahead into the cell. Ian looked inside.

"Oh. My. God."

CHAPTER TWENTY-TWO

LIGHT IN THE DARKNESS

Tuesday afternoon

PENNY GRABBED the scissors out of Veronica's hand as she continued to frenziedly slash at her left wrist, tossing them onto the floor. They clanked and skidded across the floor. Turning on the cold tap she thrust Veronica's hand and wrist under the water, thankfully noticing that, although there seemed to be plenty of blood, the damage wasn't serious.

"I'm sorry, I'm sorry, I'm sorry... You weren't supposed to find me..."

"I'm glad I did," answered Penny as she covered the deep scratches with a wad of clean paper towels. "Come back to my office and I'll dress that for you. I've got a small first aid box with some steri-strips, bandages and stuff. We'll get a doctor to have a good look at you later, let's just keep things calm and quiet for now. Come on, lovey."

"I'm sorry, I'm sorry..." Veronica was crying now as if she'd never stop and Penny quickly got her back to her office, assuring people they passed on the way that all was under control. Thankfully Veronica's wounds didn't need stitching, but it was the deep psychological wounds Penny was more concerned about. Seeing that the woman was shivering, Penny took an old cardigan that was hanging on a hook and draped it around her shoulders.

"I was so cold," Veronica whispered, "so very cold."

Then, just as Penny was taping a bandage in place around Veronica's wrist, the door burst open.

"Pen ..." Ian started, "sorry, I thought you were on your own."

"What's up?" Penny saw that Ian was very calm, very serious and very in control. That meant there was a crisis.

"I need to speak to you urgently about the Pastor," Ian nodded towards Veronica, a puzzled look on his face when he spotted the bandage, "but alone."

"What's he gone and said now? What's he done?" asked Veronica, turning to look directly at Ian. Penny laid a hand on the woman's shoulder to keep her seated, and indicated to Ian that they could speak just outside her office door.

"Try and stay calm now Veronica, I'm only just by the door, I won't leave you. Take some nice deep breaths and I'll be straight back." As soon as Penny stepped outside her office, making sure she had a clear view of Veronica through the door window, Ian ran a hand through his hair and exhaled loudly.

"What's up, Ian?"

"You won't believe this," he said.

"Try me." Penny still watched Veronica, who sat quietly now with her arms crossed.

"It's the Pastor."

"What about him?" Penny furrowed her brow, perplexed; surely there couldn't be anything any worse?

"He's dead."

"He's *what?*" Penny's eyes widened, expressing her incredulity.

"Dead."

"He's dead? How? What the…"

"Just before twenty-five past one John sounded the alarm. It was the Pastor's cell. He'd hung himself. Did a quick job of it too."

"What? How? Where was everyone?"

"He'd been checked on every fifteen minutes, maybe more, according to procedure. He'd still managed to take off his shirt, tie the sleeves..."

"Yes, yes. Were all the checks recorded?"

"Yep. All as it should be."

"Thank God for that. Well, this is a turn up for the books! I would never have graded him as a suicide risk. I've got that wrong, haven't I?"

"None of us saw this coming so don't stress over it. The police surgeon's there now, the rest of the crew's on its way. I've relieved the WPC, she's pretty upset."

"Okay. Good. Carry on then as you seem to have it all under control. I'll have to leave it with you for now as I've just found Mrs Pratt in the ladies toilet trying to cut her wrists."

"You're joking!"

"I wish I was."

"What the hell's going on here today, Pen? You gonna be able to tell her about the Pastor? She's gonna have to be told."

"I know. The sooner the better I suppose, though God knows how she'll react to this. I know she claimed to hate the sight of him, but you never know. You just never know..."

"No, you don't boss. None so queer as folk. Right, I'll get off then and leave you to it."

"Keep me up to date please, Ian. It's going to be a long day."

"Will do. By the way," Ian thrust a hand into one of his trouser pockets, "this was on the floor in the Pastor's cell. I haven't had a chance to read it yet. He was writing it just before he topped himself so it might be significant."

"Okay, I'll deal with it when I've got a moment." Penny took the screwed up sheet of paper from Ian, holding it tightly in one fist. She then returned to her office to find Veronica calm and quiet. She didn't know where on earth to begin and so decided to give her the news immediately and then deal with the fallout. She quickly stuffed the paper Ian had given her into her handbag. She was eager to know what was written on it, but that would have to wait.

"Veronica. I've got some more bad news I'm afraid." Penny looked at the woman, wishing she could give her a hug but knowing that here, in the police station, she had to keep a professional distance. That didn't stop the flood of pity she had for her though. "I'm so sorry to have to tell you this but your, er, husband, has just been found dead in his cell. I'm so sorry." She spoke slowly and clearly, trying to maintain eye contact with Veronica, trying to make sure she was taking in what was being said.

"Dead? Anthony? He's dead?" Veronica looked at Penny, not aghast but... hopeful? Was that an accurate interpretation of the look on her face? Surely not. Yet, why not? Theirs had not been a happy union and from the little contact Penny had had with the man, he was deeply unpleasant.

"I'm so sorry," Penny repeated, for surely that was still the right thing to say in these circumstances?

"I'm free. I feel free! Maybe you won't fully understand but it's like you've lifted a ton weight off me. How did he die? A heart attack? It must have been quick. Or was it a stroke?" Veronica was whispering, obviously eager to know the details.

"No. He hanged himself. It was very quick by all accounts." Penny spoke softly and gently, as the situation demanded, for she was still unsure of Veronica's reactions. The woman was too calm, and it was the calm, quiet ones who needed watching the most in her experience.

160

"Like Judas Iscariot," Veronica mused, "who betrayed Jesus before hanging himself. So Anthony also betrayed Jesus by hurting His people. Now he's died the same way, by hanging himself. Yet he won't have done it because of any sense of remorse. He won't have been the slightest bit sorry."

"Veronica?" Penny watched the woman become pensive and glassy eyed, yet there were no tears. "That's a serious observation."

"But can't you see? All the people he's judged over the years as being wicked and evil, and all the time it was *him* who was the evil one, him all along. Now he's finally done us all a favour, although I can tell you that was not his intention. He's merely saved his own skin with no thought for anyone else." Veronica paused here before continuing. "I must go to Matthew! Can I? Can I see Matthew? He has to be told and I think it should come from me."

"Of course you must see Matthew. Give me ten minutes to sort a few things out and I'll take you there myself. One of my support officers will sit with you while I'm getting ready." *Phew*, thought Penny, it comes to something when a man does his family a favour by hanging himself. And what a legacy to leave behind – a trail of misery and unhappiness.

Mike answered the door to find Dr Emily standing there staring at her shoes. She was, in fact, wishing she'd worn her little black ankle boots as the day was chilly and she did feel the cold around her feet. There again, it had been nice and warm in the car with the heater on. She was also thinking about adding prune juice to her shopping list as she'd had a guts full of chewing All Bran and prune juice was known to set you free. Apparently, a small glassful should do it. There again, Isobel had passed on an interesting recipe for All Bran cake which deserved a try. As soon as she realised the door was open she lifted her eyes, ceased all thoughts concerning bowel movements, and greeted Mike.

"Mike! I hope you don't mind an unannounced visit but I had the most peculiar feeling about Hayley."

"Dr Chatwith! How odd that you should turn up, but come in, quickly, we have quite a surprise for you." Dr Emily noticed that Mike was smiling and felt instantly relieved that nothing bad had happened to Hayley. She followed Mike into the living-room where Hayley was finishing eating what looked like a slice of toast. She was eating! Hayley was eating and smiling!

"Hello Hayley," Dr Emily smiled warmly, "I was just passing and wondered how you were feeling after yesterday?"

Hayley swallowed before answering. "Absolutely fine. I feel fine. It's only just happened, as if someone flicked a switch and – hey presto – I started to talk again. I was even hungry and had some toast." Hayley smiled shyly and looked completely different from the wreck of a woman Dr Emily had met only the day before. "I can't believe I feel so different so suddenly. It's like a miracle, like some pile of crap has been lifted off me."

"It's amazing. We're so pleased," continued Mike, "you wouldn't believe it but there isn't even any sign of the weakness she had in her arm and leg. It happened all of a sudden. Like someone clicked a light on inside her head!" The man was understandably excited and Dr Emily could not help but share their joy.

"My word," said the doctor, "I'm very rarely lost for words but I'm as near to speechless as I'm going to get! This is wonderful news and I'm very happy for you both. May I sit down?"

"Yes, yes. Shall I make you a cuppa?"

"No thank you Mike, I won't, but I would like to stay and have a little chat if that's alright with you both?" The pair of them were like a couple of kids with a Christmas present and Dr Emily desperately didn't want the sudden improvement to be temporary. She was fascinated by what had happened psychologically to bring about such a flight into health and wanted to hear all about it. As the three of them continued to chat, her mobile rang. She fished her phone out of her bag and saw that it was Penny. "Do you mind awfully if I answer this one? I do apologise."

"Dr Emily?" Penny's voice sounded hurried and urgent, "I'm in a mad rush here as I'm just about to take Veronica Pratt to her son's house. I wanted to let you know that the Pastor has committed suicide…"

"What? How?" Dr Emily pressed the phone closer to her ear, hoping Mike and Hayley couldn't hear what was being said on the other end.

"Hung himself in his cell just before twenty-five past one today. Kind of complicates things, as you can imagine. Can I come with you tomorrow to see Hayley Bishford? She'll have to be told."

"I'm here with Hayley at the moment. Would you like me to tell her now or wait until tomorrow?"

"Tell you what, Dr Em, as you're already with her, I'll drop Veronica off, make sure there's somebody with them all, then I'll call straight round. Can you still be there?"

"How long?"

"Forty, forty-five minutes tops?"

"That's fine. See you shortly then." Dr Emily finished the call, placed her phone back in her bag, then turned to Hayley, who, like Mike, was wearing a puzzled expression. "The police have some news about Pastor Pratt," she explained, "and Inspector Whistle is going to call here in about forty minutes' time to bring you both up to date. Shall I be here when she arrives?"

"Yes, please, don't go if the police are coming." Hayley spoke quietly and pleadingly, all previous excitement gone as she started to twirl a section of her hair with the thumb and forefinger of her right hand. She was extremely anxious. "I said I didn't want to see the police at all."

"It'll be fine, Hayley. I'm here, so please don't be at all anxious. Any chance of that cup of tea after all Mike?" Dr Emily would concentrate on keeping Hayley as calm as possible, for who knew what she'd have to deal with once the young couple heard about the Pastor's suicide?

"Tea on its way! In fact, we'll all have one. You fancy a biscuit with yours, Dr Chatwith?" Mike and Hayley exchanged a knowing grin.

"I shouldn't really, but go on, why not!" Dr Emily settled back on the settee, crossing her legs and making herself comfortable.

Penny and Veronica turned into the street where Matthew and Tracey lived and cried out in unison when they saw the ambulance parked outside. They shot a questioning glance at each other but were silent as Penny parked the car. They got out quickly, knocked urgently on the door, and it was Dave who answered.

"Dave?" Penny spoke immediately, "what the hell's going on? This is Matthew's mum." Pointing to Veronica, Penny was already through the door.

"Am I glad to see you! They're fine," said Dave, "at least they are now. They weren't when we got here but we've managed to calm things down. I've got a couple of their church friends on the way over; they shouldn't be long – the kids gave me their number. I wasn't going to leave them on their own."

The scene in the living-room was too normal for what had been planned and attempted only a short while back. Although they had obviously been crying, Matthew and Tracey were

164

seated quietly together now on the settee, each holding a mug of tea.

"What's happened? Why's there an ambulance?" Veronica looked from one to the other.

"It was me. It was all my fault. It wasn't Tracey at all. I can't accept what's happened Mum, I can't live with something like this. We planned to – I planned for us to take a bunch of pills and opt out. Go and be with Chloe. All I wanted to do was anything, anything, that would stop this pain. I can't cope. I cannot, cannot cope with this... Then we had a bit of a fight. Me and Tracey. She tried to stop me, tried to get the pills off me, but I wouldn't stop. Dave and Roger turned up then. They got here, they stopped me..."

Nobody uttered a word until Penny spoke quietly and gently. "Oh Matthew, Tracey... You're not *supposed* to be coping with what's happened, how *can* you accept it? Not yet. Not ever. It's early days, far too early, and it's okay not to be okay. You need to grieve and that takes time."

"Mum? What made you come here anyway? Is Dad still at the station?"

"Well, yes, your Dad is sort of still at the station." Veronica hardly knew how to proceed, or even if she should, until Penny nodded, indicating that she should come out with the news they had brought.

"What does that mean? Mum?"

"It's not good news Matthew. Maybe I should come straight out with it, but..."

"What?" Matthew interrupted, "Not good news means he's on his way to prison, right? Well, all I can say is 'hallelujah!' I didn't think anything could cheer me up, but this does. What did he do? Something serious I hope. Get him locked up for good!"

"No Matthew. He's not going to prison. In fact he's not going anywhere on this earth ever again."

"What d'you mean, Mum?"

"He hung himself in his cell and by all accounts did a good job of it as it was over very quickly. He's dead. Your father is dead, Matthew."

The room was silent, everyone holding their breath, waiting to see how Matthew would take this latest news. The young man looked at Tracey, then back at his mother, then in turn at Penny, and Dave, and Roger. Seconds felt like elastic minutes until he eventually spoke. "D'you know? I feel nothing but relief, as if a dark shadow has been removed from my life, as if I can breathe, even with losing my Chloe. It's like someone's taken a whole ton of crap off me so that I can start to think, to grieve, to... to... I don't feel at all upset about Dad. Or sad, or any of the things I maybe should be feeling because my Dad's dead. It's a relief, such a relief that he can't spoil Chloe's death, or her funeral, or her memory. He can't spoil any of that now. Mum?" Matthew looked at his mother, wanting her to say that she understood what his short speech was all about. As indeed she did.

"I know what you mean," Veronica told her son, "I feel it too. Relief. An inexplicable relief. The ability to breathe, even in the middle of unbearable tragedy. It's as if some tangible wickedness has departed from us. Only God knows how much any one of us can bear and I don't believe we could have grieved for Chloe if your father was still alive. He was a dark man, Matthew. He was the evil that needed to be consigned to the pit."

"When did he do it?" It was Tracey who asked.

"Round about twenty-five past one today. Lunchtime." Penny answered.

"But...?" Tracey turned to Matthew, a look of astonishment on her face, "That's near enough the time we were going to, trying to... and I tried to stop you but couldn't and then Dave and Roger..."

166

"That's *soooo* freaky!" added Dave. "I noticed it was just before twenty-five past one when I got this feeling that you two weren't okay and we decided to call in. The feeling was *that* strong. I couldn't ignore it."

Everyone in the room went quiet, each looking from one person to the next.

"Even freakier than you think," put in Veronica, "that was almost the exact time Penny found me in the ladies toilets in a terrible state. She stopped *me* doing something self-destructive too."

"Hey," said Matthew. Quietly. Thoughtfully. "Maybe this is God looking out for us all."

"Except for your Dad, Matthew. Except for your Dad. Seems we were all rescued except him."

Or all rescued *from* him, thought Penny. Is that what this man's death had achieved? Was this its purpose? That is, the removal of wickedness from the lives of others?

"All the times I've wished him dead," said Tracey, "d'you think…?"

"No!" replied Penny emphatically. "Your wishes had nothing to do with him choosing to take his own life."

"Did us having Chloe push him over the top?" Matthew wondered out loud. It was again Penny who replied without hesitation.

"No. That's rubbish Matthew, of course it didn't."

It was only a matter of minutes later that Tim and Gloria turned up, anxious for the young couple who were suffering so much. This enabled Penny to leave Matthew, Tracey and Veronica in safe hands and after being told of the latest happenings, Tim assured Penny that they would stay for as long as necessary. All night if that's what was needed. Dave and Roger chatted briefly to Penny outside on the pavement before setting off in their ambulance. Penny then made her way to the Bishford's house, wondering what on earth she would

167

find when she got there. Dr Emily said there was good news. Like what? She would soon find out. A bit of good news would not go unappreciated on a day like this!

Penny could not believe the difference in Hayley Bishford when she eventually arrived at the Yellow House. She remained pale and painfully thin, but she was laughing and talking, hardly recognizable from the woman Penny had found outside the tunnels less than a week ago. Was it really less than a week ago? So much had happened since then and Penny couldn't help shedding her police persona and questioning God's hand in this particular case. Even where the Pastor's suicide was concerned.

The kids, Daisy and Mikey, had gone to a friend's house for tea that day and Penny had found herself intruding on laughter and a lively discussion about, of all things, dunking biscuits. Penny guessed that it was Dr Emily who stood up to greet her.

"Penny? It's so good to meet you at last. We've spoken so many times over the phone. I'm Emily."

"Dr Em! It's good to meet you, too. Hayley? Mike?" Penny shook hands with all three of them in turn before she sat down and got straight on with the reason for her visit.

"I'm glad Dr Emily is here with you today, Hayley, as I need to update you on what has been happening concerning Pastor Pratt. I believe you have a right to know. It's okay," Penny smiled briefly here, "I don't need to ask you any questions in an official capacity at the moment. I'm just here to pass on some information. A courtesy visit, if you like.

"Now, the Pastor was arrested yesterday as a result of forensic evidence which suggested a serious crime had been committed and he was subsequently detained at police headquarters. I'm afraid that earlier today Pastor Pratt was found dead in his cell." Penny paused here to let her words sink in. "He had taken his own life."

168

Mike gasped audibly and reached for Hayley's hand. She turned to face her husband and uttered in hushed tones, "Then I'm free. I'm finally free." It was hardly the expected reaction and Penny and Dr Emily closely observed the young couple, expecting some terrible, emotional explosion to happen at any second. It didn't, and all remained calm. Yet should they be surprised that Hayley expressed relief at the man's death? Even his wife and his son had spoken of feeling relieved and free.

"When did he do it?" demanded Hayley. "Please tell me when he did it, I need to know!"

"The recorded time of death is approximately 13:23." Penny whispered the answer to Hayley's question, aware of the increasingly obvious psychic significance of this information. Mike uttered another gasp. Dr Emily sucked in a breath.

"But that's almost exactly the time Hayley started to feel suddenly better! It's as if she's been delivered of some evil because he died. What sort of a hold did he have over her?"

"I'm not sure, Mike," said Dr Emily, "but it's almost exactly the time I felt I *had* to come here."

Penny was next to speak. "There have also been other truly extraordinary coincidences surrounding the time of the Pastor's death."

Silence descended. Comfortable, peaceful silence.

After several minutes,

"How is Mrs Pratt?" This from Hayley.

"Umm. I don't know quite how to answer that," Penny replied, "the poor woman actually seems relieved at her husband's death for it was not a happy union from what I've found out. She's reeling at the bad news about their only grandchild, so she's having a pretty rough time."

"Grandchild?" Hayley looked at Mike. "We didn't even realise they had any children, never mind a grandchild."

"They had only the one child," explained Penny, "a son. I would guess he's in his early twenties now. He and his partner had a little daughter, fifteen months old, who died from meningitis only last week. As you can imagine, the parents and Veronica, Mrs Pratt, are distraught."

Hayley put a hand to her mouth. "Oh my God, I can't imagine how they must be feeling, that's terrible."

"That's so awful," agreed Mike, "but I can see why the Pastor kept quiet about an unmarried son with a kid. Blimey, can you imagine it Trace? His only child living in sin, over the brush, it must have nearly choked him."

"Well," said Penny, "the biggest surprise of all is that Pastor and Mrs Pratt aren't married either. Apparently went through some sort of wedlock ceremony at a community they were involved in. It's not a marriage acknowledged by the law of the land."

"Wow!" exclaimed Hayley, just as Penny realised she should have kept her mouth shut. "That is so hypocritical after all he preached about living in sin. Well, well!"

"Hey, that's off the record mind. Forget you heard that." Blimey, she could lose her job over this little slip. No good crying over spilt milk though.

"He was certainly a very self-righteous, judgemental man," Dr Emily joined in.

"You've met him?" Penny turned to Dr Emily.

"Um, well, not met him as such, but I have heard him preach, if you could call it preaching. I went to the service at the Sinners Chapel of Mercy last Sunday morning for curiosity had got the better of me. I wanted to know what Hayley had been listening to in church that might have influenced her. Well, it was quite a morning, I can tell you! As soon as I got there I was told to move as I was sitting in someone's seat. Then I was subjected to a dose of the gloomiest theology I've ever heard in my life, following which I was encouraged to leave before the communion service as they didn't know

170

whether I was saved or not. I was obviously one of the great unwashed in their eyes."

"That sounds like Pastor Pratt," said Mike. "What did you do then?"

"Well, in need of a little fellowship, I met a bloke and we legged it into the Black Swan round the corner!" The four of them burst out laughing. "Something must have sunk in though as by then I was so afraid of imbibing a little alcohol – fire and brimstone awaited! – that I stuck to a coffee!"

"You drank coffee? Did you dunk?" Hayley ventured, grinning. My goodness it was good to hear this little bit of humour!

"No, no. I thought it better not to partake of such hedonistic delights so soon after being judged and found sadly lacking, according to the gospel of A. Pious Pratt." Dr Emily paused here for effect. "Besides which, I was on my best behaviour."

"You mean they didn't give you any biscuits with your cuppa more like it."

"Quite right Mike, quite right. Not a ginger nut in sight." Again they all laughed, Dr Emily marvelling over this witty exchange and delighting in being its cause.

"Excuse me, but what's so funny about this? I'm laughing but I haven't the foggiest idea what you people are talking about. Do enlighten me." Penny looked from one to the other of them.

Hayley giggled as the younger voice of Lizzy emerged and spoke. "Dr Emmy dunks biscuits in her drink and then scoops out the soggy bits that drop off with a teaspoon when she thinks nobody is looking. She is the world's bestest dunking shrink!"

Again there was laughter. Real laughter? Or only an attempt to lighten the seriousness of the afternoon's business? For if any one of them had stopped to think, which they didn't, they'd have realised how extremely odd it was to be sitting together, enjoying themselves and laughing, only hours after somebody they knew had committed suicide. Yet it did not feel as if anything tragic had happened. Instead, the atmosphere was one of light and peace, as if darkness had scattered, had been eradicated from a situation where once it had been in control. Hayley was not the woman she had been even yesterday, such had been the lifting of heaviness, sickness and despair. She was no longer the hounded, tormented, menaced creature of a few days ago. Again Penny thought the Pastor's death had rescued two more people, Hayley and Mike. God was most surely at work in His usual mysterious way. What other explanation was there? What would happen next? What did it all mean? What was her part in all this?

"Right!" announced Penny, rubbing both hands together. "While it's good to have a smile and a laugh, I need to get serious again. Obviously the case against Pastor Pratt no longer exists and so I will need to tie up all the loose ends sooner rather than later. I'll particularly want to know what part Mrs Pratt played in whatever went on between you and the Pastor, Hayley. We can leave it for today, but I do want to talk to you pretty soon."

"What was the case against him?" Hayley was suddenly anxious and afraid. Penny glanced across at Dr Emily with a questioning look. Dr Emily returned the look with a nod, as much as to say go ahead, tell Hayley what has happened.

"Okay, Hayley. We arrested him on suspicion of raping you following forensic evidence and a witness account."

"But he didn't rape me!"

"Then did he attempt to? There were carpet fibres on your clothes and his. You have injuries indicating a struggle. You managed to scratch him. A neighbour heard you screaming and saw you run from the chapel."

"And Lizzy did tell me that you had been raped again," Dr Emily added softly. "I hope you understand that I had to pass that on to the police. You did give me written permission to do so."

"But he didn't try to rape me. Well, at least not physically." Hayley had tucked her feet beneath her and was starting to curl up on the chair, to retreat.

"Then what did he do to you Hayley? Please tell us what happened."

"Oh my God! It's my fault he killed himself! It my fault, it must be, it has to be…"

"No, no, no!" exclaimed Penny, although she'd sort of been expecting this to happen. "It is absolutely NOT your fault. Remember he'd had some bad news and might have felt responsible himself. Plus, we don't yet know of any contributory factors that might have driven him to take his like. But one thing we ARE sure of Hayley, listen now, it was NOT your fault."

"Is Mrs Pratt blaming me?"

"No. She is not. You're going to have to believe me when I say that she is as relieved as you, probably more so, that the Pastor is dead." Penny sighed deeply. "Look, this is quite an unusual situation so I'm going to suggest something completely different and out of the ordinary as far as police procedure goes. How about we all meet up and discuss what's happened? The four of us here, Mrs Pratt, even the Pratt's son and his partner if they feel it might help them to talk, and I'm guessing they will. We're all connected by what's happened to the Pastor in some bizarre, dare I say spiritual, way. The timing of events coinciding with the time of his death is extraordinary to say the least. There's a whole mix of darkness and light going on and I think it would be useful to meet as a group and put it all together. What does everyone think? You two up for it?" Penny looked questioningly at Mike and Hayley, who both nodded. "How about you, Dr Em?" Another nod of assent. "Okay. Let me get hold of the Pratts and see what they think of the idea. Call it group therapy if you like. We have our shrink!" Penny smiled at Dr Emily who did not return the facial expression, being somewhat miffed at being called a shrink again. Why did the term ruffle her even when used affectionately? It shouldn't. But it bally well did!

"Where would we all meet?" This from Dr Emily.

"I haven't a clue at the moment," replied Penny. "Leave it with me and I'll get back to you all. I'll leave you now, get back to headquarters, make a few calls and hopefully let you know what's happening later this evening."

CHAPTER TWENTY-THREE

PENNY

Tuesday evening

S LAMMING THE FRONT DOOR shut behind her, Penny leaned against it briefly, closing her eyes for a few seconds, before picking up the post, going into the kitchen and putting the kettle on. Migmos began weaving in and out of her legs, meowing for food, the phone started ringing, and she noticed that the heating hadn't come on as timed. Blimey, it was cold! Welcome home! And she hadn't taken her coat off yet.

It didn't take Penny long to feed the cat, ignore the phone, sort the heating, and get herself seated in front of the television with coffee and a slice of toast. Although hungry, she couldn't be bothered to make a meal. It was after six o'clock and she was tired. What a day! She began to flick through the small pile of post that had arrived that morning. Mostly adverts, but oh my gosh, there it was, the letter she'd been waiting for from the university, telling her if she'd been accepted to study there that September. Being a mature student she hadn't needed to go the UCAS route but had instead gone through a series of gruelling interviews. Here now, in her hand, was a decision that could change the rest of her life. Tearing the envelope she held her breath as she scanned the brief communication. It was short and sweet. 'Pleased to confirm... offer of a place...

September 2005… yours faithfully, Dr R Preston.' There was a bit at the bottom she had to sign and return if she wanted to accept, which she most certainly did.

"Yes!" she squealed. "Migmos? I've done it! Yes, yes, yes! I'm going to Uni!" The very next thing Penny did was to go over to a desk in the corner of the room, open a drawer and take out a sealed envelope. She placed her letter of resignation in her handbag ready to hand in the very next day. Then she reached for her phone and quickly punched in a number while Migmos sat grooming herself in front of the fire, oblivious to all the excitement now that her stomach was full of trout in jelly.

"Ian? It's me, I've had the letter, I've been accepted at Truffleton University to start this September."

"Pen, that's great news! I don't have to keep your secret any longer then?"

"Well, keep it quiet for just a bit longer. You fancy coming over? A chat and a takeaway? I can't have a quiet evening now, I'm too excited."

"Yeah, okay. Be there about seven? Fish and chips do you? I haven't eaten yet, couldn't be bothered to make anything."

"Splendid! See you shortly. I'll leave the back door open for you." Penny sat back, grinning from ear to ear and looking forward to sharing her excitement with Ian. She had always wanted to go to University and do the student thing and she had never felt so excited in her life, even more excited than when she had joined the police force. That had never been her first choice though. Her father had been a copper and always insisted he would never take orders from a female officer. Well, Penny took that on as the ultimate challenge. As an emerging feminist back then she was out to prove him, and the establishment, wrong, for women could make excellent police officers and easily rise through the ranks. Well, it hadn't exactly been *that* easy, but Penny had succeeded and had certainly risen high enough to give orders to men! Content enough, she had been good at what she did, excelling in promotion exams and working well with her colleagues. But it simply wasn't what she wanted to be doing for the rest of her working life. She'd had enough of being the one in charge, the one responsible for important decisions. She wanted to go in another direction, to follow her heart and do something she was even more interested in. What she had chosen was certainly something completely different.

For Penny, the road ahead was about to curve acutely. At forty-five she wasn't too old either. Mind you, her father had been so proud of her in the end, and she wondered now what he would make of her decision to jack it all in. But hey, she needed to stop thinking and make a few calls, find out if Veronica, Matthew and Tracey were agreeable to meet up with Dr Emily and the Bishfords. She was hoping to arrange the meeting for the following Thursday morning, in the interview suite behind the main station buildings. It would be quiet and relaxed there.

"Yoo hoo! I'm here!" Ian clattered in through the back door and Penny rushed to give him a hug and relieve him of a bundle of fish and chips. "Salt and vinegar's already on," said Ian, "let's eat out of the paper, save on the washing up." They were silent as they opened the food and shared it out between them. Migmos took a quick sniff of the air, detecting a fishy aroma, but settled back down having decided that vinegar was an undesirable intrusion so stuff the fish! She sighed deeply, the way cats do after making important observations and decisions.

"Say something Ian, you're too quiet."

"I'm thinking. Selfish I know, but I'm gonna miss you. You still sure you're doing the right thing? It's one hell of a big step."

"Never been so sure of anything in my life. I'm more sure about this than I was about joining the force. It's the right decision at the right time in my life. I've been a cop for twenty-five years, Ian. I want something different, this is my chance, and I'm going to take it. I'm not even sure about where it'll take me after three years of study, but that's the exciting bit."

"Hmm. How will you manage financially, if you don't mind me asking?"

"To be honest, it won't be that bad. I'll get a lump sum and pension from the force, I don't have a mortgage and I have money in savings from my late Dad's house. I'm also entitled to a small education grant. One thing I will do, to bring in a bit more cash, is take in a lodger, housemate, houseguest, whatever you call it. I'll get a proper contract drawn up where we share the bills etc. It'll be okay. If not I'll go and work in McDonald's!"

"You serious about that, Pen?"

"What, McDonald's?" Penny laughed.

"No you nitwit! Taking in a lodger."

"Oh yes, dead serious. I'm sick of living on my own anyway, if I'm honest. I'm gonna be picky about who I let live with me, but I want some company. I'm lonely Ian, I don't seem to make or keep friends. Maybe the job puts them off, I don't know."

"Then let me move in with you."

"You?"

"Yes. Why not? What's so shocking about that? I'm in the same situation as you. Single and lonely. We get on well, trust each other, why couldn't it work?"

"You've taken me by surprise, that's all. I was thinking it should be another woman, but…"

"I'm a bloke? Is that what's bothering you?"

"Don't be daft, you know that doesn't bother me. It's just… Let me think about it and let you know, okay? You've thrown it at me all of a sudden and we both need time to think it through."

"I'm not suggesting it for wrong reasons, Pen, to try and take advantage of you in some way. It's not that. I really think it would work."

"Okay, I'll come out with the real reason. You already know I'm a Christian. I'm the sort that won't live with a bloke outside marriage. Go on, have a laugh!"

"But we'd be sharing a house, not living as if we were married!"

"Yes, but..."

"No buts, Penny, I just don't get that."

"Well you wouldn't, would you? You keep your particular brand of Christianity secret, so you won't get teased in work. Remember how you confided it to me and asked me to keep schtum?"

"Penny! I can't believe you said that! Just because I don't go to church every week and do a daily reading it doesn't mean I..."

"I'm sorry. I didn't mean to... Look, I'm sorry. Let me get my head round the idea and get back to you on it. I've got three months' notice to get through anyway as I don't start Uni until the end of September."

"Fair enough. The chips are getting cold." Ian's expression oozed some of the glumness he felt at the thought of Penny leaving the force. He'd be partnered with somebody new, have to go through all that 'God of the handcuffs', 'Saint Ian to the rescue' stuff ... and worse. Boy, it was tough being a lapsed Anglican. Trouble was, it had been even tougher when he'd been un-lapsed!

Penny sensed, correctly, that it was time to change the subject and they chatted generally while they ate their supper, comfortable with each other and enjoying being together. Penny was surprised to find herself rapidly warming to the whole idea of having Ian share the house with her. The house was big enough for them each to have their own space as Penny had an en suite bedroom, there was a spare downstairs sitting room, a large spare bedroom next to the bathroom, and they'd only be sharing the kitchen. He could certainly afford the rent, was trustworthy, and she wouldn't be worried about her own safety or that of her house. Perhaps he could even tidy the garden up? And to be honest, she did really like him. Did she more than like him? Yet what was she thinking? She'd only known him closely for a matter of months since they were partnered together for work. It had been a good partnership though. The best. Yet how would she really feel about it? Dare she even acknowledge that it was the judgement of the people in church she was afraid of? For there would certainly be whispers of disapproval when it was discovered she had a man in the house to whom she was not married, even if they *weren't* up to anything! Aw stuff it! When did Inspector Whistle get so bothered about what other people thought? She deliberately stopped her thoughts and concentrated on the last few chips nestling in the gloriously vinegary paper.

"Righty ho!" Ian crumpled all the empty fish and chip papers together and took them into the kitchen. "Talking shop, what's next on the 'to do' list concerning one A. Pious Pratt?"

"The usual reams of paperwork, waiting for the coroner's report, plus I'm arranging for everyone involved to meet up and talk through what's happened."

"Is that such a good idea, Pen? The young couple have just lost their kid mind."

"I'm well aware of that, I know what you're saying Ian, but I've got a hunch, a gut feeling, that it'll work in this particular situation. I don't know how, or why, but I have to give this hunch a chance. If it's a disaster it'll be down to me and I'll sort the fallout, but don't forget we've got Dr Emily, she's a good psychiatrist and facilitator."

180

"Dr Em okay with it?"

"Yes, she's fine with it – retiring soon, so she has the time to devote to anything that may develop. You never know, we might all meet up once and that's it. Else it'll become a regular support group for however long it's needed. It's hardly normal procedure, but who knows? I have to try this."

"Oh well, go with it then. Let me know how it turns out. When's the first get-together?"

"Thursday, and yes, I'll keep you up to date. You know? There's something 'other worldly' about the Pratt case."

"What d'you mean, Pen?"

"Well, take the Pastor. He's virtually a caricature of an overzealous, fundamentalist preacher from the dark ages. Hellfire and brimstone. Sin and lust and the wrath of God. To hear him speak, it's as if he was driven by something, something not of God that was overplaying its hand, being too ridiculous yet retaining threads of credibility. There was some*thing* about him."

"Oooh! Demon eyes! Get out the garlic!"

Penny ignored Ian's interruption and continued. "Then take the timing of his death which coincided with me finding Veronica cutting her wrists, Dave and Roger turning up at Matthew and Tracey's place just as they were going to take an overdose, Hayley's sudden improvement, Dr Emily feeling constrained to go to the Bishford's... All this happening at almost exactly the same time. There has to be a link and, dare I say it, a supernatural one."

"Yes, when you rattle it off like that, I can see there are some bizarre coincidences. I don't know about supernatural though, remember I'm a straightforward, bog standard ordinary copper. I don't usually consider the possibility of guardian angels flitting about keeping everyone safe from whatever forces drove some jerk to hang himself!"

Penny raised her eyebrows and smiled knowingly. "Interesting theory Ian, very interesting!"

"Get away with you!"

The two of them lapsed into silence for a few moments until Penny got up and made a pot of tea which she brought in on a tray with two mugs, milk and sugar. As soon as she sat down she flew straight back up again and reached for her bag.

"Eh? You got ants in your pants, Pen?"

"No, I just remembered something. That piece of paper from the Pastor's cell, I stuffed it into my bag and forgot all about it. I guess we'd better take a look at it, as it could be a suicide note. I'll need to pass it on anyway. It's remiss of me not to have already done so but what with Veronica..."

"Don't worry, Pen, we can sort it. What does it say?"

Penny opened up the single sheet of paper and smoothed it out, noticing the pencil writing on both sides. The first side she looked at contained a list of words, each beginning with a capital letter, each word describing something dark and negative.

Destruction, Hatred, Violence, Blasphemy, Lust, Wickedness, Murder, Idolatry, witchcraft, Jealousy... The list went on and on. A long list of terrible words, their upper case beginning suggesting they were names, proper nouns. Penny went cold for she had an idea of what the list meant. They shouted at her exactly what was going through the Pastor's mind and no doubt had been for some time. What she was thinking would also explain what had happened to Hayley last Thursday morning, and so many times before that as well. She turned the paper over to find a suicide note, the like of which neither Penny nor Ian had ever come across before, and they'd read a few in their time as coppers.

"Pen? Come on, what is it? Read the damn thing out to me, I'm in suspense here!"

So Penny read the note out loud,

182

"The Lord has ordered me to be with him immediately and I go joyfully and willingly from this sick and evil generation. I have been a faithful and obedient servant but none would hear my words. The demons I fought were of the higher echelons of the spirit world (see over). I fought to pin her down and struggled with her as she screamed and thrashed in my arms like pure wickedness. The lord has decided I must leave you all to the fight. I now send the demonic to punish you all, knowing that there will be no help for any of you. I shake the dust off my sandals, released even from fear for you who are bound by the chains of Satan himself and of hell. My struggle was with Satan himself. I fought bravely but the lord has chosen to relieve me of the task. I choose now to enter heaven and partake of my salvation. I shall miss nothing and nobody."

Penny and Ian looked up at each other open mouthed and silent.

"What d'you make of that?" Ian asked.

"Spiritual rape." Penny spoke so softly that Ian barely heard her words.

"What? What d'you mean?"

"I've come across this before Ian, although not as severe as this."

"So *did* he actually rape Hayley Bishford? Even if he didn't, we could still have had him for assault and false imprisonment, although reading that," Ian pointed to the piece of paper Penny still held in her hand, "I'd seriously be thinking he could plea insanity! He was a real nut job but we've got plenty of evidence that he injured her, had her pinned to the floor, held her there, had her screaming her blasted head off... she more or less admitted being raped. If he didn't rape her, or attempt to, then what the hell *did* he do to her, Pen?"

"I think I know," said Penny, ever so quietly. "In fact, I'm pretty certain I know."

CHAPTER TWENTY-FOUR

HAYLEY

"**SO, HAYLEY**, how are you feeling now that we've had a serious talk about what's happened?" Dr Emily was still at the Bishford's but would shortly have to leave, having spent the last couple of hours discussing the Pastor's suicide. "I want to leave you with the absolute fact that he, and he alone, was responsible for the decision to end his life. Nobody... nobody is at fault here. It was his decision, his responsibility and all the blame lies with him."

"I understand what you're saying," Hayley answered, "but I need to get my head around it. What's helping at the moment is how much better I'm feeling, and that's only been since almost the exact time of his death. Like I've said a dozen times or more in the last few hours, it seems that his death has been my cure. Like he had to die for me to survive. I don't get it! It's like *he* was the evil one, not me, and when he went, so did whatever was making me ill. He took the badness with him. He hurt me terribly, but I know he didn't rape me..."

"Who did rape you, Hayley? Are you able to tell me yet?"

"You still want me to tell you rather than Lizzy?"

"I think I do," Dr Emily said, "I believe it would be helpful to you, Hayley, if you could acknowledge whatever happened yourself instead of dissociating and becoming Lizzy. Perhaps the time has come when you, as Hayley, are able to bring those memories out into the open and deal with them."

"As well as dealing with the Pastor's suicide?"

"You're stronger than you think, Hayley."

"Am I?"

"Look, you must be pretty tired now. We all are, so we'll leave things there today but we certainly need to discuss this further. I'll call in tomorrow morning as planned, and then we'll have the group meeting on Thursday that Penny's arranging. You have my contact numbers so don't hesitate to ring me at any time if you need to or want to. I mean that."

"Okay," said Hayley. "Thanks for today, you've been really kind."

Dr Emily stood up to leave, putting her jacket on and fishing about in a pocket for car keys. "Try and get some sleep tonight, and stay as strong as you are now. You're doing amazingly well. I'll see you tomorrow."

Mike, who had been putting the kids to bed after their arrival home, was coming down the stairs as Dr Emily was leaving. "Bye Dr Emily!" he called.

"Bye bye Mike, see you tomorrow."

The door closed.

"She's not a bad old bird, is she?" Mike commented. "I like her actually. She's a bit of a fusspot though, and not at all how I expected a shrink to be."

Later that evening, when the kids were fast asleep, Penny rang to confirm that a group meeting had been scheduled for Thursday evening and were they both still willing to be part of it. Mike confirmed that both of them wanted to be there.

"I can't imagine what the Pastor's son will be like," said Hayley.

"No, nor me," replied Mike, "pity it's in such lousy circumstances, could have been quite interesting."

Hayley slept fitfully that night. The recurring dream recurred but with a difference. This time it wasn't Pastor Pitchfork who was on top of her, it was Uncle Dan. She was

185

fifteen, the same age as Lizzy, he was heavy and smelly, hurting her, damaging her as Pastor Pitchfork looked on in judgement and called her names. She stared at the damp patch on the ceiling and screamed.

CHAPTER TWENTY-FIVE

MATTHEW AND TRACEY

Tuesday evening

"**H**ANG ON, I'll ask them." Tim took the phone from his ear and addressed Matthew and Tracey. "It's Penny. She wants to know if you two, and you Veronica, would be willing to meet up as a group with the Bishford's and Dr Emily this Thursday evening."

"Who are the Bishford's?" asked Matthew.

"Who is Dr Emily?" asked Tracey.

"Why?" asked Veronica.

Tim spent some minutes on the phone, listening, before speaking again. "Seems you are all closely involved with the Pastor and will all have issues concerning his sudden death. Penny thinks it would help you all to get together and talk things through. Veronica, you already know Mike and Hayley Bishford so you can give Matthew and Tracey their details. Dr Emily Chatwith is the psychiatrist who has been helping Hayley and who does referral work for the police. Penny says will you think about it and let her know as soon as possible." Tim finished the call by assuring Penny he would call her back shortly.

"Mum? You know this Mike and Hayley? What have they got to do with Dad's death? What's going on?"

Veronica took several minutes to explain about how the Pastor had been seeing Hayley, trying to help her, and that it had all gone wrong, culminating in his arrest.

"Well, how the hell would it help me and Tracey to talk to them? I'm not sure I even want to. Why should I? Come on, it just ain't going to help. That won't help me, will it?" Matthew was surprisingly angry.

"It might not," put in Tim, "but it could very well help *them* to talk to *you*. Hayley must be feeling pretty guilty over your Dad's death since it occurred so soon after his arrest for attacking her."

"But we don't know them from flaming Adam! I'm not sure I want to be with strangers at the moment, I really don't get it." Matthew sat back and crossed his arms.

"For starters," interrupted Gloria, "Hayley will need to know, from the three of you, that you don't blame her or hold her responsible for what happened."

"What?" exploded Matthew, "Blame her? Hold her responsible? Shoot'n'balls! I'm bally well thanking her, not blaming her. My kid's gone and I'm glad, yes glad, the sicko I had for a father, who told me she should never have been born, that she…"

"Matthew, don't, please…" Tracey put a hand on his arm, already crying again herself and unable to bear his pain also. "Don't put yourself through this again."

"No, Tracey," he brushed her arm off, "this has to be said. He called our Chloe a bastard, a bastard conceived in sin, said it was not God's will for her to live and that… The best thing my father ever did for me was kill himself." He couldn't go on.

"I absolutely hated your father, Matthew, I'm glad he's dead too. I hated him."

"I'm sorry, I'm sorry…" Veronica was reaching for a fresh fistful of tissues.

"Listen to me, the three of you," Gloria's voice was firm, yet gentle and calm, her eyes glassy with unshed tears as she willed herself to stay in control, "this is exactly the reason Penny wants to get you all together. The circumstances are extraordinary to say the least and you are all connected by how the Pastor influenced your lives, and not in a good way. Like it or not, you three and the Bishfords are in this together. The timing of the Pastor's death coincides with healing for Hayley and prevention of mishap to the three of you here. You're tied together, dare I say spiritually, and I think you should at least meet up and give it a go. You know of Penny from church," Gloria nodded at Matthew and Tracey here, "surely you can give her the benefit of the doubt on this? I don't believe she would knowingly suggest anything that would hurt any of you, especially not in the circumstances. I don't understand it all myself, but why not go with it and see what happens?"

Matthew sighed deeply. "Oh well, why not then? Let's all go ahead, all get together and have a party to celebrate the death of the world's greatest plonker. Why don't we invite a whole lot more of the people he's botched up over the years? There's plenty of them! We can all dance on his grave and be merry and gay. Then they can all blame me for being his son..."

"Matthew," said Tim, "this is precisely the reason for such a group. It will be a controlled and safe outlet for one hell of a lot of anger, hatred, pain, and the rest of it. Please don't take this the wrong way, but you're not the only one who's confused and in pain because of..."

"No," Matthew shot back, glaring at Tim, "but I'm the only father who's lost his little girl!"

Gloria wanted to point out that many parents had lost precious, loved children, not just Matthew, but it would have been a cruel and pointless observation at that moment. Besides which, no other father in the world had lost Chloe. There truly was no comfort anyone could offer.

Gloria quoted from the Bible, "Underneath are the everlasting arms. Deuteronomy thirty-three, verse twenty-seven." The five of them fell silent. Three of them were still falling, plunging deeper and deeper into the darkness. How far down *were* those everlasting arms?

"Why didn't Jesus save our Chloe?" Tracey's voice was barely audible.

"He did, Tracey. He did. That's why she's in heaven now. In His arms. There is no better, safer place to be." Gloria could hold her tears no longer and wept openly.

"But *my* arms are so empty…"

A hush fell over them and they sat a while in silence.

"Look," said Tim finally, "what have you got to lose? Things can't get any worse than they are now, so why not go on Thursday, see what Penny's got in mind, then decide if it's for you or not. No pressure. You either decide to go again or you don't."

"I *know* Penny," said Gloria, "and she would never do this in a police capacity, probably against the rules. She's got the Holy Spirit's leading on this. I believe that. Please, trust me, trust Penny. Go with it and keep an open mind."

"I'd like to go if that's okay with you, Matthew."

Matthew drew in a deep, long breath and let it slowly back out. "Okay Tracey, as Tim says, it can't get any blasted worse. I don't get it, but I'll go. I'll do it for you so that you won't be there on your own."

Tim phoned Penny to let her know. "Before you go, Tim," Penny had said, "tell Veronica I'll be over about ten in the morning to have a chat with her. I'll have Ian with me."

Later that same evening, after Tim and Gloria had gone home, Veronica, Matthew and Tracey sat with only the light from a small lamp illuminating the room and casting shadows. They were talking, crying, remembering, regretting… hating, blaming, and refusing to forgive.

CHAPTER TWENTY-SIX

VERONICA'S SECRET

Wednesday morning

MATTHEW AND TRACEY were still in bed when Penny and Ian arrived the following morning to speak with Veronica. The bereaved parents had stayed up for most of the night, eventually hauling themselves into bed just after five thirty and falling into an exhausted sleep. Veronica, too, was exhausted from lack of sleep and was still in her dressing gown. She opened the door to let the two officers in before opening the downstairs curtains and making a cuppa.

"Instant coffee okay?"

"Yes, thanks, that's fine Veronica. Spot of milk, one sugar. Same for Ian."

When the three of them were seated, holding their drinks, Penny spoke. Ian held a biro poised over a notepad.

"How are you feeling this morning, Veronica?" Penny began.

"Tired. Battered. Wondering how we're all going to get through the next days, weeks, months…"

"It's very difficult for you," said Penny, "and I wish I didn't have to cause you any further distress, but I do need to take a statement from you. Do you feel up to getting it over with this morning?"

"Yes, let's get on with it, for I don't suppose I'll ever feel up to it."

"Right. We'll go for it then. Now what can you tell me about what happened between the Pastor and Hayley last Thursday morning?"

"Oh dear," sighed Veronica, "this isn't going to be easy. You're not going to believe me if I tell you."

"Try me," Penny urged, "you might be surprised."

"Anthony was carrying out a major exorcism."

"What!" Ian spluttered, having just taken a mouthful of coffee. "Exorcism? Oh, for crying out loud…"

"I guessed as much," said Penny.

"How did you guess?" Veronica and Ian spoke in unison, both incredulous at Penny's reaction.

"He left a note in his cell – you can read it if you want to Veronica, it gave a list of names which he described as higher echelon spirits. He wrote of his fight with Satan." Penny spoke as if this was no more unusual than a regular, bog standard burglary.

"His fight with who? *Satan?* Are we back in the Middle Ages? This is like something out of the Salam witch trials!" The look on Ian's face was almost funny. "What the devil are you two on about? Excuse the expression."

Penny flashed Ian a sympathetic half grin before turning her attention back to Veronica. She inwardly chided herself for enjoying his discomfort and surprise so much.

"So tell us exactly what happened on the morning in question. No rush, take your time."

"Okay," started Veronica, "we had arranged to meet Hayley at the chapel because Anthony claimed she would be more open to deliverance if she was in the chapel building. Consecrated ground, prayer soaked walls. We arrived there a little before nine thirty I think and Anthony got cross when Hayley was five minutes late. He couldn't abide tardiness.

When she did arrive, the three of us sat in the front row and Anthony explained to her yet again that the voices she kept hearing in her head were demons. They were causing all her problems and she needed to be rid of them. They belonged in hell."

"Demons? Oh, come on..." Ian's eyes were about to pop out on the proverbial organ stops.

"Shush! Carry on Veronica." Penny flapped a hand in his direction, furrowing her brow and giving him one of her fearsome 'shut your mouth or else' looks.

"He got her to pray and confess all her sins, plus a few more just in case, and then asked her to give him the names of the demons who possessed her. When she kept repeating that she didn't know any names, Anthony became angrier and angrier. He said he was going to call down the wrath of God upon her. I begged him to calm down, but he wouldn't. He started shouting at her. When she got up and tried to leave, he grabbed her quite roughly."

"He physically prevented her from leaving?" Ian asked.

"Yes, he did," Veronica continued. "I was shouting at him to stop but he was screaming right up close, into her face, shaking her viciously, ordering the demons to come out of her and go to the pit."

"The pit?"

"Another name for hell, Ian. Also referred to as Gehenna. Go on Veronica."

"I had never seen Anthony so angry. He was mad. It was terrible, like *he* was the one possessed. I was getting frightened and said I was going, that if he didn't stop then I wanted no part of it. So I walked down the aisle towards the door at the front of the chapel. I glanced back and he was still screaming and he had her pinned to the floor, banging her head on the carpet over and over again..."

"Dear God!" exclaimed Ian.

"So you left the building while this was going on." This from Penny.

"Yes," Veronica responded, "I left and went straight back to the manse."

"Veronica," said Penny, "did you try to help Hayley at all, or get any help for her after you left the chapel?" She already knew the answer.

"No, I didn't."

"Why not?"

"I don't know why not. I just didn't. I was scared. I didn't know what to do."

"Has Anthony ever showed violence towards you? Has he ever hit you?" Penny knew by the length of silence following this question that the reply would be in the affirmative, but she needed to hear it from Veronica.

"Yes," she replied eventually, "he has."

"Were you afraid he would hit you again if you reported what was happening in the chapel?"

"Yes. Plus I was afraid nobody would believe me."

"Afraid nobody would believe you?" Ian couldn't keep quiet. "Forget the freaking demons, this was a serious assault you walked away from! There's a woman out there covered in bruises and scared witless!"

"Okay," Penny continued, wishing Ian would calm down but at the same time understanding his frustration, "so you went back to the manse. What happened then?"

"I got lunch ready because Anthony likes... *liked* his meals on time. He came home..."

"Can you remember the time?"

"No. But it was getting close to lunch time. Maybe around half eleven."

"What was he like when he arrived home?"

"He was hungry, said he wanted his lunch as soon as it was ready."

Ian blew out a noisy sigh, shaking his head slowly from side to side.

"What did he look like Veronica? How did he seem? What was his mood like?"

"His suit was rumpled and there was a scratch on his neck and another one on his hand. I put a plaster on his hand for him. I did ask about Hayley and he said she'd been more uncooperative than usual and the Lord had told him not to carry on. Anthony said she had become extremely difficult and had run out of the building. I assumed Hayley was okay and had gone straight home."

Ian still couldn't resist butting in. "So you assumed Hayley was okay after being shaken roughly and having her head repeatedly banged onto a hard floor?"

"Yes. I did."

"Did either you or the Pastor attempt to contact Hayley to see how she was? You'd been seeing her for two years – surely you would have been concerned?"

"No," said Veronica.

"Why not?" asked Penny.

"Anthony insisted she was to be handed over to Satan…"

"Oh, pur-leeeez!" Ian was finding this all extremely difficult and again Penny flapped a hand in his direction, trying to keep him quiet. She needed to get the whole story out of Veronica.

"Go on, Veronica."

"Hayley was to be handed over to Satan so that she would come to her senses. Anthony said the Lord had instructed him he was to have nothing more to do with her."

"How convenient," said Ian.

Veronica continued, "She's always been okay before. Well, sort of okay, although Anthony has never been as angry with her as he was last Thursday. Never had her on the floor like that. Well, not too often anyway…"

"So this wasn't the first time he'd tried to exorcise her?" Although Penny was utterly horrified that this could happen in 2005, she knew from experience and Christian contacts that exorcism was indeed being practiced in many charismatic, fundamentalist settings. Even in some mainstream denominations. How many of those exorcisms, if any, were actually necessary was anyone's guess. Penny held a morbid fascination on what drives someone to set themselves up as an exorcist, and why does someone like Hayley go along with it? What were the psychological processes at work?

"No," said Veronica, "this wasn't the first exorcism. He's been seeing her for about two years, as you already know."

"Were you always present?"

"Nearly always."

"And what would go on?"

"Mostly Anthony would talk to Hayley and get her to tell him everything about herself. Everything. Then she had to confess her sins. Then he would read scripture to her and command the demons to manifest themselves and come out of her."

"Was he enjoying it all?" Ian still had bulging eyeballs. Surely what had been happening was nothing more than an exaggerated power trip.

"Yes," said Veronica, "I believe he did enjoy it. He liked being needed and being in control. He told Hayley he was the only one who could help her because of the condition she was in. He liked that power and control over people and over demons. Jesus had authority over the demons so this put Anthony in a special and unique spiritual position."

"Did he, at any time, suggest that Hayley consult her GP?"

"No."

"Did he seek help and support from anyone else? A fellow minister, doctor, psychiatrist, counsellor…?"

"No, he didn't, because he believed he was the only one who could deliver Hayley. He told her that doctors and psychiatrists wouldn't be able to help her as they would not believe or understand what was going on."

"How did you see your role, Veronica?"

"Just as a chaperone I suppose. I was there as prayer support as well, praying for Hayley."

"Did you agree with what your husband was doing? Did *you* believe Hayley was possessed?" This, thought Penny, would be an interesting answer. Veronica hesitated before replying.

"I knew Hayley had problems, and I believe in demons, but I think true possession is extremely rare. Maybe people like Hitler, or Jack the Ripper... but not a housewife in Truffleton, looking after two little kiddies. Surely not. Hayley was, is, so quiet and gentle. So no, I never did believe that Hayley was possessed."

"Did you tell Anthony that?"

"Yes, but he kept telling me that he was the one called by the Lord, I was wrong. He had the power of discernment, not me, and what he was doing was right. He *knew* Hayley was possessed and he was the one called to drive the demons out of her. Full stop."

"And you went along with that?"

"What choice did I have? He was an extremely difficult, awkward man and not many would dare to confront or contradict him. I was afraid of him."

"Veronica," Penny took in another deep breath and exhaled slowly before continuing, "what was your relationship with Hayley like?"

"I don't know her that well. I think, hope, that she guessed I didn't like what was happening or how Anthony was treating her. I'm nervous about meeting her tomorrow. I don't know how she'll react to me."

"Let's go back now to the beginning. When the Pastor began seeing Hayley. Why did he begin counselling her?"

"She had a few problems."

"Like what?"

"She began having difficulties taking communion after she had joined the fellowship. She said the bread and wine made her feel sick and she didn't want to partake. Anthony said that wasn't normal, which it wasn't, and asked her to come to the manse and speak to him about it. He thought he could help her. When she said that she'd been interested in witchcraft many years ago, that explained why she was having difficulty with anything Christian. Then when she said she was hearing voices in her head, well, Anthony put two and two together and…"

"Made five?" suggested Ian.

"No!" Snapped Veronica, "the voices were extremely blasphemous, it's a common assumption in Christian circles…"

"In *some* Christian circles," added Penny.

"Well, okay, but some believe that anyone who hears voices is possessed. That's what Anthony believed about Hayley."

"Jesus heard voices," Penny whispered, unheard by the other two people in the room.

"So he spent two years trying to get rid of *demons*?" asked Ian.

"Yes. He did."

"What was happening to Hayley all this time?" Ian wanted to know.

"She was getting worse."

"And the two of you carried on without sending her to a doctor?" Ian remained cross.

Veronica looked at him pathetically. "Battles often get worse just before the final victory. The enemy will exert one final effort. The night is darkest before dawn. Anthony believed Satan was getting stronger in Hayley because he knew his time was up, and so Hayley was getting worse."

"This would sure sound good in a court of law!" Ian commented, somewhat sarcastically.

"Do you think your husband raped Hayley?" Penny at last asked this question.

"Yes. I know he did."

"What?"

"Not physically. Well not as far as I know. But what he did to her over two years was, was... violating, intrusive, humiliating... oh, I can see it all more clearly now, all of a sudden, now I'm released from him... Wouldn't you call that rape? Spiritual and emotional rape?"

"Okay. Let's leave it there for now. You may well be right, but it's not for us to imply anything psychological comes close to a traumatic physical assault second only to murder in English law. Ian? If you can get a statement written for Veronica to sign that would be helpful. Leave me here with her for half an hour while you do that, and chase up the coroner's report on the Pastor's death. That's being rushed through at a rate of knots thank goodness. Then we can think about lunch."

"Will do. Thanks for the coffee, Mrs Pratt. You take care now." Ian got up and made his way out of the room. The two women remained silent until they heard the click of the front door closing. Veronica was the one who then broke the silence.

"I know what you're going to ask now. You want to know what Anthony was blackmailing me about."

"Well?"

"Do I have to tell you?"

"No. You don't. I can't force you to tell me anything you don't want me to know."

"Even if a crime was committed and I should be in jail?"

"Only you can decide if you want to tell me. Why do you say you should be in jail?"

"Anthony has held this over me for so long, never let me have a moments rest, keeping me on edge, taunting me, calling me evil, reminding me… Now that he's gone and can't torment me with it any longer, I still can have no rest. I'll never rest, I know that now. Doesn't scripture tell us there is no rest for the wicked? So it must be for me. Perhaps now is the time for me to unburden myself, for prison cannot be worse than the emotional blackmail I've been punished with all these years. I've lived with it constantly for many long years. Maybe I should be dead as well?"

Penny was wise enough and experienced enough to know that then was the time to use one of the well-known tools of interrogation. Silence. It worked, too, for Veronica spoke again after only a short pause.

"I killed two people."

"You *killed* two people?" Blimey! Penny had certainly not been expecting to hear *that*!

"Yes. My parents."

CHAPTER TWENTY-SEVEN

DR EMILY

DR EMILY had decided against prune juice for breakfast as she didn't particularly want to be set free that day. She settled for the gentler ministrations of bran flakes, having decided against the endless chewing of a portion of All Bran. As if all this decision making first thing wasn't enough, Doodle was being a positive pain, having refused her usual Caesar in jelly, yipping non-stop until Dr Emily gave in and threw a Delidog Delight onto the kitchen floor for her. "I've spoilt you, haven't I? Now be quiet while I get ready. I've got another busy day today." There was Hayley to visit, then back to Angel's Rest for a light lunch and to wait for Richard Preston to pick her up. Oh, but that was the most interesting part of the day! She was so excited. What should she wear? Would he even notice what she was wearing? Yes, yes, she told herself, of course he would notice, silly woman. Out with the glad rags! Half way through the bran flakes the phone rang. "Botheration!"

"It's me, Penny."

"Hello dear, how are you? What can I do for you?"

"Two things. I understand you're popping in to see Hayley this morning?"

"Yes, I am."

"Right. Tell you the truth, I'm having my doubts about this group get-together tomorrow and wonder if you could sound Hayley out for me? I'm particularly worried about how she'll feel meeting up with Veronica."

"I'll certainly do that Penny, but don't go worrying about the group. It's not a bad idea at all and I'm sure the two of us can steer everyone towards a positive, healing encounter. I've got a good feeling about it." Beside which, it would be absolutely riveting! Dr Emily could hardly wait to get all these people together, hear their accounts and study their interactions and reactions.

"Then I hope your good feeling pays off, I really do. I've gone on a hunch with this, as you know, and it's certainly not usual police procedure. Also, could *I* come and have a chat with you? Alone? Completely off the record?"

"Penny, yes, of course you can. When? How soon?"

"Today any good? I really need to talk to someone before tomorrow, if you've got the time."

"Well, I'm going out at two this afternoon, I'm out this morning visiting Hayley, but how about you come here for lunch? We'll have about two hours."

"That would be brilliant! Thank you so much."

"Not a problem my dear. I'll look forward to seeing you later." Drat it! That's the trouble with bran flakes; leave them for a minute or two and they go soggy in the milk. Should have had toast. Never mind, these things are no doubt sent to try us. What did Penny want to talk about that was so urgent? Splendid! The day ahead promised to be both busy and interesting. Now, what was she going to wear? Better dress tidily now, for she'd have no time to change with Penny coming for lunch.

Dr Emily spent close on two very useful hours with Hayley that morning. It had been hard work and Hayley still had a long way to go, for although she'd had a sudden flight into health, there was still a host of mental health issues to work through. At least Hayley was able to acknowledge physical hunger and eat small amounts of food. It was good progress.

"Are you still hearing voices, Hayley?"

Hayley had gone into much detail about the voices she heard in her head, explaining that the Pastor had managed to convince her they were demons who needed to be exorcised and sent to the pit. (Dr Emily had managed to keep a straight face and appear unshocked but, for heaven's sake, surely exorcism went out with the dark ages?) Hayley had also taken great pains to point out that Lizzy and Little Lizzy were separate persons. They were not her.

"Who are they then?" Dr Emily had asked.

"I don't know. Maybe they are demons after all, like the Pastor said they were. Then I do need to get rid of them!"

"Why do you think they might be demons?"

"Because he said,… the Pastor said they must be and…"

"Hayley, I do not believe they are demons. You are NOT possessed, despite what Pastor Pratt told you. Try and see the Lizzies as younger versions of yourself, caught in a time trap if you like."

"What d'you mean?"

"How can I put it…" Dr Emily raised her face to the ceiling while she thought in double quick time. She then lowered her head and looked at Hayley. "Lizzy is fifteen. You've already told me that something horrible happened to you at fifteen. You didn't like it so your mind created another person for it to be happening to. It's called dissociation and is a well know psychological self-defence strategy. It enables you to survive far more psychologically sound than you would otherwise have been. Do you understand what I'm saying?"

"Yes, sort of, but what about Little Lizzie? She's only three."

"You tell me about her."

"I can't!"

"Okay. Tell me about the other voices you hear."

Hayley had gone on to describe a group of male voices who were always in the background of her life. Whispering, talking, sometimes shouting, always commenting on whatever she was doing, telling her what to do, laughing at her, swearing copiously... Scatological, vile, blasphemous tormentors. No wonder it had been easy to convince the poor woman she was possessed!

"Have they always been blasphemous?"

"No. Only since I started going to church."

"Right! That suggests to me that they were reacting to where you were and what you were doing. If they were demons, wouldn't they have always been blasphemous?"

"Yes, but they wanted to hide the fact that they were demons!"

"Hayley, wouldn't they have hidden even more in the presence of an exorcist who was trying to get rid of them? Yet you tell me church made them worse."

"I don't know."

"I want you to think about all this. For now, I want to help you find coping strategies that will make life a lot pleasanter."

"What? Are you going to get rid of the voices then?"

"I honestly don't know if anyone or anything can stop you hearing voices, but while you've got them, we need to find the best way for you to cope with them. Trying to get rid of them hasn't worked and has actually made them worse. For the time being, let's find ways of coping that will ease this terrible depression and blackness you speak of."

"But nothing works, and I don't want to be drugged up to the eyeballs!"

"My dear, I'm not suggesting we drug you up to the eyeballs! I would like you to see your GP. I'll contact him myself, and we'll get you started on a mild antidepressant. You need to trust me that this *can* help. Now have you got an MP3 player or an iPod?"

"Mike has an MP3 player he hardly uses."

"Then get some of your favourite music on it and plug it into one ear only if you're not alone, two ears if you are. You might find that very helpful. Some voice hearers even find that plugging one ear with cotton wool can help. These are ways of telling yourself that your ears don't want to be disturbed by any bad voices you're hearing. It's worth a try. It's also a way of telling the voices that you don't want to listen. Another thing you could try is..."

Dr Emily had been able to leave Hayley with a few nuggets that day which she hoped would be helpful. She'd also remembered to ask Hayley how she felt about meeting Veronica again.

"I honestly don't know."

"Do you blame her for how the Pastor treated you?"

"If I'm honest, yes, I do. I'd like to ask her a few things, that's for sure. She was always just there, in the background, not saying anything, going along with him... Yet there *were* times when I sensed she wasn't happy with it all. She was always *too* quiet, as if she was afraid of him. Yes, I believe she was! I've been worrying that she blames me for his death. I was frequently accused of wearing out the saints! But then, shouldn't it be *her* worrying about *me* blaming them both for... Oh, I don't know. It's all so complicated..."

"Do you think it would be *useful* to meet with her again?"

"Yes. Maybe. There's plenty to talk about I guess, and I'd be interested to meet their son. I can't imagine Pastor Pratt being a father!"

Dr Emily had left Hayley then, giving herself enough time to pop into Tesco for some lunch items, arriving home just before noon. She could hear Doodle yipping as soon as she opened the front door, and made a fuss of the little dog as soon as she was inside. Dr Emily then went into the kitchen and made some cheese rolls, pouring crisps into one bowl and cherry tomatoes into another. She then set out two mugs ready for coffee, and placed a few small cakes on another plate. That would do! Just as she was checking the time by her watch, she heard a car draw up outside and guessed, correctly, that it was Penny.

"We meet again, Penny! It's so lovely to see you dear, do come in."

"What a lovely little cottage! Have you lived here long?" They hugged briefly.

"Not very long. My late husband and I shared the big house next door which my daughter and her partner now share. I hardly need all that space now and I'm quite content in smaller surroundings. Do sit down. I'll bring in our little lunch and we can chat and eat. I'm eager to know the latest on the Pastor Pratt case!"

Lunch was perfect, the coffee hot and welcome, and the two women were soon talking easily together.

"What I really wanted to talk to you about was something Veronica has confided to me. I'm in a bit of a quandary because, as a police officer, I should be reporting an historical crime, a very serious one too, and yet the poor woman is traumatised enough as it is. She's lost a grandchild, the Pastor's hung himself, I honestly don't know what to do. She's confessed to a crime. I'm waiting for the case notes to be dug out of police archives so I can find out what's been recorded, but I'd really like to get it off my chest. What I'm trying to say is, will you be my shrink for an hour and can you keep it confidential?"

Shrink? That word again! It really did ruffle the Chatwith plumage, but Dr Emily quickly forgave and forgot, her curiosity aroused. Doodle had jumped up and settled on her lap and she gently petted the little animal as she urged Penny to spill those extremely intriguing beans.

"Penny, we are two professionals here. What you tell me will stay with me, I promise. What has Veronica told you?"

"*Phew*, where do I start? First of all they weren't really married."

"Not married? Well, colour me pink, I'd never have thought that, what with him being the holier than thou preacher that he was. Gosh! I *am* surprised."

"It took me by surprise, too," continued Penny. "Turns out the two of them went through some sort of cult wedding ceremony but never legalised their union. According to the law of the land they are not married."

"Goodness! I'm not easily surprised and shocked, but..."

"Yes, I know. As if that wasn't bad enough it appears he's virtually ostracised his son because he's living with a girlfriend and they had a child."

"That's certainly a case of the pot calling the kettle black. How bizarre!" Dr Emily paused in the fussing of her Doodle while she digested this information. You never knew people, did you? She'd guessed the Pastor was a self-righteous, hypocritical, opinionated jerk, but unmarried? Well, well."

"Out and out hypocrisy if you ask me, made all the worse by his so-called Christian faith."

"Yes. Absolutely." Doodle had successfully nudged Dr Emily's hand back into action, once again revelling in the attention.

"There was quite a scene between the Pastor and Mrs Pratt when I took her to the station to break the news to him about Chloe. He got quite heated and went to grab her across the table, threatening to tell us something about her. Seems he's been blackmailing her for nigh on twenty years."

"Blackmailing her?" Again Emily ceased petting Doodle as she paid attention to the riveting information from Penny.

Thoroughly annoyed, Doodle jumped off Dr Emily's lap, went and curled up in her bed, and gave Dr Emily a rather pathetic look before sighing deeply and closing her eyes. "Tell me more," prompted the doctor. This was getting more and more interesting – like something out of a crime novel.

"Well," continued Penny, "after the angry words between the two of them I took Veronica back to my office to calm down. I couldn't help asking her why she had stayed so long with the Pastor seeing as he wasn't even her real husband, and especially because of the thoroughly unpleasant man he was. That didn't make any sense to me. It didn't add up."

"It's obviously something pretty serious he was blackmailing her over then?" said Emily. This was truly edge of the seat stuff!

"Murder!" exclaimed Penny.

"Murder? Good heavens above!" Edge of the seat? On the floor more like. Dr Emily's eyes were wide open, for the events of the last six days kept getting more mysterious, bizarre and extraordinary by the minute.

"Veronica told me that, about twenty years ago, she had murdered two people. Those two people were her parents."

"Oh my word! Why? How? Why did she do it? What happened?" Dr Emily was now sitting bolt upright, almost holding her breath as she waited for Penny to continue.

"Turns out Veronica was one of two children. She has an older brother she hasn't seen for close on thirty years as he left home at fifteen. Parents were both heavy drinkers and so home life wasn't good and it sounds as if both kids were pretty neglected, left to their own devices. Anyway, Veronica was in town one Saturday and met Anthony Pratt. He was handing out leaflets, recruiting for some religious community he was part of. When she took him home, her parents hated him on first sight, warning Veronica to dump him quick. However, Veronica was young, eighteen I think she said, unhappy at home, wanting to leave, wanting to kick out at her folks… usual teenage stuff. She told them she was going to join this religious community, sounds like a cult to me, whether they liked it or not, and would probably end up marrying Anthony."

"What was the name of this cult? Did she say?"

"Yes. The Community of Saintly Followers, believe it or not. Anyway, to cut a long story short, Veronica joined them and went on to take part in a communal wedlock ceremony. Sounds more like an excuse for sex if you ask me. She and Anthony set up home together within the commune, then when Veronica found out she was pregnant, they went to tell her parents the good news."

"Oh dear," commented Dr Emily.

"Oh dear indeed! There was an almighty row, Anthony stormed out, Veronica stayed behind to try and calm things down with her parents. That didn't happen, things went from bad to worse and a lot of stuff got said. It was getting late and her parents, quite drunk by then, went up to bed, ordering Veronica to be gone by morning, or else, and never come back. As she was leaving to return to the commune, Veronica noticed her mother's cigarette, still lit, in the ashtray beside the settee. She picked it up, placed it under a cushion and left the house." Penny paused here for just a few seconds. "Both parents were killed in a house fire that night. The papers reported it as a tragic accident."

Dr Emily very rarely struggled for words, but she did then. This was serious, serious stuff.

"Oh. My. Dear. Lord. That poor woman."

"Poor woman? Why d'you say that Dr Em? I don't know *how* I should be feeling."

"Poor woman? Well, if you think about it, that must have been a profoundly dysfunctional relationship she had with her parents for it to even cross her mind to do something like that. She must have felt utterly desperate and abandoned by them, at the end of her tether, if not off the end of it. It could even have been something she did subconsciously, not realising what the consequences could be. There again, it could have been a wicked, calculated act done to cause the most damage. But to kill? I don't know Penny, I don't really. I can't imagine how she must have felt when she heard about the fire and its devastating consequences. Good grief, and she's kept it to herself for so long."

"Not quite kept it to herself, Dr Em. She did tell Anthony what she had done as soon as she was back with him."

"Ah yes, the blackmail. I see. He's held it dangling over her like a sword of Damocles ever since."

"Yes, he has."

"What a thoroughly wretched situation."

"Yes, it is Dr Em, and I can quite understand the relief she expressed at his death. It's all so horrible. What am I to do about it?"

"It's a tough one, that's for sure. The thing is Penny, what's to be gained by bringing this out into the open after all this time? Have you been able to check any records yet about the fire?"

"No. Ian, my DS, is doing that for me now. If he wonders why I want to know about the fire then he's been wise enough to say nothing. He probably thinks I just want a few background checks on the Pratts."

"Then you must do nothing at all until you have the full picture. Veronica is already traumatised by everything that's happened this last week and I don't see any point in taking this further at the moment."

"I'm glad you said that and I do agree with you. My main worry is that if she once became unbalanced enough to start a fire, could the same happen again while she's so stressed out? Two deaths. Two funerals to get through. Is she any danger to herself or to anyone else?"

"I understand where you're coming from, but don't forget, this is something she did close to two decades ago. As far as we can know, she hasn't done anything similar since, and if anyone has suffered and been punished for an act of wrongdoing, then she has. She's been in hell, believing that she killed her parents, plus living with someone who was blackmailing her over it. Please don't think I'm excusing her Penny, I'm not, but I can't help feeling that she's had punishment enough. As to the stress she's under, you've got a point there, let me sus her out tomorrow. She certainly needs to be seen by her GP so I'll get her going in that direction. If she refuses, then I'll… but let's take it one step at a time."

"Sounds sensible. You've confirmed my inclination not to bring the whole sorry episode out of the closet. You didn't mind me talking to you, did you? I'm in the wrong job! I should be able to cope with this sort of stuff."

"No. Of course I don't mind. I'm glad you did as a matter of fact as I'll be in a better position to deal with anything Veronica might come out with tomorrow when the group meets. I hope it's helped to get it off your chest, and please don't worry, I'll keep this confidential."

"Thanks Dr Em. It's been really bothering me, but if I mention it in work then another case has to be opened and… I don't think that should happen at this moment in time."

"I believe you're wise to hang back, Penny. You also need to take care of yourself in all this. Please do ring me or call at any time you need to talk."

"I appreciate that. Thanks again. Well, I must be on my way. Thanks for the lunch as well – just hit the right spot!"

As Penny got up to leave, there was a sharp knock on the door.

"That'll be my date. I'm having an afternoon out," said Dr Emily.

"Good for you," Penny replied, "enjoy yourself."

Dr Emily opened her front door to let Penny out and allow Richard Preston in. She could hardly have expected what happened next.

"Penny?"

"Dr Preston!" exclaimed Penny, "I didn't know you two…"

"Emily, my dear." Richard Preston shook Emily warmly by the hand before turning to Penny and offering her his hand also. "Emily and I met only recently, and now we are off for an afternoon jaunt. We shall, no doubt, put the world to rights in pleasant surroundings!"

"How do you two know each other?" Dr Emily was surprised and curious. "Don't tell me you've arrested this gentleman in the course of your career, Penny." The three of them laughed.

"No, no. I haven't arrested him, but that doesn't mean he's not guilty, just that we haven't caught him at it yet." Again they all laughed, which felt so good after the serious business over lunch. "Dr Preston interviewed me recently and has since offered me a place at University. I start the end of September."

"Penny, you have rendered me speechless yet again. So you're going to study Theology?"

"Yes. I am. It is a bit of a surprise I suppose and I'll tell you all about it when we've got time. Now, I must leave you lovely people to your afternoon out as I have to get back to HQ. Dr Preston, do fill Dr Em in on all my details, she's dying to know!" Penny smiled warmly at Dr Emily, deciding that she very much liked and respected this older woman who possessed a quiet dignity and deep wisdom that was both humbling and reassuring.

"I certainly shall, Penny. It's Richard, by the way."

"Splendid. Thanks Richard. See you both again soon. Bye now." With that, Penny was on her way to her car and Dr Emily was ushering Richard into the cottage.

"I shan't keep you a moment. I just need to pop upstairs and get my coat, then we can be off. Oh, and that's Doodle by the way," pointing to the little dog, "don't worry if she gives you the once over. I have told her to be on her best behaviour." On hearing her name, Doodle trotted over and began to sniff Richard's shoes and introduce herself with a few Yorkie yips.

The drive to the Buds'n'Blossoms garden centre was not a long one and Dr Emily listened with interest as Richard explained how he had met Penny during the University interviewing process. "I must admit," he confided, "I do feel a little uneasy about her transition from top cop to undergraduate. It's a huge step to be taking, yet she does seem pretty sure she's doing the right thing. I guess only time will tell. How do you come to know her?"

Dr Emily had gone on to explain her connection to the police in her capacity as a consultant psychiatrist. "I've known Penny for years via the telephone but it was very recently that we finally met up. I knew she was thinking of leaving the force but had no idea of her intended destination. What does she plan to do with a degree in Theology?"

"She doesn't know herself yet, which is another reason I shall observe her progress with great interest. Honestly, Emily, there isn't much you *can* do with a degree in Theology unless you want to teach or go into the church. She's a capable, highly intelligent woman and she'll have no difficulty keeping up with the work, but three years isn't a long time. What, then, for our former Inspector?"

The garden centre was well laid out, pleasant, and had a lovely restaurant which they were soon entering. The busy lunch hour was coming to an end and so there were plenty of tables free. Answering his question, Dr Emily assured Richard that coffee would be fine as she had eaten lunch with Penny. She made herself comfortable as Richard went off to order their drinks. He wasn't long.

213

"Here we are," he announced as he set the tray on the table, "coffee and complimentary biscuits."

"Thank you, Richard. It's very nice here I must say. I haven't visited since they rebuilt and added the restaurant."

"Yes, it's very pleasant. I often come here at the weekend and bring a newspaper. It gets me out of the house for a few hours." They were both quiet as they shook packets of brown sugar into their drinks and stirred. "Have you by any chance heard the rumour about Pastor Pratt, our hellfire preacher?"

"I don't know about any rumour," Dr Emily replied, "but I do know he's no longer with us, if that's what you mean. That's partly why I was having lunch with Penny. We were discussing something to do with the case."

"So, to come right out with it, is it true that he hung himself in a police cell?"

"I'm afraid so."

"Good heavens! Why was he *in* a police cell? It was only Sunday that we were sat in that Godforsaken place listening to him."

"It's a long and complicated story..." Dr Emily found herself pouring out as many details as confidentiality would allow. Well, okay, maybe a few more as well, but then the Pastor's death would be public knowledge very soon and would certainly be reported in the press. "Penny is getting everyone directly involved to meet together tomorrow evening. Group therapy, mutual support, tea and biscuits... The happenings at the exact time of the Pastor's death are certainly unusual coincidences, supernatural even, and Penny's hunch is that we need to be together and discuss it. We all seem to be in the grip of some cosmic battle – God versus the devil himself. Hence the bizarre coincidental happenings, both good and evil."

"Interesting observation, Emily – in Biblical Hebrew, also referred to as the language God spoke, there is no word for coincidence. Make of that what you will. Anyway," they were both unwrapping their biscuits, "I'd love to be a fly on the wall when you all meet tomorrow."

"Yes, I'm quite looking forward to the challenge of steering everyone through the various traumas," Dr Emily was ready, biscuit poised above the remaining coffee in her cup, "and maybe we could use your skills to explore the theological aspects." She plunged the biscuit energetically into the warm liquid.

"Emily!" Richard leaned over the table and whispered loudly. She could tell by the expression on his face that he was truly appalled and embarrassed. "How could you?" She quickly withdrew the biscuit, thankfully not too soggy, and placed it in the saucer.

"Do forgive me, Richard, I'm so sorry." His standards of public etiquette obviously exceeded her own and Dr Emily was instantly mortified. How could she have so forgotten herself in public? She had shown herself up and struggled to think of anything she could do or say to put this right. She looked up dejectedly as Richard continued to speak.

"Don't you know," he whispered conspiratorially, "that when your drink is half finished, a dunk cannot be a true dunk, due to the fact that there is a distinct possibility of the biscuit hitting the bottom of the drinking vessel? There is absolutely no guarantee that the depth of remaining liquid is adequate for the degree of dunk required to obtain maximum pleasure. Also, consider the temperature of the dunking medium and the problems in timing exactly how long the biscuit should remain submerged without over sogging." Richard grinned. Dr Emily was instantly delighted and picked up the thread.

"What, pray, would you recommend a dedicated dunker should do in such dire circumstances?" She grinned back, eyebrows raised questioningly, both of them enjoying the silly banter.

"Ah! I am pleased to tell you I have studied this dilemma and come up with two solutions. The less adequate one demands that you break off a little of your biscuit, like so," which he proceeded to do. "You then place it on the teaspoon, gently tip the cup towards you, and lower the spoon slowly into the liquid." Having done that, Richard slurped the soggy mess off his teaspoon much to Dr Emily's delight and the interested stares of the couple at an adjoining table. "Splendid!" He uttered, for all to hear.

"What about the other solution?" prompted Dr Emily.

"Easy. I buy you another coffee!"

Later that evening, back at Angel's Rest, Dr Emily was sitting with Doodle on her lap enjoying memories of the afternoon with Richard. They had definitely connected and had planned another outing for the following Wednesday, which was the University's usual half day. "Oh Doodle, it's so good to have some male company after all these years. I'm not betraying Henry, am I? No, of course I'm not," she answered herself, "he'd want me to be happy. It's been a long seven years." She was jogged from her thoughts by the phone ringing.

"I thought you'd be interested to know," said Penny on the other end, "we managed to dig up the records concerning the deaths of Veronica's parents, Mr & Mrs Woodson. They certainly did die in a house fire that night, but it was definitely started in the bedroom, almost certainly caused by one of them smoking in bed. Fire damage to the ground floor was minimal, so Veronica did not cause the fire that killed her parents. The cigarette end she placed under the cushion obviously went out. The seat of the fire was the couple's double bed."

"I see," said Dr Emily, "this will undoubtedly be reassuring to Veronica and assuage a little of her guilt. At least she can know that she was not responsible for their deaths but she still has to cope with the fact of her intention to destroy the house with them in it. That's never going to be easy."

"No, it won't be easy for her. Another thing, too – apparently Pastor Pratt knew all this as the results of the inquiry were passed on to him. Veronica was in too much of a state and it was left to him to give her the news, which he didn't. Instead he left her believing the fire was entirely her fault and that she had got away with it. The withholding of vital information was quite deliberate on his part."

"That was wicked!"

"Sure was, Dr Em. At least I'm glad now that I kept Veronica's confession to myself. And obviously I won't be taking it any further."

"Sure, but I am extremely concerned about Veronica's present state of mind. I will get her to her GP as soon as possible. I can't offer to see her professionally myself as it would compromise my therapeutic relationship with Hayley."

"I understand. I'm popping over to see Veronica this evening, see how she is. I'll tell her to get to the GP. How did your afternoon go, by the way?"

"Richard and I had a wonderful time! He's a very interesting man and we didn't stop talking. I understand he'll be one of your lecturers later this year."

"Yes, he will be. How do you come to know him if you don't mind me asking, Dr Em."

"Remember I told you I'd gone to the Pastor's chapel last Sunday? Well, Richard was there, on a field trip, doing research for some papers he's putting together. We both sat in the back row, not enjoying the service at all, and ended up together in the Black Swan afterwards."

"That's a good one," laughed Penny, "out of the chapel, straight to the pub!"

"I do assure you, Penny, we needed it after what we'd been through in that place. We did only drink coffee, mind you."

"Was his preaching as over the top as I imagine it was?"

"Oh yes! And more. Never heard anything like it."

"Oh?" Penny was interested.

"Very legalistic, judgemental, intolerant… It was more like a rant. I'd love to know how he kept anyone *in* his congregation, unless they're all like him. Perish the thought."

"Perhaps we'll find out more tomorrow when we all get together."

"Yes, I'd love to. See you tomorrow then. Bye for now."

Doodle stirred and Dr Emily closed her eyes in thought.

"Doodle? Life is getting so very, very interesting."

It was about to get a whole lot more interesting!

CHAPTER TWENTY-EIGHT

THE GROUP

Thursday evening

"**V**ERONICA!**" Penny called out as she spotted the woman in the corridor. "Come into my office for a minute. I'm glad you're early as I need to tell you what I've been able to find out."

"Matthew and Tracey are already next door in the whatsit suite," Veronica said. "The three of us came in the car together."

"Excellent! They'll be fine over there for ten minutes. Come on in." Penny closed the door behind Veronica and they both sat down, Penny noticing just how pale and drawn Veronica was. Hardly surprising in the circumstances.

"Have you made an appointment to see your GP yet? Did Dr Emily or I mention it?"

"Yes, I'm going next Tuesday."

"Excellent, right, so that's in hand. I've actually got some good news for you today, if you can call it good news."

"Good news?" The woman's eyes looked straight at Penny, red rimmed, tired, speaking the two words as if they could not possibly mean anything.

"Maybe 'good' is the wrong choice of word, but listen, Veronica, I've done my bit of research and found something out. That is, you were not responsible for the fire which killed your parents. The report clearly states that the fire started upstairs, in their bedroom, in their double bed. They had been smoking in bed and both had sky high blood alcohol levels. The spread of fire to the downstairs also indicates clearly that the fire began on the upper floor. This means you were NOT responsible for their deaths. It was not your fault, Veronica."

"Not my fault?" Veronica looked at Penny, perplexed, confusion written all over her face. "But Anthony told me the fire started downstairs, behind the cushion where I had left the cigarette."

"Then he should not have told you that because it didn't. He was told to tell you the investigation found that the fire began in your parents' bed. You didn't kill your parents, Veronica." Penny came round and sat on the edge of the desk, taking hold of one of the woman's pale hands. "They were drunk out of their minds and careless with a cigarette. Look at me? You didn't kill them!"

"But I meant to. I wanted to."

"I know, I know, but you *didn't* and you *have* to make that count for something now, else do you torment yourself for the rest of your life?"

"But Anthony said… he could have told me, but he didn't. How could he have done that to me? How could he?" Veronica whispered the words, a quiet desperation showing in her expression. What could Penny say to her? Veronica continued, "He held it against me all these years when he could have told me."

"I'm so sorry, Veronica."

"I hate him! I hate him now more than I thought it possible to hate another human being. I absolutely, utterly, completely detest him. If he was still alive then I would kill him. I would kill him with my bare hands." The words were spoken quietly and chillingly.

"Veronica…?" Penny was disturbed by the venom in the woman's words and the look of almost insane madness in her eyes. In those few moments she began seriously to fear for the woman's sanity, wondering if a doctor should be called in urgently to assess the situation.

Meanwhile, in the building next to HQ, a non-uniformed officer had shown Matthew and Tracey into a large, comfortable lounge where easy chairs were gathered around a coffee table. The couple sat in adjoining chairs and looked around the room which was pleasantly decorated with the intention of creating a non-stressful meeting place, intended as it was for the victims of crime.

The door opened and another young couple were shown into the room. The officer, not knowing the situation, left them to introduce themselves, which they hesitantly started to do.

"Are you Matthew Pratt?" Mike spoke first, offering his hand. "I'm Mike, Mike Bishford, this is my wife, Hayley." Matthew then introduced Tracey and there were more handshakes.

"I'm so sorry to hear about your little girl," said Hayley.

"Thing is," said Mike, "you can always have…" Hayley caught hold of his arm quickly, to shut him up. She then spoke directly to Tracey. "They don't want another baby. They want Chloe." That said, the two young women put their arms around each other, hugging briefly, and although they could not know it then, a firm and lasting friendship had begun.

"I'm sorry my Dad messed about with your heads," said Matthew, looking at Mike and Hayley, now sitting opposite. "He messed with everyone's heads. That's what he did in life."

"I thought you might blame me for his death," Hayley whispered, almost afraid of what the answer to that would be.

"Blame you? More like thank you!" Matthew responded feelingly.

"Yes," Tracey agreed with him, "it might sound sick, but we're not the slightest bit sorry he's gone if the truth be told. Some of the things he said to us, and about Chloe, were more than unforgiveable. He was a pig of a man and believe me, we won't be missing him."

"But what he used to say to me sounded so plausible. I went along with him, believed what he told me..."

"That was how he was, Hayley," Matthew explained, "he'd back everything up with verses from the Bible, and he had the sort of charismatic personality that got people to latch on to him. He was like some blasted cult leader on a power trip, with a freaky ability to control people. He was a brainwasher."

"Dr Emily said I would need to be debriefed, like a deprogramming."

"Hayley love, that's not a bad idea if he's been at your head." Matthew spoke bitterly, then dropped his head. "We all need deprogramming from that freaking jerk. Let me guess that he told you – Satan was in your head, together with hordes of minion demons, and he was the one person in the whole world appointed to make you better. He could help you, you needed him, don't go near anyone else."

"How did you know?" Hayley looked from Matthew, over to Mike, and back to Matthew again.

"Huh! Self-appointed exorcist my father was. He enjoyed telling people their heads were sick and full of evil spirits. He got off on power trips commanding demons to..."

"Matthew, stop," pleaded Tracey.

"It's okay," said Hayley, "I don't mind. He did try to exorcise me." She wanted to hear more of what Matthew was telling her.

"He did it everywhere he went, Hayley, I'm only sorry you got messed up in his games."

The four of them lapsed into silence.

Several minutes passed.

The door opened.

In came Dr Emily.

"Hello everyone! Hayley, Mike," then she looked over to the other young couple in the room, "I'm guessing you are Matthew and Tracey?" They both nodded in the affirmative. "Good! I'm Dr Emily Chatwith, consultant psychiatrist, but please, all of you, call me Emily, or Em if you like." She proceeded to take off her coat and make herself comfortable in one of the chairs. "I see they haven't provided us with any refreshments yet?"

"No," said Matthew, "and I could murder a strong coffee."

"Me, too," said Hayley.

"Might warm us all up a bit more. It's freezing out there this evening." Mike went on to explain how he'd had to scrape frost off the windscreen before setting off after their babysitters had arrived. Chat about the weather continued for several minutes. Mundane small talk, but helping everyone to be together. It was past seven o'clock when the door opened again and Penny ushered Veronica into the room ahead of her. "Sit over there, Veronica, you already know everyone. I'm off to rustle up a tray of hot drinks, I won't be long." When she had left the room, Veronica turned immediately to Hayley and Mike.

"Don't worry. Please don't worry that I blame you for what happened because I don't. He did it to all of us. Messed us all up."

"But I am sorry..." said Hayley, close to tears.

"No. Don't be. It's okay. It's me who should be apologising to you. I should have tried to stop him..."

"Stop Dad?" Matthew butted in, "there was not a chance in hell of stopping *him* when he got something into his head, you know that Mum. He was a raving lunatic. Should have been locked up years ago."

Dr Emily joined in. "You're all connected in different ways to the Pastor and there's plenty to discuss and unpick. I'm understandably picking up on a lot of terrible hurt and pain. It's good to acknowledge that."

"You know something?" It was Matthew who spoke again. "You're right, there's a lot of hurt and right now I'm almost wishing he *wasn't* dead so I could tell him exactly what I thought of him, make him listen for once, see him behind freaking bars, 'cos that's where he should be."

"You want to hurt him as he hurt you," spoke Dr Emily, softly.

"Yes," replied Matthew, "I do. But I won't get the chance now." He banged the fist of one hand into the palm of the other, his anger very real.

That was the moment Penny returned, holding the door open for the officer to carry in a tray of steaming mugs which was placed on the table. "I know you all like coffee, so coffee it is. There's one without milk for Hayley. Help yourselves to sugar or sweeteners." Penny waited for her colleague to leave the room, closing the door behind her, before officially opening the meeting.

"Okay everyone, thank you all for coming. As you may already know, I've gone out on a hunch that meeting as a group will be beneficial to each one of you. Five of you here have been traumatised by Pastor Pratt and I'm hoping that sharing those experiences in a controlled way will be therapeutic. It'll help each one of you to come to terms with his sudden death as well as his terrible influence on your respective lives."

"So this is group therapy?"

"I hope it will become very much more than that, Matthew. The coincidences surrounding the time of your father's death are quite extraordinary to say the least, plus, each one of us, in this room, would describe themselves as a Christian. This is a unique fellowship in many respects. Let's see where this takes us." Penny paused before continuing. "First of all I have some news that will take all of you by surprise, as it did me. Before Veronica and I left my office where we had been chatting prior to coming here, I had a phone call from the coroner's office."

"Don't tell us, the swine's risen from the dead. I blasted knew it!"

"*Shush*, Matthew!" Tracey gave him a look.

"The Pastor's cause of death was not hanging," announced Penny, bracing herself for the inevitable responses.

"What?"

"Then how did..."

"...told he was found hanging by his shirt ..."

Several mugs clattered onto the table as excited chatter filled the room.

"Listen up, everyone!" Penny waited for them all to calm down. "The police surgeon who saw the Pastor in his cell shortly after it happened was concerned that the degree of tension, abrasion, etc., on the Pastor's neck was not sufficient to cause death by hanging. It was noted at the time that death was remarkably quick and also the method used was poorly executed, excuse the expression. A Post Mortem examination has revealed that he died from a ruptured aortic aneurysm."

"What's that?" asked Tracey.

"It's a weakness in the biggest blood vessel in the body. This weakness causes a bulge which can rupture, and the results are nearly always fatal. It could have happened at any moment and according to the pathologist would almost certainly have happened within a few weeks, if not sooner."

"So he would have died a few weeks from now anyway? Is that what you're saying?"

"That's correct, Matthew, he could have collapsed and died at any minute. He didn't have long to live. It was a massive aneurysm."

"Did the stress of being arrested cause it to rupture?" asked Hayley.

"I'm going to be perfectly honest with you," replied Penny, "we don't know, but as far as you are concerned that hardly matters in the light of the fact that it was me, not you, who arrested him. You are in no way responsible for what happened. He had this condition and would have died soon anyway."

"In other words," put in Matthew, looking across to Hayley, "even if the stress of the arrest did bring it on, you still did us all a massive favour."

"But…" stuttered Hayley.

"If I can just come in here," Dr Emily was eager to speak, "Hayley is bound to feel a huge amount of guilt at the timing of your father's death, Matthew, and I'm not sure telling her she did you a favour is entirely helpful."

"Yes," agreed Hayley, "I do feel so guilty. He was arrested for doing something to me that he didn't do. Next thing is, he tried to hang himself. How else am I supposed to feel!"

"Penny?" Dr Emily glanced at the Inspector, indicating that it was her turn to speak.

"Hayley," Penny leaned forward, "with the evidence we had we would still have arrested the Pastor for a serious assault against you and for false imprisonment, and we would have gone ahead with that whether you had wanted us to or not. He committed a serious criminal offence and deserved to be in that prison cell, that's the law. It was *his* fault, and *his* fault alone."

"I know, but…"

"This is something you and I will work through one to one," Dr Emily added.

"In that case, why am I here?" asked Hayley.

"Because," said Penny, "I believe it will help you enormously to hear that the Pastor's family does not blame you in any way for his death, however you may feel. It's important for you to grasp this – you are in no way responsible. The only responsibility lies with the man himself."

"We're not blaming you for God's sake woman," this was Matthew speaking, "we're thanking you!"

"But that's my point," wailed Hayley, "you're thanking me for driving him to commit suicide!"

"But he didn't kill himself!" Tracey joined in.

"He tried to!" Hayley was becoming too distressed and it was time for Dr Emily to jump in and calm things down. "Let's all take a deep breath here. It doesn't so much matter that the Pastor would have died anyway; it matters to Hayley how he *intended* his death to come about. I will point out here that an aneurysm of that size didn't just happen. It would have taken a long time to develop, and lifestyle factors such as diet and exercise would be contributory factors. Anyway, what will help for now, as I'll be working alone with Hayley about this anyway, is if you can all share how you feel about the fact that the Pastor is dead, not how he died. Just share how the fact he's no longer alive affects you. Veronica? Would you like to go first?"

"Okay, I'll go first. To be honest, the first thing I felt was relief, especially since what happened with Chloe. It was like a weight being lifted off my shoulders for, apart from everything else, I don't think I could have tolerated him being around for the funeral."

"If he had so much as *thought* about coming to Chloe's funeral," Interrupted Matthew, "I'd have killed him myself with my bare hands."

"You and me both," agreed Tracey. "It's a huge stress off our shoulders now he's not around and I know it must sound awful but we're all so relieved he's gone. We can't help it."

"Do you have a date for little Chloe's funeral yet?" asked Mike.

"No. They haven't released her yet." Matthew put his face in both hands and stifled a sob while Tracey began to cry silently. "You know something? This is the absolute truth. If my father was still alive I think I'd go mad, have a nervous breakdown, go freaking, overboard nuts!"

"Tell us why, Matthew." Dr Emily spoke calmly.

"Because of what he put me through, what he put Mum through for years, what he said about me and Tracey, what he said about Chloe… He said Chloe was the product of sin! It was not God's will for her to live, that her death was punishment for me…"

Mike and Hayley gasped audibly, horrified, their hearts going out to this troubled man who was in so much pain.

"Matthew," said Dr Emily, "I cannot stress enough how wrong your father was to say those things. They were wicked, wicked words and you know that, despite your understandable anger. Chloe was born out of love, in the image of God. Chloe was a child of God! That is fact. That is the truth. Nothing, I repeat nothing, your father ever said can make that any different."

"I know Dr Em, but it doesn't stop hurting." Matthew now banged a fist into his chest. "I can picture his smug face when he heard that she had died. What sort of a father is that? He wasn't a man…"

"He was an excuse for a man and a father Matthew, even by what he put my wife through, which is nowhere near what you've had to put up with." It was Mike who spoke again. "But I'm begging you mate, don't let him spoil Chloe for you, don't let him do that to you. She was your kid, you loved her, she'll always be yours. Don't let him take any of that away from you or knock you down any further, mate. He's gone and he's not worth it."

"Tracey," Hayley said, "you'll never get over losing Chloe, I cannot imagine how you must be feeling… but please don't let that man spoil your memories. He's gone. Let him take his evil words with him."

"Are you glad he's gone as well?" Tracey turned to ask Hayley.

"It hasn't sunk in yet, I can't get my head round it. One thing though, I didn't know how I was going to get away from him even though I wanted to and wasn't exactly chained to him. It was like he had cast a spell on me and I had become addicted to his help, only it wasn't help. He convinced me that I needed him and kept saying he was the only one who could help me. Mike and I came to realise what was happening but were somehow powerless to break away. Then, at the moment of his death, I got dramatically better. What the hell does that mean?"

"Probably that he took with him the bit of hell he was keeping you in," said Matthew. "That's what he did to people, he cast a spell on them, put the heebie jeebies on them, anything to get his power kicks. You're not the first person he's made worse and damaged by his so-called God appointed ministry."

"Really?" Hayley was amazed at what she was hearing.

"Oh yes," put in Veronica, "what Matthew says is right. You are not the first one Hayley. We moved from place to place over the years because we had to. Things went wrong, Anthony got too deep with his blasted exorcisms, people started to complain but couldn't do much about him. What would the police have done about an accusation of exorcism? He believed he was untouchable."

"Amazing!" whispered Penny to Dr Emily, giving her a discreet thumbs up, for the meeting was going better than she could have expected. They both sat back in silence, hardly needing to interrupt, as the two couples, and Veronica, continued to talk and share. Hayley had gone on to ask what Chloe was like and there were even smiles as Matthew and

Tracey spoke about the little girl who had given them so much. They were even able to say how thankful they were to have had her, albeit for a tragically short time. There was not a dry eye in the room. Thankfully Penny had thought to put a box of Kleenex on the table.

An hour and a half later and nobody wanted the meeting to end.

"Look," said Penny, "we don't want to overdo it on our first get-together. The room's booked for nine, so I can give you another fifteen minutes but I'll have to be on my way. I'll leave you with the capable Dr Em. Shall we meet again next week? Same time, same place?" They all agreed that they would. It had been so helpful to talk and, for the two young couples, to get out of their respective houses for a few hours.

Penny hugged the four females and shook hands with Matthew and Mike before she left. "Don't forget, any one of you, my phone's always on and if I can't answer straight away then I'll get back to you as soon as possible."

The Group, minus Penny, chatted generally until it was time to vacate the room. Deep psychic wounds had been cohesive in bonding strong friendships that evening. Confidences were shared and trust was laying down the foundations of a truly unique, healing fellowship.

What did the future hold for them all?

PART TWO

June 2005

So *did* anything good come out of the events following the arrest of Pastor Pratt? It's certainly true that not everyone involved lived happily ever after, for that's not how real life is. Fairy tale endings are for fairy tales only and, almost four months on, there continued to be much suffering, yet also much joy...

... and a few surprises along the way!

CHAPTER ONE

DR EMILY

Dr Richard Preston's usual parking space outside Angel's Rest was occupied by a largish white van bearing the words, 'Molly and Mutley's Short Bark and Sides – Mobile Dog Grooming'. As he drew up alongside and got out of his car he could hear Doodle yipping away inside the van. It was hard to tell what sort of a 'yip' it was, for the little dog always sounded the same to him. Grinning to himself, he made his way to the front door and knocked, even though the door was not closed. He then pushed it gently and went inside. "Hello," he called out, "Only me!"

"Richard! Hello, it's so lovely to see you, as usual." They hugged briefly in greeting, as they always did these days.

"I see you've got the real deal in to see to Doodle this Sunday?" He tilted his head in the direction of the white van.

"Yes, she needs the full works this week and I'm not very good at trimming her all over. She's having her anal glands squeezed as well."

"A treat indeed. I'm so glad I'm not a dog."

"Yes, so am I, Richard dear," replied Emily, oblivious to the amused expression on Richard's face. "She shouldn't be much longer, then we can have our little tea." As predicted, it was barely minutes later that a friendly young lass appeared carrying a distinctly shorn, clean smelling Doodle, who was being mollified with one of her favourite chews. She eyed her owner with a most pathetic look that said, 'Try having your anal glands squeezed on a sunny afternoon!' As soon as she was deposited on the floor she trotted off into the garden, presumably to ensure her rear end was still in good working order.

"Oh dear, I'm in the dog house now. Did you see that sulk?" Emily chatted away whilst paying the dog groomer and bidding her farewell.

"Can't say I blame her," said Richard, "I wouldn't take too kindly to having my… Anyway, do you want a hand in the kitchen?"

As was their habit of late, Emily and Richard spent a pleasant afternoon together, ate a delicious tea, and went to St Matthew's for Evensong. Afterwards they returned to Angel's Rest where followed the always enjoyable discussion on matters theological, psychological, political, and anything else that popped up during their animated conversations. Emily's newly acquired coffee making machine continually dripped a wonderfully aromatic, surprisingly good decaffeinated blend. Better for bowels and wouldn't add to insomnia! Too soon, Emily had wished Richard goodnight before curling up on the settee with Doodle who, with the onset of hunger, had forgiven Emily the humiliation of the dog grooming session.

The late evening was pleasantly warm and Emily felt so comfortable and peaceful as she relaxed, finding her thoughts going over her recent retirement. Oh, how her feelings and expectation had changed, for she no longer dreaded the time ahead, no longer feared boredom and loneliness, old age, the lack of structure and routine to her days... And really, that was all because of Pastor Pratt, believe it or not.

'The Group,' as they had come to call themselves, had been a roaring success, proving Penny's hunch to be correct, for which Penny was very relieved and glad. Emily now ran that one evening a week, still a Thursday, as well as having embarked on intensive psychotherapy with Hayley and joining the choir at St Matthew's. Then there was part-time locum work to fit in. She had also surprised herself by taking an interest in gardening and was enjoying the care of her first batch of tomato plants. The front door was surrounded by pots overflowing with flowers and she was even thinking of having a pond.

Then there was Richard.

Where were things going with Richard? Where did she *want* things to go? "Doodle? I need to be honest with myself here, don't I? I more than like him, I know that, but he once said he didn't want another woman and I always said there could never be anyone after Henry. But..."

Darn and blast it! If she *was* being honest with herself, then she *did* want things to go further with Richard. They were seeing each other every week now, going to St Matthew's together (couples who pray together stay together?) and she'd been to his home several times for Sunday dinner. He had even been approved by Isobel, Emily's daughter, who, together with her partner, got on very well with him. It made perfect sense for her and Richard to be a couple. Well, perfect sense to Emily, that is. Seven years *was* a long time, surely Henry would be glad for her to find romance again? He could never be replaced and nor would she want that, besides which, Richard was different in many ways. She'd not gone looking for him, he'd simply happened. What was so wrong with that? Absolutely nothing! He'd held her hand a few times and that had felt so good, so right. Had it felt the same for him? They hugged every time they met, many hugs progressing to a brief kiss. He was certainly affectionate, but did he only see them as companions and close friends?

"Oh, stop thinking about it too deeply woman!" Emily said out loud to her canine friend, "It's early days yet, early days." The grandmother clock ticked on, chimed eleven, then Emily roused herself to make her bedtime drink, all the while thinking about Richard. "I need to change the subject, Doodle, else I shall never get to sleep. What will be, will be." Oh, but it was exciting! She felt like a lovesick teenager all over again, and why not? Sixty wasn't old these days and she had plenty of energy and life left in her. Indeed, retirement was not so bad after all. Who would have thought that she'd end up too busy to go to work anyway?

Lying in bed a little later, Emily's thoughts turned to Hayley and she wondered what their session the following morning would be like. After the euphoria of Hayley's dramatic improvement at the time of the Pastor's death, Hayley was having difficulties again. That wasn't surprising after what she'd been through, but at least the return of speech and full use of her limbs appeared to be permanent. It was going to be a long, slow job if the psychotherapy was to have lasting results, and there was no reason why it shouldn't. Haley was an intelligent woman who showed tremendous insight into her mental state.

Hayley participated extremely well in The Group on a Thursday evening too, despite her almost crippling shyness, and had made a real friend in Tracey. And vice versa. The two of them were now meeting for a coffee morning once a week, neither of them having had such a close friendship before. And who had brought them together? That creepy Pastor Pratt.

It had been fascinating to hear what had been found out about the Pastor as well. All that writing, found at the manse, which even Veronica had been unaware of, in which he had recorded details of the many exorcisms he had carried out over many years. All had failed due to the lack of cooperation, commitment, or wickedness of the person being exorcised. Such was the man's ego and drive for power and control that he appeared totally unable to accept that he just might be the one getting something wrong. Goodness, he'd been one messed up, confused man. You could almost feel sorry for him, but only almost. Plenty of other people were just as messed up, confused, ill or abused, yet didn't cause such damage and unhappiness to the people around them. Nor did they ever seek such control and power over another. Emily knew this for a fact as she'd worked with enough messed up people. Had the Pastor been mad? Or bad? The debate over that very point continues in medical schools, law schools, police colleges… and probably many other places. Society awaits an answer, plus a cure that might not exist.

Emily's thoughts then wandered to the other members of The Group. Matthew and Tracey were still struggling but that was only to be expected. Chloe's funeral had been utterly heart-breaking and as Tracey had so far been unable to find a job, she had too much time on her hands to think. Matthew had returned to work in a call centre and was managing okay as far as that went. Let's face it, with the parents he had, he wasn't doing badly at all! The Sally Ann had been a considerable support, that was for sure, and had given much help over the past few months. Emily was very impressed with them. She would send another donation for they did sterling work.

After Chloe's funeral, Veronica had moved back into the manse, giving the young couple much needed time to themselves. It was Veronica, out of all of them, whom Emily worried about most. Not that she wasn't concerned for Hayley and the others, of course she was, but Veronica? It was a worry. The woman had Emily's psychiatrist's antennae on red alert and that usually meant trouble. She would have another chat with Penny about her, and also phone Veronica's GP yet again and voice her concerns.

Still awake, Emily thought what a funny old world it was. All in all, though, she was happy and content. Her thoughts turned to tomorrow. What should she have for breakfast? Stuff the prune juice! She'd been set a little too free and had no wish to repeat the experience. She had to be out by nine so toast and coffee would do. Nice and quick and easy.

Her mind then went through her wardrobe, deciding what she would wear, bearing in mind the weather was rather warm at present. Maybe she would wear a thin cardigan in case it was a little chilly first thing. There again, she would be in the car, then in Hayley's house. Well, she could always take the cardigan and leave it on the passenger seat if it was not needed.

Where were her K Skip sandals? asked the *tic tock* of the bedroom clock as it carried her into a restful sleep...

CHAPTER TWO

PENNY

"**P**ENNY, will you marry me?"

"Ian! Is this some sort of a joke, or what?" They were in the kitchen in Ian's house, washing up after a very pleasant Sunday dinner together. Ian had yet again broached the subject of him moving in with her and, yet again, Penny explained that she would not feel comfortable living with a man. When she'd thought about taking in a lodger for financial reasons, she had thought only of sharing with a woman.

"No. I don't make jokes like this, I'm deadly serious. Penny, please, marry me?"

"Why? Just so you can move in with me like you've been suggesting for the past few months?"

"Don't be daft, you know that isn't why I'm asking you. Haven't the last four months meant anything to you at all?"

"Of course they have, more than you'll ever know, but why do you want to marry me?"

"Why not?"

"Because, for starters, less than five months ago you told me you'd been through a few girlfriends and were crap at relationships and didn't want another one and... don't you think that's maybe just a bit of the 'why not'?" Penny was frustrated, wanting Ian to say the one thing he hadn't yet said to her, to tell her he loved her. "You said you'd never feel comfortable with another woman, vowed never to have one in your life again…"

"Yes, I had written off having another woman in my life but that was before I met you! Obviously I hadn't met the one meant for me! I thought that was pretty easy to work out!"

"Yes, and I also know that, since I've been looking to take in a lodger, you've suddenly seen it as a good idea for us to live together. How the hell do I know you're not just fancying a bigger house and somebody who'll do all the washing and cooking, someone to share the bills with? Maybe…"

"Penny, for God's sake, you know that isn't true! We've talked about this before. Don't forget I'll continue to earn my salary while you're in Uni, so I'll actually be the bigger earner anyway. The financial benefits are on both sides. Look, let's not argue, please, but come on, we can hardly bear to be apart these last two months! This can work, I know it can."

"We haven't even had sex! I know I, well,… but the thing is, most men would at least have tried it on a bit more by now."

"…so maybe I'm not most men! Maybe I respect you enough to wait until you're ready. Maybe I'm sensitive to what happened to you all those years ago. Maybe I like the fact that you're so faithful to the God you believe in and won't have sex outside marriage. Hey! That's rather something in this day and age. I might not agree with it and it doesn't mean I've not wanted you, but I've respected that. Hell, we've just about done anything and everything a couple can possibly do in bed without actually…"

"But why d'you want to marry me?" Penny's voice had risen several decibels.

"Because…"

"Because what?" Penny was almost squealing at a level only dogs could hear.

"Because I love you!" Ian squealed back. "I absolutely adore you and everything about you, and I want to live with

238

you for the rest of my life. I love your face, your crazy hair, the sound of your voice, the way you care, you dribble when you sleep, the sun shines out of your sweet little backside..." He took her in his arms and spoke more gently now. "I love you, my Penny." Her reply was smothered in a kiss, tender, non-demanding, but nonetheless genuine in the depth of emotion it contained. At last he had said those words, 'I love you' – and when Penny eventually caught her breath, she buried her head in his shoulder and had never felt so safe in the whole of her life.

"Ian?"

"Yes?" He was smoothing the back of her head with one hand, the other still clasping her close, for he felt he could never be complete without her.

"Of course I'll marry you!" Upon which he picked her up and swirled her around, both of them giggling with excitement and joy.

"Thanks boss!"

"Put me down, you idiot, and get these dishes finished, and be quick about it!"

"No way, boss," said Ian, "these dishes can wait. I've got my mind on other things."

"Have you now!" Penny laughed as Ian caught hold of her, propelling her into the living room and towards the settee where he lay her down tenderly.

That was over a week ago, and Penny's left ring finger now proudly displayed a beautiful, three stone engagement ring. At least it did when she wasn't in work. Penny had decided to keep things quiet at HQ about their engagement as she only had another two months' notice to work through. It wasn't exactly forbidden for two officers to fall in love, as long as they didn't work closely together. Penny didn't want them split up before she finished.

Old Mrs Whistle had smiled her sweet smile when Penny made her monthly visit and gave her the good news.

"Mum? You remember Ian?" She went on to explain about the engagement and how happy they were. Yet, as had become the norm, Old Mrs Whistle didn't answer. Nor did she recognise who Penny was. Only that sweet, vacant smile which sent Penny running from the room in tears.

"How did it go at the nursing home? How's your Mum?" Ian had asked later that evening.

"It went how it always goes. I talk, she ignores, I cry... I told her our news. Her response? Zero!"

"I'm so sorry love, it's hard for you. Come here." She went willingly into his arms, enjoying the feeling of being held and comforted and safe. "When are you going to tell The Group about us?"

"Oh, I'm bursting to tell the world, but I don't want work to find out just yet."

"Confession time," said Ian, "I've had a word with the Chief Super about us and..."

"Ian!" Penny drew away and looked him straight in the eye.

"Listen, listen. As you're already working your notice, he's happy to leave us partnered, especially as you'll be taking annual leave out of your notice in any case. It'll be easier not having to keep quiet..."

"Well, thanks a lot for going behind my back! How's that going to look with..."

"Penny, you're leaving! I did what I thought was right for both of us – we're both dying to share the news. Please don't be mad at me, it's not a big deal, honestly, there's plenty in work who'll be tickled pink for us."

"Oh Ian, I'm sorry. I'm just frazzled after the visit to Mum."

"I know, love, I know..."

"I love you, Ian," said Penny. And she did. With all of her heart.

Later that evening they were back at Penny's house, sitting on the settee, both reading. Migmos, the traitor, had taken to curling up next to Ian as often as she could. Mind you, that was only since he had bought her fresh salmon. 'Fresh salmon for a cat?' Penny had scolded him, laughing. Was he after brownie points? If so, were they to be awarded by the cat, or by Penny?

"So, Pen, you going to tell The Group tomorrow?"

"Yes, definitely, I can't wait. I know they'll be pleased for me, even though they've all got so many problems still. How Tracey and Matthew got through that funeral I'll never know. That little white coffin! Utterly heartbreaking. It makes you count your blessings, that's for sure."

"Yes, it was pretty grim. I thought Gloria was brilliant the way she spoke during the service. First Sally Ann funeral I've been to. Matthew didn't go to his father's funeral, did he?"

"No. Who can blame him for that? The Pastor had said some evil things, and I mean evil. God alive, we've been cops long enough, heard it all, but that man spouted the purest venom I've ever heard. It wasn't just the words he spoke either, it was the look on his face, the way his voice trembled, the chilly atmosphere, the heaviness wherever he was... Veronica says the only reason *she* went to the funeral was to make absolutely certain he was six feet under. *Phewee!*"

"How's Veronica, The Vulture, doing these days?" They laughed, remembering Hayley's nickname for Veronica.

"Out of all of them, she's the one who worries me most. Worries Emily too."

"How come? She still acting strange? I thought she was seeing a doctor."

"She says she's seen her GP and is taking his advice, but I'm not convinced. Her behaviour seems way out, erratic, and it's more than just strange – the woman seems haunted, for want of a better word. Like she's not under her own control."

"It's still early days after a double bereavement; I guess she's entitled to act a bit weird in the circumstances."

"I suppose you're right, but she still bothers me, rattling around on her own in that big house."

"Gloria and Tim still coming to see us at the weekend?" Ian changed the subject to a much happier one.

"Yes. I've told them our possible dates and Tim is dead chuffed to be marrying us."

They went on to discuss details of the wedding. There was so much to do even though they were planning to keep the wedding small and quiet. Ian was hoping to rent out his own house as soon as he'd moved into Penny's, bringing some of his own stuff with him so that, in addition to some decorating and renovations, the house would be 'theirs' rather than Penny's.

There was also Penny's leaving party at HQ to look forward to, then the start of University, and soon it would be their first Christmas as man and wife. There was so much to look forward to.

Penny slept soundly.

CHAPTER THREE

HAYLEY AND MIKE

"**B**OTH KIDS ASLEEP at last." Mike came downstairs, looking and sounding as tired as he felt. "Fancy a last cuppa and an early night?"

"Sounds good to me," said Hayley, "I'm over at Tracey's for coffee in the morning, then there's The Group tomorrow evening. I could do with an early night."

"Yes, The Group. I hope Matthew's calmed down a bit. God, I can understand his anger but he's so vicious at times. Mind you, Emily's spot on in the way she deals with everything."

"She's been brilliant, Mike, with me as well. I never thought I would talk the way I have but I do feel better for doing so."

"You seem a lot less depressed these days. I only wish I could take those voices out of your head though."

"Yeah, so do I." They smiled sadly at each other.

Mike made them both coffee, black and no sugar for Hayley, who was still in the grip of anorexia. Emily was keeping an eye on her which was so reassuring, and having opened up to what had been going on in the exorcisms it was little wonder she had lost her appetite.

Worryingly, Hayley had not been Pastor Pratt's first victim, merely one of many, all women, all vulnerable, who had fallen into his web. Caught in his deadly trap, they became worse and worse, more and more ill, only confirming the Pastor's initial diagnosis of demonic possession. Having convinced himself of this diagnosis, Bingo! He was off on another ego boosting power trip, supposedly controlling the planet's cosmic evil by attempting to exorcise the poor souls unfortunate enough ever to have met him. Physically and verbally abusing them, not to mention their emotional and spiritual welfare, he'd spouted hatred into their fragile minds and left a trail of misery and despair. It had indeed been spiritual and emotional rape. "That man ought to be strung up!" Mike had uttered at one of The Group's meetings. That had been met with silence. Mike had not realised what he said. Nobody had disagreed with him though.

Thankfully, Hayley had Emily now. Tracey was a good friend, too, and they had vowed to stick together. With Mike and Matthew they even met up as a foursome once a month and Tracey enjoyed concocting supper for them all.

Hayley had even grown to like and trust Penny, realising that it had been the position, rather than the person, that had scared her initially. Gosh, it had been quite a revelation to learn that Penny was a committed Christian, and what a help she had been in making safe all the Bible verses the Pastor had used against her. Penny was able to give context to whole bible passages, thus returning Hayley to a safe and loving Father.

"You okay to get the kids off to school tomorrow? I'm in early again." Hayley assured Mike she would be fine. The supermarket had been good about the time he'd taken off to be with her, but Hayley knew he was glad to get back, finding the hustle, bustle of the big store easier than looking after her and two kids!

As for Mike, believing The Group wasn't for him, he'd been surprised to find himself enjoying the contact. Veronica though... well, Veronica was nuts according to Mike. He hoped her nuttiness was of the harmless, eccentric kind for she sure came out with some scary stuff, but… It was fascinating in a perverse way, he mused, but that woman seriously needed help. Or should that be 'needed serious help'?

"Hayley?"

"What? I'm trying to get some sleep."

"Sorry love, but I was wondering if you think Veronica should have stayed at Matthew's rather than move back to the manse. Or why don't Matthew and Tracey move into that big house with her? She's on her own. They're struggling with the rent and bills. Wouldn't it make sense for them all to live together?"

"Put it this way Mike, if Veronica was your mother-in-law, would you want to live with her?" Hayley sniggered and shuffled into a more comfortable position, all the while thinking Mike was right about one thing, it wasn't good for Veronica to be on her own so much. Of all of them, Hayley thought Veronica seemed the most traumatised. Crikey, hadn't Matthew gone nuts when they'd discussed her 'non-marriage' one Thursday! She couldn't blame him, especially as the Pastor had virtually disowned him for living with his girlfriend, then claiming Chloe should never have existed and was sin incarnate. Tracey had had quite a bit to say about that too. Good for her! He was a wicked man was Pastor Pratt. A thoroughly wicked man.

Hayley had been pretty cut up and confused over the Pastor's death at first, but it was The Group who had helped her most to sort out her head. Oh, the guilt she had felt, and still felt over his death! She was still certain that the stress over his arrest had caused the aneurysm to rupture, even though she'd been assured it was going to happen anyway, and soon. And as The Group had pointed out, the suicide note had spoken of nobody but himself. There had been no consideration whatsoever of how his actions would impact on his family or his congregation. He'd been a self-seeking, dangerous individual and the world would not miss him. Fine. But the fact remained that he was arrested for what he did to Hayley. Would she ever get that out of her mind?

Mike was already snoring when Hayley's thoughts moved back to Veronica. She didn't understand why on earth that woman had stayed with such a man when it would surely have been so easy to leave him. She wouldn't even have needed a divorce. Veronica had mumbled about the Pastor holding something against her, but surely it couldn't have been that bad?

She wondered how Tracey would be feeling tomorrow, caught in the daily battle with bereavement. What was that like? If anything happened to Daisy and Mikey…

The sleeping tablet she took in conjunction with an antidepressant finally kicked in and Hayley felt herself drifting off to sleep. Tomorrow was another new day, another new start. She moaned as she turned over, the seven stitches in her arm, where she'd cut herself because the voices told her to, were still very painful and sore, but at least they were holding her together.

Everyone in the Yellow House slept peacefully that night.

CHAPTER FOUR

MATTHEW AND TRACEY

HOW ABOUT Stickleback-Fagend?" Matthew suggested. "What?" said Tracey, as the two of them fell about laughing, which was a change after so many tears. The laughter was short lived, however, feeling like a betrayal of Chloe's memory, so soon after her death. But laugh they had, as they were trying to decide on a new surname for Matthew who was desperate to no longer be a Pratt.

He'd asked Veronica if he could use her maiden name but she'd thrown a fit, forbidding him to even mention her parents. Matthew knew that they'd died in a house fire before he was born, but why wouldn't she speak of them? Why were there no photos? He sensed there were long buried secrets and he longed to find them.

Anyway, he was going to change his name by deed poll, which wasn't that difficult to do. His surname felt like more of an insult and he needed the psychological distance changing it would create between himself and his late father. He was going to do everything possible to make sure he was never again associated with that man. How the hell had his mother stuck it for so long? But therein lay another long story for there was more to his mother than met the eye. She held secrets, of that he was certain, and although she'd snapped at him, "leave it Matthew, just damn well leave it!", that had only whetted his appetite to know more.

"How about something ordinary that can't be messed with?" Tracey went on.

"Like what?"

"Williams? Thomas? Jones?"

"I don't know, Trace, don't you think they're a bit *too* ordinary?"

"I've got it!" announced Tracey, suddenly, "Davidson! Matthew Davidson. I had a teacher called that and he was okay, he was nice."

"Actually, that sounds good, yes, I don't mind that. Put it on the list."

Sitting up in bed, the two of them continued to make a list of possible surnames. It had been a terrible few months and how they had got through Chloe's funeral neither of them knew. It had been a blur of excruciating agony the like of which they hoped never to experience again, and the heartache had continued every day since. Tests had revealed that Chloe, as suspected, had succumbed to a virulent form of meningitis, despite having been vaccinated. How cruel was that? They would never forget her, simply wanting to be able to cope with the overwhelming grief. Never, ever would they forget that little white coffin...

The arguments had started immediately after the funeral, many of them stirred up by Tracey who was keen to get pregnant again as soon as possible.

"You can't replace her! For God's sake, it'd be as if she never existed!"

"I'm not trying to damn well replace her! Can't you even try and understand? I want..."

Yet Tracey hardly knew herself what she wanted as the jury was still out as far as the experts were concerned on whether it was wise to embark upon another pregnancy so soon after losing a child. It worked for some. For others? Well, nothing repaired the hurt. But then, it wasn't about forgetting, or replacing; it was about living in spite of tragedy, and remembering in a less raw way. Emily had wisely urged both of them to consider if, so soon after Chloe's death, another baby might be compared and found lacking, for that baby could never be Chloe, who would be perfect for evermore. There was a lot to think over, and in Matthew's opinion it was far too soon to be thinking of another pregnancy.

"Tracey," Emily had said, "you're at home, alone while Matthew is working, and suddenly there is so much less to do. No wonder you long for another baby to fill that place."

"What am I supposed to do?" Tracey had asked, "I was a useless thickhead before Chloe, now I'm back to being a useless, freaking thickhead again. Being a Mum was the only thing in my life I was good at, something I did well, the only thing I got right, and now you all tell me to wait? Why should I damn well wait? What for?"

The Group had been quiet following Tracey's outburst, fearful of saying the wrong thing. Matthew had leaned forward, head in hands, silent as Tracey had continued.

"What the hell is my life about if I'm not a mother? Tell me! Come on all you clever dicks, tell me!"

"How about me?" Matthew looked up at this girl he loved and felt like slapping her across the chops. "Remember our plans before you got pregnant? We wanted to be a couple, set up home, even get married. Two homeless failures, that's what we were, but we were going to make it. Together. You wanted to go into nursing, remember? You could do that now, build a life, get our own place..."

"That's like Chloe was some sort of inconvenience."

"No, that's not how I'm seeing it at all, and you know it. It's about making sure we give the next baby the best we can. Not making do in a poxy rented dump and worrying about every bleedin' penny!"

"So things and money matter more than a baby, do they?"

"Don't be stupid, of course they don't. I'm just not ready yet, Trace, I can't do it. Please, give me some time, I'm not ready for another baby. Not yet."

Some of the rows had been nasty and prolonged, the making up cautious and slow. Yet tonight they had laughed! A candle had flickered in the darkness and both secretly hoped it would never be extinguished.

"I do love you, Matthew."

"I love you too, Trace. Who said that it was better to have loved and lost than never to have loved? We've lost enough, but please don't let's ever lose each other." Matthew snatched the list of surnames form Tracey's hands and tossed it onto the floor as he took hold of her, kissing her and moving himself gently on top…

As always happened after they had made love, Matthew fell into a deep sleep, one arm draped over Tracey's waist. She lay there, quietly mulling over the events of the last few months. She was looking forward to seeing Haley tomorrow and hearing all about her latest session with 'Emily the Dunking Shrink' as she called her (behind her back, mind you). Daisy and Mikey would be breaking up soon for the long school holidays and the two women had made lots of plans to take them swimming, to the park, to McDonald's… There was that new community farm just outside Truffleton which the kids would love. Tracey found that she was looking forward to that as well. Then The Group was due to meet tomorrow evening. Thank God it would be a busy day as she needed to get her mind off herself and have a rest from being alone with too many thoughts and too much time to dwell on them.

It was a long time before Tracey felt herself relax enough to hope that sleep was a possibility. As she eventually drifted off into slumber land, her last thought was, "How the hell do I tell Matthew I'm already pregnant?"

As Matthew snored, Tracey slept fitfully.

CHAPTER FIVE

THE GROUP

HAYLEY AND MIKE were almost late arriving at Angel's Rest, the new venue for The Group.

"Sorry folks, in-laws late for babysitting duties," Mike explained. "Where's Veronica Matthew? What's with the posh cake?"

Matthew said that he'd had a call from Veronica saying she couldn't make it that evening as she had a doctor's appointment.

"A doctor's appointment?" queried Emily, "In the evening?" She caught Penny's eye across the room, both of them exchanging a knowing look of unease and disbelief.

"She sounded okay on the phone, just explained about the appointment and said she was going to take a couple of paracetamol and curl up in front of the TV with tea and toast," added Matthew.

Again Penny and Emily looked at each other as professional wisdom informed them that the doctor's appointment didn't exist.

The posh cake? They all looked at the wonderful fresh cream Pavlova piled high with juicy, red strawberries that took pride of place on the coffee table, next to a pile of dishes and an assortment of cutlery.

"That, Mike," Emily explained, not giving away how niggled she felt about Veronica's absence, "is not a posh cake.

It is a Pavlova, which, as those of us possessing culinary skills are aware, is an absolutely spiffing dessert named after the Russian ballet dancer, Anna Pavlova."

"So what's the difference between that and a posh cake?" Mike was enjoying the exchange.

"The difference being, the meringue and strawberries are low enough in fat and calories for your lovely wife to join us in celebrating good tidings of great joy."

"Which shall be to all people?" continued Tracey.

"Indeed!" added Emily, smiling widely.

"The fresh cream isn't exactly lacking in calories and fat, though," Hayley piped up.

"Quite correct," replied Emily, "and when you are truly on the road to recovery, you will learn that fresh cream is actually the best part of any Pavlova. In the meantime you must scrape it off a few strawberries, and nibble those with a little fat free meringue."

"I will indeed!" Hayley laughed, not minding the reference to her eating disorder. She was also rather touched that whoever had provided this celebration dessert had thought about her and wanted her to be able to take part and share in something special. These were good people she was with. What was the celebration about anyway? She was certain none of them had a birthday just yet.

"Come on then," said Mike, "who's responsible for the Pavlova. Own up!" He looked around at the people he now regarded as good friends. Emily, Penny, Matthew and Tracey. Even Ian had come this evening. He was okay, was Ian. As pre-arranged, it was Emily who made the announcement after dramatically and formally clearing her throat and patting her little grey bun.

"I would like to formally announce," and here she paused for effect, looking from one to the other, "the engagement and forthcoming marriage of Inspector Penny and Sergeant Ian!"

The room erupted into joy and congratulations, the women taking turns to hug the happy couple, the men hugging Penny and shaking Ian's hand. Everyone was smiling and speaking all at once, and Emily could not have been more delighted to have this happening after all the hard work of steering everyone through the last four months. Doodle contributed by yipping loudly and racing around everyone's ankles. While this was going on, Emily had retreated into the kitchen and phoned the manse. Veronica had answered, chatting away as if nothing was amiss before lying through her teeth about getting the time of her GP appointment mixed up. Emily was not fooled and managed to whisper to Penny that she would not leave things until the morning, she would visit the manse after the meeting. Penny was relieved as it meant she didn't have to!

It was a good fifteen minutes of excited chatter later before Emily announced she was about to serve the Pavlova. It was a large one, just right for a warm evening, and Hayley and Tracey brought in drinks, sandwiches and crisps from the kitchen. Whoever would have thought group therapy could be so much fun? But then, it was far more than group therapy, they all knew that.

"I think," said Emily, "it would be a rather nice idea if I took Veronica a piece of the Pavlova. It's such a shame she's not with us this evening. I can pop over when we've finished, tell her the good news and see how she is."

"Yes, that'd be good Dr Em. I wish she could have been here this evening, too, and I guess we're all a bit bothered about her," said Matthew, helping himself to a plate full of food.

"She seems worse than she did a few weeks ago," added Hayley, "while the rest of us are making a bit of progress, she seems very distracted somehow. Not her usual self."

"I think we all would agree with that," put in Penny, "I'm glad Dr Em will be seeing her this evening. It'll put all our minds at rest."

Emily spoke again, "Yes, I'll certainly call in later, ask how her appointment went. Right then, unless anyone has something they desperately need to discuss tonight, how about a bit of a debate instead?"

"Eh? About what?" asked Matthew, who was scooping up the last bit of Pavlova from his plate while hoping for seconds.

"Well," continued Emily, "how about we discuss cosmic synchronicity? The psychology and theology of coincidence?"

"Crumbs," said Tracey, "that's a bit deep isn't it?"

"Eh?" Mike looked at his wife who was equally perplexed and still nibbling away delicately at her third strawberry.

"Yer what?" asked Matthew, displaying a mouthful of half chewed ham sandwich.

It was only Penny who grasped what Emily meant. "You mean try and work out why things happen when they do, especially when they all happen at the same time and it appears a bit freaky. Like so much stuff happening the exact minute the Pastor died."

"Exactly!" replied Emily. "Just think about what was going on at that exact moment he died. Let's make a list. Hayley had a sudden improvement in her health. I was utterly constrained to pay her an unplanned visit. Matthew and Tracey were in serious trouble. Two Paramedics *knew* they needed to check in on them. Veronica was trying to harm herself. Penny suddenly *had* to find her and stop her. All this at exactly the same time! Now, how do we begin to explain that sort of coincidence?"

What followed was a lively and animated discussion, everyone taking part and having their say, all of them appreciating the chance to try and find a reason for those finely timed events. Had Penny and Hayley been closest to the answer with their theory of a spiritual battle between good and evil? Was the Pastor himself demonised? Then, at the time of his death those dark forces were unleashed, seeking to destroy Veronica and Matthew, his closest kin. In response, God had dispatched those guardian angels to prompt the help, in the form of Penny and the two paramedics that had rescued them. At the point of the Pastor's death, Hayley was released from those dark forces of his which had held her captive and robbed her of speech and full mobility. Far-fetched? Unbelievable?

"How else can we explain it?" Penny had asked.

"How else indeed," Emily added, thoughtfully. There followed a profound silence, lasting maybe a full minute, in which every one of them in that room felt a Presence far, far greater than themselves; utterly good, unconditionally loving. A peace which passed all understanding wrapped around them and they were comforted. They were also called. Were they willing?

…and what were they being called to do?

Ian provided the answer by speaking and clicking them all back into earthly mode, the ticking of the grandmother clock easing them gently back into the present, urging them unremittingly into the future, whatever it might hold.

"I've got a referral for you guys," Ian announced.

"A referral?" Emily looked and sounded as surprised as the rest of them felt.

"Yes, if it's not too soon and you think you're up to it. A lady, a single mum who's just moved here from up North, has been seeing an Anglican priest for eighteen months. He's spent most of that time trying to exorcise the poor woman and she's in quite a state. She desperately needs the kind of support only folk like you lot can offer. That's if you agree."

"Oh hell, so my old man wasn't a one off? Bloody hell! Sorry, but it's enough to make a saint swear."

"How did you come to know about her?" asked Emily.

255

It was Penny who replied. "Ian and I met her at the Sally Ann a few weeks ago, you might have spotted her." Penny looked across to Matthew and Tracey, marvelling afresh that these young people would go anywhere near a church after their dealings with Matthew's father. God certainly had a soft spot for injured sheep!

They were all in agreement that this lady needed The Group and it was decided that Penny would invite her to join them, then let her decide if she wanted to continue. It was essential not to put her under any pressure, for the woman had been controlled and manipulated enough having gone through a totally unnecessary ministry.

Was this referral the beginning of what The Group was called to do? To minister to those who had been harmed by 'church'? Was this the purpose for which they had been brought together? It is said that when the devil overplays his hand, which he inevitably does, then God brings forth help and goodness in abundance to those who seek, however flimsily, to follow him. "All good things work together for good to those who love God and are the called according to His purpose." Is that what was starting to happen here? Only time would tell.

The Group then continued with general conversation until Mike and Hayley announced they would have to leave in order to relieve their baby sitters.

Suddenly, Penny stood up and announced that she wanted to close the meeting in prayer.

"Is everyone okay for me to pray? I feel we've moved on to another level this evening. We all claim to be Christians, even Ian," at this they all laughed, "so let's acknowledge God in a big way. He was here tonight, we all felt His presence, so let's pray together now." The room fell silent and even Doodle, sensing the seriousness of the moment, hurried into her basket and lay down quietly.

Penny prayed for peace and healing and understanding. She gave thanks for The Group and for being able to share her joy with them. She asked God to guide them as they embarked upon a ministry to those who had been harmed supposedly in God's name, for another injured sheep was about to join them... "and may the peace of God, which passes all understanding, guard our hearts and our minds... God bless us and keep us faithful and trusting in Him. Father God we love you... Amen. And amen."

What an evening it had been! The seven of them didn't want it to end but were soon all on their way home. Emily finally locked her front door and went to wash the dishes which she always insisted on doing, despite frequent offers of help. But then, deciding they could wait, she picked up a dish containing a slice of Pavlova, wrapped it in tin foil, snatched up her car keys and closed the front door after her.

Penny and Ian were almost home when Penny broke the silence in the car.

"Ian?"

"Yes, love?"

"When I prayed this evening, I prayed for all of us, but I couldn't pray for Veronica. It wasn't that I forgot she wasn't there; in fact I had her especially in mind for prayer. I just could not pray for her."

"What d'you think that means, if anything."

"I don't know. I really don't know."

CHAPTER SIX

VERONICA

THERE WAS NO ANSWER when Emily arrived at the manse and rang the doorbell, so she knocked hard on the door, waiting several minutes. When there was still no reply she used her mobile.

"Veronica? Hello, it's Emily. Look, I'm actually stood on your doorstep. I come with tidings of great joy, plus a slice of Pavlova! Can I come in?"

"Um. I'm actually in bed. It is after nine o'clock you know!"

They chatted briefly but Emily could not make Veronica open the door if she didn't want to. Nor could she break in! Was the woman really in bed? It was possible. It was also possible that something was seriously amiss, yet what could Emily do? She eventually had no choice but to return to Angel's Rest, whereupon she informed Penny of her continuing unease before eating Veronica's Pavlova.

Veronica had indeed been in bed when Emily had called.

The hours passed so slowly. It was the middle of a long, sleepless night and Veronica had honestly, truly, damn well had a gutsful. More than a blasted, damn gutsful if anyone were to ask her. Which they didn't. Well, that was a bit unfair she supposed, as The Group were always concerned and asking her how she was. Emily and Penny phoned several times a week and she'd even been to a few services at the Sally Ann. That had been a bit of a shock – people laughing and having fun in church, clapping to the music and shaking timbrels. Could that be right? Yet the preaching was straight from the Bible, the only thing missing was an emphasis on sin and hell. And it did say in the Psalms to make a joyful noise unto the Lord, but that was something she had never done.

"Sad b***h!"

Where did that come from? That word? B***h. That didn't only refer to a female dog, that was swearing which she would never do.

"You go and roast in the flames of hell, you murdering..."

Who said that? Was that Anthony, telling her that her punishment was imminent? For she *would* be punished, Anthony was always telling her that. "Thou shalt not commit murder." But she hadn't! Penny told her she hadn't.

"But you planned to, intended to, wanted to, desired to kill, kill, kill,... murderous cow..."

Where did that come from? Oh, what the hell was the point any longer! She would never know a moment's peace, maybe she was guilty of too much and could never be forgiven or redeemed. And why hadn't she gone to The Group tonight? Why lie about an appointment when she knew she'd feel better for going, if only temporarily. Cutting her nose off to spite her face she was. That was pointless too. Everything was pointless. Too much pointlessness...

Anthony. She deserved the same as he was getting. She deserved to roast in the fires of hell, that lake which bubbled for eternity...

"Roast, you b***h!"

That word again! Everyone else was doing well except her. They were all so pleased with their prattling and chatting and talking. Healing and hoping. Loving and living. Choosing blessing and not cursing. Choosing life and not death. Happy, happy ending.

"What do *you* choose, Veronica? Make your choice, lady. Do you choose life?

Or do you choose death?"

She sat on the edge of her bed, steely with determination…

…and struck the first match.

CHAPTER SEVEN

DAVE AND ROGER

"**I COULD HAVE** done without a week of nights at the moment," said Dave as they waited in the drive-through for their coffees and burgers.

"Yeah, me too," agreed Roger as he took their order from the service window and passed it to Dave before moving into their usual parking spot. Unwrapping their burgers they proceeded to enjoy their supper break. The coffee was hot and much appreciated.

They had barely finished when another call came through. Fiddlesticks and monkey bottoms! Never two minutes to chew your food properly!

"Yeah, yeah, okay, got that. We're on our way."

"What we got this time, Rog?"

"House fire. Police and fire brigade are on their way."

What was left of two coffees sloshed in cardboard containers as Roger swerved out of the carpark and onto the main road...

THE END

15948524R00149

Printed in Great Britain
by Amazon